IMAGE
OF THE BLACK
IN CHILDREN'S
FICTION

IMAGE
OF THE BLACK
IN CHILDREN'S
FICTION

====

DOROTHY M. BRODERICK

====

R. R. Bowker Company

New York & London 1973
A Xerox Education Company

XEROX

813.009
B78i
83761
July 1973

Published by R.R. Bowker Co. (A Xerox Education Company)
1180 Avenue of the Americas, New York, N.Y. 10036
Copyright © 1973 by Dorothy M. Broderick
All rights reserved
Printed and bound in the United States of America

Library of Congress Cataloging in Publication Data

Broderick, Dorothy M
   Image of the Black in children's fiction.
   Based on the author's thesis, Columbia University, 1971.
   Bibliography: p.
   1. Children's stories—History and criticism.
2. Negroes in literature. I. Title.
PN1009.Z6B7   813'.009'352   72–1741
ISBN 0–8352–0550–9

CONTENTS

PREFACE

The *Image of the Black in Children's Fiction* is a historical, literary, and critical analysis of the portrait of the black that emerges from children's books published between 1827 and 1967. The early books studied were listed in Jacob Blanck's popular juvenile bibliography published by R. R. Bowker Company in 1938, *Peter Parley to Penrod: A Bibliographic Description of the Best-Loved American Juvenile Books, 1827–1926*. The later titles are from the 1909–1968 editions of the H. W. Wilson Company's *Children's Catalog*.

The doctoral dissertation on which this book is based was begun in the spring of 1968, defended in the summer of 1970, and accepted at Columbia University in February 1971. A lengthy inquiry occurred early in the research period as to whether Negro or black would be used in writing the dissertation. A famous historian said to me, "I was a Negro before these kids were born. I'm not about to become black." The question was asked of a number of other people, and a wide range of responses showed clearly that there was a generation gap as well as a political consciousness gap. I decided, finally, to use "black" as the designative noun because it represented the first time that black people had decided for themselves what they would be called. If the term loses favor at some future time and changes it will again be because black people wish it.

Although the cutoff date for books analyzed represents a time-lag and many improvements have been made in presenting black characters in children's books in the past half-dozen years, the overall image of the black in books published since 1827 to date would not differ very much from the image that emerges in this book. The study might have revealed improvement in the black images were it not for the erratic nature of the subject headings assigned to juvenile fiction in the *Children's Catalog*. For example, *The Egypt Game* by Zilpha Snyder (1967) and *Jennifer, Hecate,*

Macbeth, William McKinley, and Me, Elizabeth, by Elaine Konigsberg (1967) are not listed under the heading "Negroes—Fiction." The best of the picture books available at the cutoff date were not listed under any of the subject headings used for this study (i.e., "Negroes—Stories"; "Negroes —Fiction"; "Slavery—Stories"; "Slavery in the U.S.—Fiction"), so they, too, could not be included in the sample of books analyzed.

Too many of the children's books about blacks—both those books in the study sample and books published since the cutoff date—have "tolerance" as their "theme." Tolerance is a placid attitude, not to be confused with love, understanding and acceptance. "Be kind to your black-skinned friends" is the message being continually transmitted, and to this day there are too many well-intentioned adults who seem unable to recognize the condescension involved in such a message. The tolerance represented reeks of superior-inferior relationships. Thus we have the image of the "good master" of slavery days replaced with the image of the white "liberal do-gooder" of more recent times. If that charge seems too harsh, I ask the reader to return to it after reading the text and see if it does not then appear a quiet understatement.

There is little to be happy about in the following chapters. But the study is offered not to beat the dead horses of the past (would that racism were dead!) but to provide an analysis that may possibly help us to avoid repeating past mistakes. It is written by a white for other whites—those whites Malcolm X talks about at the end of his *Autobiography* when he says there is a place for whites to help—with each other.

Many friends and associates helped and encouraged me throughout this project. I acknowledge with special thanks the special strengths of Augusta Baker, Margaret Harris, Marjorie Jones, Elizabeth Miller, and Mary Woodworth. For Frances Henne, teacher, dissertation adviser, and friend, no words are adequate to express my appreciation. Madeline Miele, my editor at Bowker, provided many of the ideas that helped restructure the dissertation into what we both hope is a combination of sound research and readability. Marion Odomirok, freelance editor and friend, is responsible for much of the book's clarity. The point of view and opinions are mine.

DOROTHY M. BRODERICK

Dalhousie University
Halifax, Nova Scotia
March 1973

IMAGE
OF THE BLACK
IN CHILDREN'S
FICTION

1

INTRODUCTION

Many people in the United States became aware of the "Negro Problem" in the 1950s following the Supreme Court's famous school desegregation ruling. Yet historical research shows that black people—and some whites—have been raising their voices against the basic injustice of American society for centuries. The difference in public awareness can probably be attributed to the electronic revolution that has brought instant information to large numbers of people. In earlier protests the medium used was print, a medium that reaches only a small percentage of the population, even today.

The immediacy of the television screen served to radicalize both whites and blacks, and the Civil Rights movement gained momentum. It is a far different experience to read about lynchings than to see before your eyes the police dogs, fire hoses, and clubs used against demonstrators.

While most black protest recorded in such titles as *The Black Power Revolt* and *Black Protest* concerns social and political injustice, there have been literary critics who concerned themselves with the image of the black in literature. These critics recognized that literary images reflect the most acceptable ideas within a society, as opposed to the images presented in mass media and in pulp magazines, which are more popularly held, but less socially approved of.

Writing in *Dial* (1916), Benjamin Brawley observed that the Negro offered great opportunities for American writers. Brawley pondered what Victor Hugo might have done with such possibilities. Furthermore, Brawley stated that the Negro situation offered an "opportunity for tragedy, for comedy, for the subtle portrayal of all the relations of man with his fellow man." Yet, he noted, "with the Civil War fifty years in the distance, not one novel or one short story of first rank has found its inspiration in this great theme."[1]*

* All references will be found in the Notes section at the end of the book.

1

Brawley's article prompted one George Greever, a northern white living in Virginia, to write a letter to *Dial*'s editor. Greever's letter is representative of a point of view still found among unknown numbers of American citizens. After disclaiming any real knowledge of Negroes because he was deprived of contact with them in childhood, "those formative years when one's powers of observation are so keen and active," he states:

I have talked over the very question we are here discussing with Southern college men whose opportunities to know have been better than mine, and I am fain to acknowledge that they do not think as I do. The negro, most of them say, is light-hearted, irresponsible, careless; he lives in the present, like a child or a beast; he does not aim high or persist; he is fond of big words and gay colors; he wants to strut, to display himself, rather than to be; and therefore, seen against the background (or the foreground, if you will) of a civilization which he apes with fantastic imitation, he is a subject for comedy, not for tragedy. . . . The tragic hero has been through the ages a person of exalted qualities and usually of world eminence.[2]

In ignoring that a good many of the great European and American novels of the nineteenth century dealt with the tragic fate of the ordinary man, Greever showed that his literary knowledge was as defective as his knowledge of the black.

While such generalizations as Greever's may be expected in letters to the editor, it was disheartening to find so many of his distortions repeated by John H. Nelson in *The Negro Character in American Literature* (1926), the first full-length scholarly study on the subject. One of Nelson's points was that Europeans did not write about the Negro because they did not really know him. On the other hand:

Americans, through the sad and unfortunate institution of slavery, have perforce associated with him as have no other whites. From this association they have themselves received much—something, no doubt from his carefree, irresponsible temper, his irrepressible good humor and musical talent, his unconscious philosophy that the present moment is the all important moment; something, too, from the social and political agitation his mere presence has raised. Gradually he has affected American civilization; gradually, too, he has himself changed from an uncouth savage to the more sophisticated and genial individual of today; and gradually he has won favor as a literary subject.[3]

For white writers like Nelson the portrait of the black as found in the works of George M. Cable, Thomas Nelson Page, Joel Chandler Harris, and Thomas Dixon was a true re-creation of the essential nature of blacks. It wasn't until the appearance in 1933 of "Negro Character As Seen by White Authors" by Sterling A. Brown that these portraits were labeled for what they were and are: stereotypes.

After observing that "the Negro has met with as great injustice in American literature as he has in American life," Brown proceeded to categorize the major stereotypes, seven in number: "(1) The Contented Slave, (2) The Wretched Freeman, (3) The Comic Negro, (4) The Brute Negro, (5) The Tragic Mulatto, (6) The Local Color Negro, and (7) The Exotic Primitive."[4] Brown's analysis of the black image in this and other articles is the basis upon which most critics have worked in the following decades.

Whether the literary critics were viewing the black image as reflecting truth or as stereotyping, there was one point of agreement among them all: children's books were of no importance. Brown could label Thomas Nelson Page an "author of Ku Klux Klan fiction"[5] without mentioning *Two Little Confederates*, which is still bringing Page's message to the young long after adults have ceased to read his books.

In *The Negro in American Fiction* (1937), Brown did include one paragraph concerning children's books in which he pointed out that "Negro children have generally been written of in the same terms as their mothers and fathers, as quaint, living jokes, designed to make white children laugh." He observed further that there was some small trend toward writing about black children with "sincere and informed sympathy," and cited five books that reflected this trend: *Araminta* (1935), *Jerome Anthony* (1936), *Popo and Fifina* (1932), *You Can't Pet a Possum* (1936) and *Sad-Faced Boy* (1937).[6]

The sincere and informed sympathy of which Brown speaks was to be replaced after 1945 with a distortion that was in many ways as bad as the earlier stereotypes. This distortion took the form of imposing white middle-class values upon black people and teaching the doctrine of "we are all alike" to the white readers for whom the books were obviously intended.

So pervasive and insidious was this doctrine that when David Gast undertook his doctoral dissertation, "Characteristics and Concepts of Minority Americans in Contemporary Children's Fictional Literature," he found joy in concluding:

Recent children's literature generally contains complimentary stereotypes of present-day American Indians, Chinese, Japanese, Negroes, and Spanish-Americans. Middle-class Anglo-American virtues make up the new stereotypes imputed to these minorities by the authors of the literature. Traditional non-complimentary stereotypes have largely disappeared from the literature. The image of the Negro in children's fiction represents an almost exact reversal of traditional Negro stereotypes with one exception—Negroes are musical.[7]

Gast never questioned whether "middle-class Anglo-American virtues" were an improvement; he never asked whether positive stereotypes are that much better than negative stereotypes. Inherent in his study is the attitude described by Vine Deloria, Jr. in *We Talk, You Listen:*

A generation ago white children were taught to look directly at black people and pretend that they didn't realize that they were black. Viewing such behavior today with our experience of the civil rights movement behind us, it appears to be the most unsophisticated and racist behavior imaginable. But *at the time* it was a sincere effort by an ignorant white populace who were truly concerned about equality to express equality by pretending that differences did not exist.[8]

One of the questions often discussed in literary circles is whether it would be possible to write a book about a black without identifying him as such. The answer is a resounding, NO. In considering this question Morris Beja has said, in "It Must Be Important: Negroes in Contemporary American Fiction," that "to ignore their racial plight is to deny the quality of their existence, to commit the one unpardonable sin."[9]

The truth of Deloria and Beja's point is shown clearly in Jesse Jackson's *Call Me Charley.* Tom Hamilton, the major white character, is depicted as totally oblivious to Charley's race. By seeing Charles as just another boy, Tom is not only of no help to Charley, he actually increases the problems Charley faces as the only black boy in the school and neighborhood. Toward the end of the book, Tom's parents deliver him a stern lecture on his responsibility as a white to speak out and stand up for Charley, since the way things are, speaking out and standing up by the black himself will have no impact upon racially discriminating whites.

Thus Jackson presents us with a vivid picture of the schizophrenic dilemma of the do-gooder white and the dependent black. Teaching children to be color blind may seem a good idea, but as long as being black is the single most important fact of a black man's life, then the real harm that comes from pretending we are all alike far outweighs whatever good can be attributed to this romantic wishful thinking.

The two assumptions underlying Gast's study—that middle-class-Anglo stereotyping was good and that we are all alike—and the limited size of his sample—sixteen books about blacks—contributed to the decision to undertake a full-length, historical study. The major question involved in the undertaking concerned which books to study.

While interesting, there seemed little to be gained in hunting up such statements as the following from the original edition of Laura Lee Hope's *Bobbsey Twins:*

Flossie's dolls were five in number. Dorothy was her pride, and had light hair and blue eyes, and three dresses, one of real lace. The next was Gertrude, a short doll with black eyes and hair and a traveling dress that was very cute. Then came Lucy, who had lost one arm, and Polly, who had lost both an arm and a leg. The fifth doll was Jujube, a colored boy, dressed in a fiery suit of red, with a blue cap and real rubber boots. This doll had come from Sam and Dinah and had been much admired at first, but was now taken out only when all the others went too.

"He doesn't really belong to the family, you know," Flossie would explain to her friends. "But I have to keep him, for mamma says there is no colored orphan asylum for dolls. Besides, I don't think Sam and Dinah would like to see their doll child in an asylum." The dolls were all kept in a row in a big bureau drawer at the top of the house, but Flossie always took pains to separate Jujube from the rest by placing the cover of a pasteboard box between them.[10]

Authors, editors, and librarians could always dismiss such an example on the grounds that they were no party to the mass-produced series titles. It seemed essential, therefore, to have a sample that carried both implied and expressed establishment approval.

Since its inception in 1909 the *Children's Catalog* has been an accepted tool for purchasers of library books, and the books it recommended between 1909 and 1968 were selected to study the black image in children's literature. During this period the *Catalog* listed forty-nine books that were considered valid for the study. (Major exclusions were books set in non-African foreign countries and *Uncle Tom's Cabin*, the latter on the grounds that it has been analyzed ad infinitum by critics of adult literature and by historians.)

The historical perspective for the study was obtained from the books

brarians, social workers—will tend overwhelmingly to be white. Not only do these people have authority over the black child, but the child learns early that his or her father and mother lose much of their strength when confronted with white authority.

In any of the books there is in fact only one occasion of an adult black speaking forcibly to an adult white. The incident occurs in *Roosevelt Grady* by Louisa Shotwell. Roosevelt is sick and Mrs. Grady takes him to the doctor, a "pink-cheeked and yellow-haired" young man. The doctor prescribes orange juice and fresh milk, and instructs them to scald the dishes, silver, and glass that Roosevelt uses. The pills are to be given at set intervals.

Then the doctor notices Matthew's clubfoot and asks why they hadn't had it taken care of? "I might be able to help it some even now, if you'll let me keep him in the hospital three months," says the doctor.

So far Mamma hadn't said much. Not anything, really. Just nodded Yes to everything Doctor Bates said. But now she looked fixing to make a speech. And she did.

"Doctor Bates," she said, "I think I'd best tell you something. We follow the crops for a living. Right now we're living in one room, all six of us. We got no clock to measure taking medicine by. We got no icebox. What we eat with, it isn't silver, it's tin, but we keep it clean. We fetch our water from a community spigot and I heat it on an oil stove.

"About Matthew's foot, his papa and I, we never knew it might be fixed. Even if we had the money to pay to leave him in a hospital, the Lord alone knows where we'll be in three months time, and He may be in some doubt Himself. Folks got to do what they can with what they got and that's what we do."[14]

Mrs. Grady is simply "telling it like it is." Had more authors depicted similar reactions on the part of black people, the result of the study would have been very different.

As it is, what the white readers primarily learned from these particular books is that blacks are lower creatures and in need of the superior white's care, so whites should be nice to black people and treat them with kindness—in much the same humanitarian way that people are expected to treat dogs and cats with kindness. That this type of thinking did not contribute to the improvement of race relations in the United States hardly needs restating.

Since the whole race-relation problem began with the introduction of black slaves into the colonies of the New World, we will begin by looking at what authors told children about the institution of slavery. From there, we will look at the major roles assigned to blacks, followed by a look at the personal characteristics attributed to blacks.

2

SLAVERY

Black poet and playwright Imamu Amiri Baraka (LeRoi Jones) pointed out the unique feature of slavery as practiced in the United States:

An African who was enslaved by Africans, or for that matter, a Western white man who was, or is enslaved by another Western white man can still function as a kind of human being. An economic cipher perhaps, even subject to unmentionable cruelties—but that man, even as the lowest and most despised member of the community, remains an essential part and member of whatever community he is enslaved in. . . . To the Romans, slaves were merely vulgar and conquered peoples who had not the rights of Roman citizenship. The Greeks thought of their slaves as unfortunate people who had failed to cultivate their minds and wills, and were thus reduced to that lowly but necessary state. But these slaves were still human beings. However, the African who was unfortunate enough to find himself on some fast clipper ship to the New World was not even accorded membership in the human race.[1]

The need to make the slaves less than human had its basis in Christianity, for accepting the slaves as human beings with souls, created by the same God the white man worshiped, would be against Christian ethics. Only if the slaves were not real people could the good Christian profess that God had intended slavery as part of his scheme for the world.

Yet there was much to be said for teaching the black the tenets of Christianity. For slave owners the idea of a heaven where all were rewarded, regardless of earthly status, was a very useful one. What the slaves could not—should not—hope to achieve on earth they could have in an afterlife. The theme is prevalent throughout many of the Negro spirituals. On the other hand, the decision to teach the slave the Christian religion did constitute an admission on the part of the owner that the slave was, indeed, a person, not merely property.

11

MORAL VIEWS ON SLAVERY

In order to dehumanize the slave within the tenets of Christianity, two basic moral defenses of the institution evolved. One method of defending slavery was to ignore the basic institution of slavery and personalize the problem as simply one of good masters versus bad masters. The premise presented was that the slave with a good master was happy and the slave with a bad master was miserable. People believed that kind treatment, not freedom, was the issue.

This view emerged early and is found in the first-published book in the overall sample, Goodrich's *Tales of Peter Parley About America* (1827). The book is simply written in short paragraphs, and its purpose was to give the youthful reader an overview of life in the United States as seen by the traveler Jenkins. In Charleston, South Carolina, Jenkins encountered his first blacks:

These negroes are slaves, and labour for the white people, to whom they belong. Jenkins saw negroes, men, women, and children sold at public auction, as we sell goods.

Some of the negroes, who happen to have kind masters, are very happy; but those who have cruel masters are wretched indeed.[2]

According to Louise-Clarke Pyrnelle, good masters and happy slaves had a grand time together. In the preface to *Diddie, Dumps, and Tot* (1882), Pyrnelle makes numerous disclaimers about what her book is not, ending with:

Nor does my little book pretend to be any defence of slavery. I know not whether it was right or wrong (there being many pros and cons on the subject): but it was the law of the land, made by statesmen from the North as well as the South, long before my day, or my father's or grandfather's day; and, born under that law a slave-holder, and the descendant of slave holders, raised in the heart of the cotton section, surrounded by negroes from my earliest infancy, "I KNOW whereof I do speak"; and it is to tell of the pleasant and happy relations that existed between master and slave that I write this story of *Diddie, Dumps, and Tot*.[3]

Despite the disingenuous denial, the author did have a view about slavery, and it reflected the second moral defense of the institution by proclaiming that slavery was not only morally right, but a natural condition. Pyrnelle's exposition of this view takes the form of a creation myth as told to the white children, Diddie, Dumps, and Tot, by an elderly slave. The children have been nodding, instead of listening, and the old man uses their nodding as the excuse to tell a story:

"Oh, yes!" said the old man, "yer may nod; dat's des wat's de matter wid de niggers now, dem sleepy-head ways wat dey got is de cazhun uv dey hyar bein' kunkt up an' dey skins bein' black."

"Is that what makes it, Daddy?" asked Diddie, much interested.

"Ub cose hit is," replied Daddy. "Ef'n de nigger hadn't ben so sleepy-headed, he'd er ben white, an' his hyar'd er ben straight des like yourn. Yer see, atter de Lord make 'im, den he lont him up 'gins de fence-corner in de sun fur ter dry; an' no sooner wuz de Lord's back turnt, an' de sun 'gun ter come out kin'er hot, dan de nigger he 'gun ter nod, an' er little mo'n he wuz fas' ter sleep. Well, wen de Lord sont atter 'im fur ter finish uv 'im up, de angel couldn't fin' 'im, case he didn't know de zack spot whar de Lord sot 'im; an' so he hollered an' called, an' de nigger he wuz 'sleep, an' he nuber hyeard 'im; so de angel tuck de white man, an' cyard him 'long, an' de Lord polished uv 'im off. Well, by'mby de nigger he waked up; but, dar now! he wuz bu'nt black, an' his hyar wuz all swuv'llt up right kinky.

"De Lord, seeing, he wuz spilte, he didn't 'low fur ter finish 'im, an' wuz des 'bout'n ter thow 'im 'way, wen de white man axt fur 'im; so de Lord he finished 'im up des like he wuz, wid his skin black an' his hyar kunkt up, an' he gun 'im ter de white man, an' I see he's got 'im plum tell yit."[4]

The story makes clear that the black man was lazy from the moment of his creation; it was this laziness that deprived him of the gifts God planned to give him and opened the door for the white man to claim him. Since the story says explicitly that God gave the black man to the white man, inherent in the tale is the idea that the blacks can never be the equal of the whites and that God deems this to be right. The black man has been spoiled for all time, and finished though he may be, it is an incomplete and inferior finish when compared to that of the white man.

That God intended slavery is also expressed by Mr. Fergus, a character in *Brady* (1960), in a statement that combines the "good master" theme with the "right and natural" position. Mr. Fergus has been sent by a segment of the church congregation to tell the minister, Mr. Minton, that his antislavery sermon is unacceptable to them and that they no longer wish to hold services with him as their minister. Mr. Fergus sums up his attitude:

"The Hebrews themselves had slaves, Thaddeus. I grant that there may be some abuse of slavery which is, indeed, an evil. But the cure for poor treatment is better treatment. Not freedom. Why, a slave doesn't have the capacity to use freedom, Thaddeus. It would be no kindness to give it to him."[5]

While the total impact of *Brady* makes it clear that Mr. Fergus' view is not that of the author, Jean Fritz, the same cannot be said of the attitude attributed to Mrs. Carroll, the slave owner, in Louis Pendleton's *King Tom and the Runaways* (1890):

She was one of the old type of Southerners who religiously believed in slavery as just and lawful, transmitted to us from the Biblical patriarchs themselves; the modern idea that the institution was harmful to the master as well as brutalizing to the slave she would have regarded as the height of absurdity.[6]

That this view, or something closely akin to it, represented Pendleton's own ideas on the subject is made clear as the book progresses. Pendleton's major black character, Jim, is shown willing to accept slavery if he can have the woman he loves, and Pendleton depicts Jim's lifestyle at the end of the war as changed only in the sense that Jim works for wages.

A scene in Amelia Barr's *The Bow of Orange Ribbon* (1886) shows how two characters can invoke religion to support opposing views. The occasion is a party attended by Alexander Semple, a Scotsman living in New York City in pre-Revolutionary days, and Batavius, a ship's captain. Batavius is home from the sea, obviously having been engaged in the slave trade, and tells Semple that "every cargo was a good cargo." Semple replies:

"I'll no be certain o' that, captain. I would hae some scruples mysel' anent buying and selling men and women o' any color. We hae no quotations from the other world, and it may be the Almighty holds his black men at as high a figure as his white men. I'm just speculating, you ken. I hae a son—my third son, Alexander Semple o' Boston—what makes money on the Africans. I hae told him, likewise, that trading in wheat and trading in humanity may hae ethical differences; but every one settles his ain bill, and I'll hae enough to do to secure mysel'."

Batavius was puzzled; and at the words "ethical differences," his big brown hand was "in the hair" at once. He scratched his head and looked doubtfully at Semple, whose face was peculiarly placid and thoughtful and kindly.

"Men must work, elder, and these blacks won't work unless they are forced to. I, who am a baptized Christian, have to do my duty in this life; and, as for pagans, they must be made to do it. I am myself a great lover of morality, and that is what I think. Also, you may read in the Scriptures, that St. Paul says that if a man will not work, neither shall he eat."

"St. Paul doubtless kent a' about the question of forced labor, seeing that he lived when baith white and black men were sold for a price."[7]

For men like Batavius, the subtleties of Semple's argument have no meaning. Morality consists of a rigid code that excludes those who differ from white, Western Christian civilization's value system. The idea that blacks were functioning human beings in their native lands, that they raised families, loved them, supported them, and that they worshiped their own gods is of no consequence to Batavius.

Semple, on the other hand, can hardly be said to have made a strong antislavery statement. His concept of morality as each man securing to himself a place in heaven has something of "the devil take the hindmost" flavor to it.

Inherent in the use of religious arguments as reasons for or against a social institution is the age-old problem of what, if any, dividing line separates a person's religious belief from his or her daily practices. For Thaddeus Minton, the aforementioned minister in *Brady*, the conflict within himself reaches the point where he must take a public stand. In the sermon he preached against slavery that causes part of the congregation to rebel, Minton stressed the sin of slavery:

You had to move slowly to keep one part of the country from being too badly hurt, but the point was, you had to move. There was no getting away from it, Minton said that slavery was a sin. He said that God had not created all white men equal; He had created *all* men equal.[8]

Minton's view, that slavery is a sin, but not so much a sin as to make it necessary for those indulging in the practice to suffer economic discomfort, is a reflection of a neat division between man's duty to God and his duty to himself as an economic being.

In all the books studied the one character with the greatest conscience conflict over slavery is not a minister or a deeply religious person—in the sense of attending church and preaching platitudes—is Huck Finn. *The Adventures of Huckleberry Finn* (1885) has at its very foundation the question of slavery. With Mark Twain the question goes beyond the problem of blacks enslaved, however; for he is concerned with the right of every person to freedom, whether it is Huck's right to avoid being civilized or Jim's right to keep himself from being sold down the river.

There are two major moments in Huck's life when he is forced to examine his conscience concerning slavery. The first occurs early in the book when Jim and Huck think they have reached Illinois, the land of freedom. Huck feels "all over trembly and feverish" when he realizes that he has helped a slave run away. He tries to pretend it hadn't been his fault, but in the end he has to acknowledge that he could have turned Jim in and didn't.

Huck's dilemma is not solved easily. As the climax of the book is reached, he is still agonizing over turning Jim in. He tries to pray:

I was trying to make my mouth *say* I would do the right thing and the clean thing, and go and write to that nigger's owner and tell where he was; but deep down in me I knowed it was a lie, and He knowed it. You can't pray a lie—I found that out.[9]

He decides to write to Jim's owner, Miss Watson, and see if after having written the letter, he will feel good enough to be able to pray. There follows one of those passages that distinguish the best of Twain's writing. It is filled with the bittersweet of life: the sarcasm that seems to ask, How dare the world make such a simple principle a matter of such agony?

I felt good and all washed clean of sin for the first time I had ever felt so in my life, and I knowed I could pray now. But I didn't do it straight off, but laid the paper down and set there thinking—thinking how good it was all this happened so, and how near I come to being lost and going to hell. And went on thinking. And got to thinking over our trip down the river; and I see Jim before me all the time; in the day and in the nighttime, sometimes moonlight, sometimes storms, and we a'floating along, talking and singing and laughing. But somehow I couldn't seem to strike no places to harden me against him, but only the other kind. I'd see him standing my watch on top of his'n, 'stead of calling me, so I could go on sleeping; and see how glad he was when I come back out of the fog; and when I come to him again in the swamp, up there where the feud was; and such-like times; and would always call me honey, and pet me, and how good he always was; and at last I struck the time I saved him telling the men we had smallpox aboard, and he was so grateful, and said I was the best friend old Jim ever had in the world, and the *only* one he's got now; and then I happened to look around and see that paper.

It was a close place. I took it up, and held it in my hand. I was a-trembling, because I'd got to decide, forever, betwixt two things, and I knowed it. I studied a minute, sort of holding my breath, and then says to myself;

"All right, then, I'll go to hell"—and tore it up.[10]

Other authors have settled for having a character give his life for a friend; but Twain's genius goes one better: the idea of giving up one's life pales as a sacrifice before the idea of giving up eternity for a friend. Best of all, the idea that God was so strong a supporter of slavery as to damn an individual who opposed the institution is made to look ridiculous.

The most succinct and unequivocal statement against slavery comes from Granny in *Shuttered Windows* (1938). (See Figure 1.) The young heroine, Harriet, is talking with her great-grandmother about their famous ancestor Black Moses. Granny has just told Harriet that "Ol' Ma'r beat e's darkies efn dey learn readin' an' writin'." Harriet responds by noting that "they keep telling us that most masters were kind." Granny says:

"Mebbe mos' of 'im was," Granny agreed, stroking Lily's head against her shoulder. "Plenty was, I knows fo' a fac'. De kind ones was kind and de bad ones was bad. But dey ain' no human, honey child, got de right to own no odder human. Case men and women is men and women in de eyes of de good Lord."[11]

AMORAL ARGUMENTS

Next to recruiting God to one's side, the best way to avoid the moral dilemma presented by slavery was to dehumanize the institution itself by talking about it as though there were no people involved in the discussion. The tone of such arguments usually centered around states' rights or the financial investment of the owners.

As with polemic writing of any era, the debate technique in which one character feeds lines to another was utilized by Susan Warner in her discussion of slavery in *Queechy* (1852). The occasion is a discussion between Fleda, the book's heroine, and a visiting Englishman, Mr. Stackpole. Early in the discussion, Stackpole points out to Fleda that England had abolished slavery, to which she replies that one cannot compare England with

Figure 1. The strength of Granny's character and a long hard life are reflected in her face. From *Shuttered Windows*, by Florence Crannell Means; illustrated by Armstrong Sperry. Copyright © 1938 by Florence Crannell Means. Reprinted by permission of Houghton Mifflin Co.

America because the English have a form of government that allows it to take such actions. America, however, must depend upon the separate states to provide remedies.

When Stackpole wants to know why the states have not acted, Fleda first informs him that the states cannot act without the consent of their citizens. Further pressed by Stackpole to explain why the citizens of the individual states have not given their consent, Fleda relies on the financial-investment explanation. She argues that for nonslave owners to vote for freeing the slaves is not really an act of generosity on their part, since it would be at the expense of others—that is, the slave owners.[12]

Not once during this entire debate does either Stackpole or Fleda refer to the human beings who are the enslaved. That Fleda is presented throughout the book as a prototype of what a good Christian should be reveals that the author did not consider social or political problems to be matters that entered into one's relationship with God.

Another example of the financial-investment attitude is found in John Townsend Trowbridge's *Cudjo's Cave* (1864). Trowbridge has one of the most narrow-minded characters, Deslow, tell the handsome, well-educated runaway slave, Pomp, that Pomp's condition is "very different from that of any white man. Your relation to your master is not that of a man to his neighbor, or of a citizen to the government; it is that of property to its owner."

Deslow is well pleased with his statement, but Pomp leaps upon it and proceeds to destroy its logic:

"I will admit your title to a lot of land you may purchase, or reclaim from nature; or to an animal you have captured, or bought, or raised. But a man's natural, original owner is—himself. Now, I never sold myself. My father never sold himself. My father was stolen by pirates on the coast of Africa and brought to this country, and sold. The man who bought him bought what had been stolen. By your own laws you cannot hold stolen property. Though it is bought and sold a thousand times, let the original owner appear, and it is his—nobody else has the shadow of a claim. My father was stolen property, if he was property at all. He was his own rightful owner. Though he had been robbed of himself, that made no difference with the justice of the case. It was so with my mother. It is so with me. It is the same with every black man on this continent. Not one ever sold himself, or can be sold, or can be owned. For to say that what a man steals or takes by force is his, to dispose of as he chooses, is to go back to barbarism; it is not the law of any Christian land. So much," added

Pomp, blowing the words from him, as if all the false arguments in favor of slavery were no more to the man's soul, to its eternal, God-given rights, than the breath he blew contemptuously forth into the mountain woods—"so much for the claim of PROPERTY!"[13]

Pomp's argument is a masterpiece of logic; but it is logical only if one accepts the idea that blacks are human beings created by the white man's God, entitled to live their own lives and determine their own destinies. It assumes that the blacks must be a party to whatever happens to them, an assumption proslavery advocates were not willing to grant.

ABOLITIONISTS

Abolitionists were unpopular people long before the fury of John Brown caused fear in the minds of many persons, both northerners and southerners. As Dale Van Every pointed out in *The Disinherited: The Lost Birthright of the American Indian*:

The north was fully as devoted to the principle of the inviolability of private property as was the south. That still rare figure, the abolitionist, was in the 1830s still universally regarded as an unAmerican anarch to be invariably and justly victimized by street mobs.[14]

Jean Fritz, in *Brady*, makes this point clear to her readers by the inclusion of an abolitionist named Moses Lowe. The reader first hears of Lowe early in the book when it is reported that Lowe had been attacked with eggs by a group of citizens in Washington, Pennsylvania, a town not far from the Minton farm in Mann, Pennsylvania. The egg throwing was occasioned by Lowe's preaching "that all slaves should be freed immediately, bloodshed or no bloodshed."[15]

The time of the Fritz book is 1838—a brief period before the beginning of William Dean Howells' *Boy's Town* (1890), in which Howells recounts his boyhood in a small southern Ohio town during the 1840s and early 1850s. Howells' book shows the evolution of a young boy's attitudes toward slavery. Early in the story Howells mentions that the boy had a grandfather who:

brought shame to his grandson's soul by being an abolitionist in days when it was infamy to wish the slaves free. My boy's father restored his self-respect in a measure by being a Henry Clay Whig, or a constitutional anti-slavery man.[16]

The town in which Howells was growing up was more in sympathy with slavery and the southern cause than it was with northern attitudes. As Howells observes, the war with Mexico was approved of by most of the townspeople:

It was already the time of the Mexican war, when that part of the West at least was crazed with a dream of the conquest which was to carry slavery wherever the flag of freedom went. . . .
His grandfather, as an abolitionist, and his father, as a Henry Clay Whig, had both been opposed to the annexation of Texas.[17]

In 1848 the Whigs nominated Zachary Taylor as their presidential candidate. Taylor had gained nationwide attention during the Mexican war, and his nomination precipitated a change of allegiance not only for "my boy's" family but for many Americans. Howells describes the political transition:

He remained an ardent Whig until his eleventh year, when his father left the party because the Whigs nominated, as their candidate for president, General Taylor, who had won his distinction in the Mexican war, and was believed to be a friend of slavery, though afterwards he turned out otherwise.[18]

This was the beginning of a realignment of political parties in the United States. Men were leaving the Whig and Democratic parties, eventually to form the Republican party. Howells describes the situation, again through the eyes of the child hero:

Among these politicians the Whigs were sacred in my boy's eyes, but the Democrats appeared like enemies of the human race; and one of the strangest things that ever happened to him was to find his father associating with men who came out of the Democratic party at the same time he left the Whig party, and joining with them in a common cause against both. But when he understood what a good cause it was, and came to sing songs against slavery, he was reconciled.[19]

Thus, Howells traced the history of political and racial thought during a very crucial period in the United States. He begins by being ashamed of his abolitionist grandfather and ends up a budding member of the Republican party and an antislavery crusader. It is questionable, however, given the

captain, "Take us home, take us to our own country, take us to our own houses, take us to our own pickaninnies and our own women."[27]

The scene is obviously designed to show how hard it is on Nolan to see men happy at the prospect of returning to their native lands while he can never return to his. Nevertheless, the scene gives the reader a small view of the conditions under which the African traveled to the United States as well as demonstrates the evils of a system that would deprive home-loving men of their families and native land.

3

PORTRAIT
OF THE HAPPY SLAVE

When the slave ships arrived in the United States the Africans aboard soon found themselves enmeshed in an ever-growing, complex organization referred to as "the peculiar institution." Uprooted from their native land, having survived a sea trip under the most inhuman conditions, the Africans then found themselves subjected to the horrors of the auction block. Not surprisingly, that initial introduction to the United States is completely missing in children's books. The authors stress that the slaves they are writing about were born on the plantations on which they are found.

As slavery developed from a casual operation into the big business it became, southern state legislatures passed "Slave Codes" that spelled out in detail what a slave could and could not do. A few of the numerous laws governing slaves will be mentioned here to show the range of behavior controlled by the state.

The slaves could not go at large, even in the vicinity of their own plantations without carrying a signed pass to show to any white man demanding to see it. Legally, slaves could not learn to read or write, be employed in setting type, or be given books and pamphlets. The slaves could not possess guns or liquor. And even if a slave were the only witness to a crime, he or she could not testify against a white person.

The master had total control in two very important areas of the slaves' life, their physical well-being and their family life. Physically, the master could beat, mutilate, or even kill a slave without interference or fear of punishment. The owner's self-interest dictated that punishment stop short of death, for each slave represented a financial investment for the owner that he did not willy-nilly throw away. The Simon Legrees of the world were viewed by other masters, if not as sadists, certainly as fools.[1]

The structure of slave family life was also under the control of the master. He could separate families on the auction block, or he could, if he wished, for his own amusement plan a gala "wedding" for a pet slave, as depicted in the marriage of Mo and Lindy in *Melindy's Medal* (1945).

Mo and Lindy were the present Melindy's great-grandparents and the story of their marriage is obviously a matter of family pride. Mo was born on a Virginian plantation owned by Mr. Bingham and was in charge of the estate's horses. Lindy was personal slave to the plantation's young mistress, Miss Lucy. As Miss Lucy's personal slave, Lindy was accorded all the privileges of the household. Lindy slept in Miss Lucy's bedroom, took French lessons, sewed, and went riding with Miss Lucy. In her specially ordered riding outfit, Lindy overwhelmed Mo, who fell in love with her immediately.

Eventually, Mo proposed to Lindy, and after some hesitation on Miss Lucy's part, the marriage was approved.

Miss Lucy fixed up this little cottage for Lindy and your great-grandfather Mo, and Miss Lucy sent away and got a special dress made for Lindy's wedding. . . .

Lindy and your great-grandfather Mo were married in Miss Lucy's own little church, and they went to live in their own cottage and everybody was very happy for two hundred and three days.[2]

At which point, Mr. Bingham died. His estate was found to be heavily in debt, and the executor told Miss Lucy that she could keep Lindy as her personal property, but Mo must be sold. Miss Lucy was horrified. After unsuccessfully pleading with the executor to keep both Mo and Lindy, she arranged for them to flee, and eventually they reached Canada safely.

The story is a good example of the tenuous nature of slave marriages since, as Stampp wrote in *The Peculiar Institution*, while marriage between whites was a legal civil contract, "slave marriages had no such recognition in state codes; instead they were regulated by whatever laws the owner saw fit to enforce."[3] However, the owner's power did have one serious limitation, also reflected in the story. Since slaves were property, if his debtors pressed him, or if he died in debt, the law could break up marriages on the auction block, regardless of the owner's wishes.

Could any person trapped in such a system be happy? If we are to believe the authors of children's books, the answer is a resounding yes.

THE HAPPY SLAVES

The fundamental characteristic of happy slaves was that they were more than resigned to their position; they accepted it without complaint, with good grace, and with enthusiasm. What kind of persons were happy slaves? They were dumb, but loyal, grateful to their masters for providing for them, and proud to belong to a man of quality. We will see more than one example of these happy creatures in our group of books.

McMeekin's *Journey Cake* (1942) offers a prototype of the dumb, but faithful slave in the person of Eli, who "was a good man. Not quick in the head, but with a strong right arm and a faithful heart, a fine slave for Master Gordon to own and a rightful husband for her [Juba] to have."[4]

Master Gordon Shadrow has gone to Kentucky to make a new home for his family, but while he is away, his wife dies. Eli's wife Juba, "a free woman of color," plans to take the family to their father in Kentucky. This does not meet with the approval of the local justice of the peace who is in charge of the Shadrow affairs in the absence of a white adult. The justice discovers the plan to leave because Eli finds keeping the secret too much for him.[5]

Throughout the book, Eli is described by such phrases as: "slow and dull and kind";[6] "He was faithful and kind, but always it was his wife who made plans and told him what to do";[7] and "Eli's slow brain."[8]

On the trail to Kentucky it is Eli's job to make the fire, and when Dulcy, one of the Shadrow children, complains about the smoke from the fire getting in her eyes, a scout they have met says, "That's cause that man of yourn likely ain't got sense enough to test whichaway the wind she blows before he sets first spark."[9]

Eli's status is equal to that of the dog, Winks. For example, on the trail Juba feeds the children, feeds herself, and only then "she fed Eli and tossed the scraps to Winks."[10]

As if the constant repetition of Eli's dumbness were not enough, throughout the book he is not given one single line of dialogue.

If not dumb, Old Balla in *Two Little Confederates* (1888), is depicted as a gullible fool in the first lengthy scene in which he appears. The theft of food from the plantation has become a real problem as the Civil War progresses; everyone is conscious of the situation. Frank and Willy, "the two little confederates," are awakened one evening by the dogs. They arm themselves with a loaded musket before heading for the hen house. There they lock up a man, despite his attempt to talk them out of it. Frank goes to get Uncle Balla while Willy stands guard.

Balla assures the boys that the man is safely locked inside for the night. Willy asks:

> "Hadn't you better take the hens out?"
> "Nor 'tain' no use to tech nuttin' out dyah. Ef he comes to, he know we got 'im, an' he dyahson trouble nuttin'."[11]

Balla brags about the security measures he has taken. The upshot, of course, is that the next morning the man is gone, so are the hens, and Balla is shown to have been simple-minded.

Loyalty to the master is depicted in a number of ways. The most shocking example of loyalty is Jim, a slave in *Diddie, Dumps, and Tot*, who is miserable over being led a merry chase by Candace, the woman he wants to marry. He is seen sitting by the creek talking to himself:

> ". . . an' ef'n I didn't b'long ter nobody, I'd jump right inter dis creek an' drown myse'f. But I ain't got no right ter be killin' up marster's niggers that way! I'm wuff er thousan' dollars, an' marster ain't got no thousan' dollars ter was'e in dis creek, long er day lazy, shif'less, good fur-nuffin' yaller nigger."[12]

Perhaps there were slaves whose self-pride was based on their financial worth to the master, but if so, that stands only as another indictment of a system that forced people to think in such terms. One does not have to approve of suicide in order to see that the reasons offered for Jim's behavior are ludicrous and vicious.

A more traditional form of loyalty is seen in *The Young Marooners on the Florida Coast* (1852) when the slave, Sam, is entrusted to go in search of the white children who have been dragged out to sea by a devilfish. The children have been living a Robinson Crusoe existence on an island when, after a hurricane, they find Sam lying badly hurt on the sand bar in the bay. Sam has a broken arm and a broken leg, and the opportunity is taken to deliver a lecture on how one sets broken limbs. The children take good care of Sam, who responds by an outpouring of gratefulness:

> "Tankee, Mas Robert! Tankee, Mas Harold! Tankee my dear little misses! Tankee, Mas Frank too! Tankee, ebbery body! I sure I bin die on dat sandbank, 'sept you all bin so kind to de poor nigger."

"No more of that, Sam," said Robert, "you were hurt in trying to help us; it is but right we should help you."[13]

Whether the children would have felt it right to take care of Sam had he been hurt in other circumstances is one of those nagging questions such comments raise but do not answer.

When Sam is feeling better, the children ask him to tell them what has been happening at home since they were dragged out to sea. As Sam begins his story, the author provides an interjection: "(For the sake of the reader who may not be familiar with the lingo of southern and sea-coast negroes, the narrative will be given in somewhat better English, retaining, however, the peculiarities of thought and drapery.)"[14]

Sam describes the scene as he and his brother William are about to set off in the boat in search of the children:

"Neither I or William could say one word. We took hold of master's hands, knelt down, and kissed them. And, somehow, I saw his hand was very wet; we could not help it, for we love him the same as if he was our father, and the tears would come."[15]

Another happy slave, Aunt Chloe, in *Elsie Dinsmore* (1867), possesses the kind of loyalty one associates with the "mother hen" syndrome. She is fiercely protective of her mistress, Elsie, and her solicitousness is such that, except for her religious commitment, she is seen as existing solely to care for Elsie.[16]

Just how much of the slave's loyalty to his or her master was based upon the relationship of master and slave and how much was inspired by the fear of Yankees is a matter of conjecture, but three authors raised the spectre of Yankee influence in a denigrating way. Another Aunt Chloe, this time in *The Story of a Bad Boy* (1870) by Thomas Bailey Aldrich, is reported by her young charge, Tom, as telling him:

"Dar wasn't no gentl'men in the Norf no way," and on one occasion terrified me beyond measure by declaring that, "if any of dem mean whites tried to get her away from marster, she was jes' gwine to knock 'em on de head wid a gourd!"[17]

A similar response is found in *The Two Little Confederates* when the mistress of the plantation is telling the slaves they can leave. Lucy Ann says, "I know I ain't gwine nowhar wid no Yankees or nothin'," and one of the other female slaves responds, "Dee tell me dee got hoofs and horns."[18]

The same scene evokes from Old Balla:

"Whar I got to go? I wuz born on dis place an' I 'spec to die here, an' be buried right yonder," and he turned and pointed up to the dark clump of trees that marked the graveyard on the hill, a half mile away, where the colored people were buried.[19]

This verbal loyalty is all the more meaningful, since the reader knows that Balla's wife has been freed and is living in Philadelphia.

Another kind of slave loyalty is expressed in *The Bow of Orange Ribbon* when black Dinorah is serving dinner while a private family discussion is occurring. The author comments upon the propriety of the situation by observing that "the slaves Joris owned, like those of Abraham, were born or brought up in his own household: they held to all the family feeling with a faithful, often unreasonable, tenacity."[20]

All the above scenes contain an assumption of loyalty that is never questioned: good slaves were loyal, period. Only once does the master actually verbalize the assumption of loyalty, and that occurs in *Chariot in the Sky* (1951) when Caleb's master is about to join the Confederate army. He tells Caleb, "We've got to leave our families and our property in the hands of our slaves. And you—you've got to stand by us in our trouble, Caleb."[21] That it might be asking too much to have the slave remain loyal to the master who is fighting the army that would free the slave never occurs to Mr. Coleman.

It would be unrealistic to argue that there were not indeed some happy slaves. The question that arises is how did these human beings come to accept slavery? How were the slaves indoctrinated to see themselves solely in relation to their masters? Some subtle and less-than subtle scenes appear in childrens' literature.

The most fully developed portrait of a young slave's education is found in Eleanor Nolen's *A Job for Jeremiah* (1940), set at George Washington's plantation. Five-year-old Jeremiah's problem is that of finding the right job for himself, and he tries his hand at helping the cobbler, the tailor, the smith, and the miller. At age five, needless to say, Jeremiah is not successful at any of these tasks.

The cobbler is an indentured servant who travels from plantation to plantation making shoes for the inhabitants. The life appeals to Jeremiah, but when he mentions this to Uncle Dorsey, an older slave, he is told that working for oneself involves great risks and a person could starve and freeze. Says Uncle Dorsey, "Lans sake, I don't see no good to that. More'n likely take all the money you make just to buy things you has to have, like what the General gives us, so where is you?"[22]

Jeremiah admits that Uncle Dorsey may be right, but he is quick to suggest a compromise. He could be a cobbler, traveling around, seeing many different places, but still be a part of Mount Vernon.

Uncle Dorsey looked scandalized. "You don't know what you's talking 'bout, boy," he said sternly. "You ain't no indentured servant, 'n' you never will be. You's a Mount Vernon servant, 'n' you'd ought to be mighty proud of it! You belongs right here 'n' you'll stay the rest o' your days, 'n' you better be mighty thankful you *don't* have to go round working for other folks that more'n likely'd treat you like dirt."[23]

Jeremiah mentions his urge to travel to Uncle 'Lijah, the gatekeeper, who tells him, "Don't you go wishing that, boy. . . . That's just hunting trouble. You just be glad you belongs to Mount Vernon, where they ain't no chance o' being sold away to foreign parts away from your Pappy and your Mammy."[24]

By the end of the book, Jeremiah has absorbed the message and says to himself, "Jeremiah, boy, you all the time knew there wasn't no chance of you finding yourself a traveling job. You all the time knew you didn't really want to go away from Mount Vernon and all the folks."[25]

A more subtle way of teaching the slave his place is shown in *Diddie, Dumps, and Tot*. The three black girls, Dilsey, Chris, and Riar, are equals to the three white girls, Diddie, Dumps, and Tot, in play situations, but otherwise the differences between black and white are conveyed by relating how, at Christmas time, "three long, white stockings, that looked as if they might be mamma's, were for the little girls, and three coarse woolen stockings were for the little nigs."[26]

On another occasion when the children are in the nursery, the white girls are playing with dolls while the black girls are practicing their sewing lessons. And while Pyrnelle devotes an entire chapter to a Fourth of July celebration that includes participation by all the plantation's populace, she also makes clear that the humans as well as the food they will eat are segregated, even in transit.

Tom Bailey relates in *The Story of a Bad Boy* that when he heard he was to be sent north he kicked his slave, little black Sam. "As for kicking little Sam—I *always* did that, more or less gently when anything went wrong with me."[27] Being used as a kicking post while denied the right to kick back hardly seems the way to instill happiness, yet the authors consistently affirmed that the slaves loved the South and their masters.

A very effective technique to make people happy with their own condition is to provide them with others to look down upon. All the happy slaves in the books are house slaves, a position that enables them to look down upon the field slaves, the overseer, poor whites, and, as we have seen, Yankees.

These attitudes are reflected in passages in which the older slaves are seen serving in the roles of mentor to the white children. For example, when Diddie, Dumps, and Tot want to go play with the children from "the quarters," Mammy tells them, "'Yer allers want ter be 'long er dem quarter-folks. Dem ain't de sohuts fur you chil'en."[28]

If the master's children were not to play with the children of the field hands, neither were they to consider just any white person their equal. After one of their wilder adventures in *Diddie, Dumps, and Tot*, Dumps protests to Uncle Bob, "I think we're heap mo' better'n we're bad."* To which Uncle Bob replies:

"Well, dat mout er be so . . .; I ain't er 'sputin' it, but you chil'en comes fum er might high-minded stock uv white folks, an' hit ain't becomin' in yer fur ter be runnin' erway an' er hidin' out, same ez oberseer's chil'en, an' all kin' er po' white trash."[29]

The natural superiority of the white child whose parents are slave owners is stated baldly, as above. It is presented more subtly as well when Mammy tells the children a story about a little white girl whom she describes as follows: "She wuz er little po' white chile, an' she didn't hab no farder nor mudder, nor niggers to do fur her, an' she had to do all her own wuch herself."[30]

On another occasion, the girls have had trouble with Miss Carrie, their

---

* A major complaint about black images in children's books is that while very young white children were depicted as speaking perfect English, adult blacks were always depicted as speaking in an illiterate dialect. In fairness to Louise-Clarke Pyrnelle, it should be noted that *Diddie, Dumps, and Tot* is the only book in the sample in which white children do not speak perfect English.

white teacher. They run to Mammy for help in avoiding the punishment they see forthcoming, but all Mammy says is, "I ain't got no 'pinion uv po' white folks, nohow."

"Is Miss Carrie po' white folks, Mammy?" asked Dumps in horror, for she had been taught by Mammy and Aunt Milly both that the lowest classes of people in the world were "po' white folks" and "free niggers."[31]

A similar view is expressed by the slave Jim in *King Tom and the Runaways*. In answer to Tom's question, "[why] you niggers and po' white people hate each other so for, anyhow?" Jim explains:

"Well, you see, Mas' Tommy, dey ain' got no lan' skacely, ner no niggers, ner no money, an' dey do de same work we niggers does; so dey ain' no better 'n we is, an' we let 'em know it."[32]

THE POSTWAR FATE OF THE HAPPY SLAVE

The special quality of bias that Pyrnelle demonstrated throughout *Diddie, Dumps, and Tot* carries through to the very end as she recounts the effects of the war upon the characters. Just as she began the book by saying she did not know whether slavery was right or wrong, so she ends with the shocking notion that the master was in no way to blame for owning slaves. The idea is conveyed as she explains what happened to Jim, the slave who had agonized over throwing himself in the creek:

He has been in the Legislature, and spends his time in making long and exciting speeches to the loyal leaguers against the Southern whites, all unmindful of his happy childhood, and of the kind and generous master who strove in every way to render his bondage (for which that master was in no way to blame) a light and happy one.[33]

Just how even the most ardent apologist for slavery could claim that the slave owner was in no way to blame for owning slaves is beyond comprehension. Surely even Pyrnelle would not maintain that owners were *forced* to enslave others.

Uncle Snake-bit Bob does not meddle in politics, so he is said to be doing very well, but those who fare best in the eyes of the author are "the three little nigs"; Pyrnelle reports "Dilsey and Chris and Riar are all women now, and are all married and have children of their own; and nothing delights them more than to tell to their little ones what 'us an' de wite chil'en usen ter do.' "

Finally, there is Aunt Nancy:

She was going to school, but not progressing very rapidly. She did learn her letters once, but, having to stop school to make a living, she soon forgot them, and she explained it by saying:

"Yer see, honey, dat man wat larn't me dem readin's, he wuz sich er onstedfus' man, an' gettin' drunk, an' votin' an' sich, tell I furgittin' wat he larnt me."[34]

Pyrnelle really out did herself by portraying Aunt Nancy as equating voting with getting drunk.

Thomas Nelson Page was more subtle in his comments. As the fall of Richmond becomes known, Page has the slaves disappearing. Then comes news of Lee's surrender:

During the following two days every negro on the plantation left, excepting lame old Sukey Brown. Some of them came and said they had to go to Richmond, that "the word had come" for them. Others, including Uncle Balla and Lucy Ann, slipped away by night.[35]

However, shortly thereafter the reader is told that "a number of old servants, including Uncle Balla and Lucy Ann, had one by one come back to their old home." The implication is clear: freedom cannot compete with the security offered by the plantation.

4

UNHAPPY SLAVES

It does not take much imagination to think of a long list of items that might make the slave express unhappiness with his or her condition. What imagination it would take is noticeably lacking in the children's authors found in this study.

For example, in the preceding chapter we were told by the author of *A Job for Jeremiah* that life for a "Mount Vernon servant" was secure and carefree. Nolen further illuminated this view in an article entitled "The Colored Child in Contemporary Literature," published in *Horn Book*, in which she explained her desire to show that Jeremiah and his sister Susannah were "persons with a consciousness of their own important place in the social and economic scheme of eighteenth century American life. This is not to say that I consider the position of 'house servant' at Mount Vernon necessarily a high or desirable goal; I do not. Under the conditions existing in the United States a hundred and fifty years ago, however, Susannah and Jeremiah were as happily placed as any of their race."[1]

Contrast that view with the description of the slave quarters at Mount Vernon as reported by a Polish visitor:

We entered some negroes' huts, for their habitations cannot be called houses. They are far more miserable than the poorest of the cottages of our peasants. The husband and his wife sleep on a miserable bed, the children on the floor. A very poor chimney, a little kitchen furniture stands amid this misery—a tea-kettle and cups. . . . They receive a peck of Indian corn every week, and half of it is for the children, besides twenty herrings in a month. They receive a cotton jacket and a pair of breeches yearly.[2]

The clothing allotment is vital information, since all illustrations in Nolen's book show Jeremiah and his sister dressed exactly like the young white masters and mistresses, complete with shoes. The cobbler, Pete James, who inspires Jeremiah's dream of traveling, is reported making shoes for all the field hands. To pass off such a picture as an accurate reflection of slave-life conditions demonstrates, at the very least, failure on the part of the author to do her homework. (See Figure 2.)

Moreover, to describe accurately the differences in the quality of existence between slave and master as Pyrnelle did in *Diddie, Dumps, and Tot* and still maintain that the slaves were happy carries with it an assumption of black inferiority. It is as if the author were saying, "Well, what can you expect from *them?* They, not being white and superior can surely be happy with less at every stage in life."

From innumerable slave narratives we know that the long hours of field work and the harsh treatment by overseers were the slaves' major complaints. Children's authors avoided facing the field hands' complaints by not having any of the major characters be field hands. Pyrnelle, for example, mentions field hands only when relating they were given the day off on the Fourth of July to hold a barbecue, or when discussing the Christmas "vacation."

With the exception of Black Moses in *Shuttered Windows* (who is murdered by his master for disobeying the law against teaching slaves to read and write), nowhere in children's books is there a portrait of a slave forced to live day in and day out with the misery of enslavement. The only method used to show a slave's unhappiness in children's books is to have the slave run away, although it stands to reason that not every unhappy slave was fortunate enough to be able to run away.

Only eight slaves run away in the children's books analyzed here, and of those, only Caleb in *Chariot in the Sky* runs away simply because he wants to be free. All the other slaves for whom a motivation is provided—six in number—do so from a desire to have some small say in what happens to them. Thus the depiction of unhappy slaves only begins to hint at the tragedy of a human being totally under the control and at the whim of another.

Chariot in the Sky begins with young Caleb remembering his running away from the Willows plantation. Caleb had listened to the stories the older slaves told about slaves being able to fly (literally) back to Africa and escape bondage, and he was consumed by a desire to be free. Caleb's trouble was that he was an amateur; his decision was made on the spur of the moment without adequate preparations or information about whom to

Figure 2. Jeremiah's clothing shows a complete lack of realism in depicting a slave's status. From A *Job for Jeremiah*, by Eleanor Weakley Nolen; illustrated by Iris Beatty Johnson. Published by Oxford University Press, 1940 and used by permission of Henry Z. Walck, Inc.

trust and where to seek help during his flight, and he was recaptured easily.[3]

Even in an otherwise sound book, this author backs off from the truth in writing for children. For instead of showing Caleb punished for his attempt to escape, Bontemps has him rewarded. In reality, the very least a recaptured runaway could expect was a severe beating. Caleb expects to be sold for his transgression. Instead, Colonel Willows, his owner, sends him to Charleston where he is apprenticed to a white tailor and allowed to live with his mother and father who are working in Charleston.

The runaway for whom no motivation is provided is fourteen-year-old Moss in *Brady*. Jean Fritz, the author, is so busy depicting Moss as just an average boy that she neglects to tell us why he ran away. It does not stand to reason that a boy who has been a slave all his life and who chooses to take the risks involved in running away can be without a story to tell— most likely a hair-raising story.

The problem with *Brady*, and it can represent a large number of other books on different subjects, is that it pretends to be dealing with a large, vital issue—slavery—while it is really about how Brady learns to keep his mouth shut and to grow into a man. It expresses, through a multitude of characters, every conceivable view about slavery. But when it comes to the heart of the matter—the slave himself—it glosses over the situation and becomes just another book about growing up with a bit of adventure thrown in. Since the focus is on the white boy's growth, it is extremely doubtful that many young readers would come away from it with any real idea of the degradation slavery inflicted upon those caught in its web.

In *The Story of a Bad Boy*, Tom relates the fate of Sam, the young slave he used as a kicking post when things went wrong with him:

Little Black Sam, by the by, had been taken by his master from my father's service ten months previously, and put on a sugar-plantation near Baton Rouge. Not relishing the change, Sam had run away and by some mysterious agency got into Canada.[4]

Young Sam's motivation is described in the same way as Nigger Jim's in *The Adventures of Huckleberry Finn* (1885). While Jim plays a major role in the book, Twain is fairly casual in describing Jim's motivation to run away in the first place. According to Jim, his mistress, Miss Watson, "pecks on me all de time, en treats me pooty rough," which he can put up with, but he is not willing that she sell him "down to Orleans."[5]

There can be little question that the fear of being sold was a sword hanging over every slave's head. Being sold contained three types of potential horror. First, for the family individual, whether child or parent, there was the separation from kin. Second, no matter how bad a present condition might be, the slave was aware that his or her next owner might be worse. Third, the slave grapevine was most effective, and slaves in the border states knew that the life of a slave on a sugar or cotton plantation was far worse than their own.

Among the runaway slaves in the children's books, the fear of separation from kin was avoided nicely by not portraying any of the runaway slaves as married or having a family. Neither of the other fears is stressed in any of the books.

Red Anne, in the retrospective story told in *Mary Jane* (1959), for example, is tired of working so hard as a slave and decides to run away. Unlike Caleb, Red Anne realizes that running away requires planning, and she bides her time while learning to read and write. While we can assume that she would have run away eventually, she does so only when she discovers that she is going to be sold. However, *why* being sold is so terrible a thought as to prompt her to action is not made clear.[6]

Strong and clear motivation is provided for Cudjo's running away in *Cudjo's Cave*. Cudjo removes his shirt and shows Penn Hapgood his back, which is covered with scars. "Dem's what you call lickins! . . . Dat ar am de oberseer's work."[7]

For Pomp, the superman prototype in *Cudjo's Cave*, the decision to run away is a culmination of circumstances that represent extreme provocation. On his death bed, Pomp's young master instructs his younger brother to give Pomp his freedom and one thousand dollars to begin his free life with. The promise is made, but with no intention of keeping it. As the younger brother says to Pomp, "You are altogether too valuable a nigger to throw away."

Pomp suppresses his despair and anger and decides, "If he uses me well, I will serve him; if not, I will run for my life." For a time, the situation is not totally intolerable, and Pomp serves as overseer on the plantation. Then comes the day when the master orders Pomp to whip a woman slave. Pomp refuses; there is a fight between him and the master, and Pomp runs away.[8]

While *Cudjo's Cave* was, on the whole, a very good book for its time (1864) and is still readable, the necessity to provide Cudjo and Pomp with such dramatic motivations for running away is irritating. Why couldn't Pomp run away simply because he had been promised his freedom and the promise was broken? Because slaves in children's books are not shown as having the same motivations and desires as whites.

Jim, the young slave in *King Tom and the Runaways*, runs away twice. He does so the first time because he knows he is going to be beaten by the overseer for having stolen a five-dollar gold piece from him. There is no question of Jim's guilt, and no doubt the incident was inserted to show that even pet slaves were thieves when given the opportunity to steal.

The second time Jim runs away is far more serious, both in motivation and in its importance to the plot. Jim mentions to "Mas" Tom that he would like to be free, and Tom pursues the subject:

"What makes you want to be free, Jim? Are you tired of playin' 'fool' for me, as Albert calls it?"

"No, Mas' Tommy, 'tain't dat," replied the negro, with an affectionate glance. "I want ter be free, so I kin hire out ter you an' save up mer wages tell I git enough to buy somebody wid."[9]

The idea of Jim wanting to be a slave owner leads Tom to offer, "Jim, I'll *give* you a little nigger to wait on you—if that's what you want." But "a little nigger" is not what Jim has in mind.

Jim's problem is that he wants to marry Venus, who belongs to Colonel Darcy, a neighbor. Mrs. Carroll, Tom's mother, offers to buy Venus from the Colonel and promises to arrange a marriage between Jim and Venus.

"Ef you des'll do dat, Miss Mary," said Jim, "I won' ax fer no freedom. Dass all I wanted wid freedom—des so I could buy Venus. Dass wut I is talkin' 'bout wen I tole Mas' Tommy I want ter buy 'somebody.' "[10]

Unhappily, the colonel has already sold Venus to a man living two hundred miles away. But before Venus can be sent off, Jim rescues her and they run away, becoming fugitives in the swamp. The remainder of the book concerns Tom and Albert's search for Jim: getting lost, being found by Jim, and eventually being rescued after a near death. As a reward for Jim's actions in saving Tom and Albert, Mrs. Carroll reopens negotiations with the up-country planter and succeeds in purchasing Venus:

But end attained, heretofore so all-powerful in its bearing upon the happiness of those most concerned, could not now affect Jim's fortunes. For, two days after she had been bought and paid for, poor Venus died of the fever.[11]

Jim's ultimate fate is similar to that ascribed to the happy slaves in *Two Little Confederates*. He remains a slave until freed by the war:

Jim early joined the black army of freedmen swarming into the towns and cities, going in search of the forty acres and a mule which he was told belonged to him. Disappointed in his endeavors to lay hands upon what remained to the last only a glittering fable, he returned after a time to the old plantation, where many others followed him, to make terms with "mas' Tommy" and begin life under the new *regime*, and where he still remains, having long ago become his employer's right-hand man. It should be added that, within a few months after the death of Venus, he consoled himself with the hand of the vigorous and cheerful Dilsey, and at last reports counted his offspring to the number of nineteen.[12]

One of the major objections to the above statement and those like it, is that it creates the impression that there wasn't any real difference between Jim's "working" for Mas' Tom as a freedman and his slave status. Yet each of the runaway slaves symbolizes the difference between having to flee and be hunted down to escape a difficult situation and having the right to simply walk away from the difficult situation as a free person could.

In contrasting the characteristics of happy and unhappy slaves, only the need of the latter to have some control over their life differentiates the two groups. The point is obvious to the adult reader, especially when all the examples, however few, are brought together for analysis. It is doubtful, however, that a child reading just one or two of these books would have any clear idea of how important being in control of one's life is to a human being.

Even the most ardent apologists for slavery understood the concept, and they showed it clearly by the viciousness of their attacks on the free black.

5

THE FREEDMAN

"Free niggers is a nuisance," says the villainous Silas Ropes in *Cudjo's Cave*, and continues, "and let me say to you, feller-patriots, that one of the glorious fruits of secession is, that every free nigger in the states will either be sold for a slave, or druv out, or hung up."[1]

Before the Civil War approximately five hundred thousand free blacks were living in the United States, over half of them in the southern states. While the northern states had legally abolished slavery, the status of a freedman in the North was far from ideal. As Pomp responds when Penn Hapgood asks why he did not flee north instead of remaining in the Tennessee mountains:

"Would I be any better off there? Does not the color of a negro's skin, even in your free states, render him an object of suspicion and hatred? What chance is there for a man like me?"

"Little—very true!" said Penn, sadly, contemplating the form of the powerful and intelligent black, and thinking with indignation and shame of the prejudice which excludes men of his race from the privileges of free men, even in the free north.[2]

In the South, free blacks were more than a nuisance. They were, in the words of Kenneth Stampp, "an anomaly." How could one argue that slavery was the natural condition of Africans when other blacks showed by their daily existence that they could earn a living, raise a family, and be comfortable living in freedom?

The presence of "free men of color" was embarrassing enough to cause southern legislatures to enact laws placing restrictions upon an owner's right to manumit a slave. In *Chariot in the Sky*, Bontemps has Ella relate the poignant story of her family. The father had saved enough money from

43

being able to rent his time to buy himself. His wife, owned by another family, was taken to Mississippi. The father saved enough money to journey to Mississippi and buy his wife and child from the owner. They returned to Nashville, but the wife died. After a time, Ella's father again purchased a slave woman for his wife. But he was unable to obtain free papers for her in Tennessee, because it was illegal by then to manumit a slave within the state's borders. When his business failed, his wife was considered part of his property, and the court ordered her sold to help pay her husband's business debts.[3]

This story has a happy ending, for the family flees to Ohio. For others the tale ended less happily. Most of the southern and border states forbade the immigration of free blacks into their boundaries. Thus, even if a slave from Tennessee were to be taken to Ohio and freed, the laws would prevent him from returning.

These legal restrictions are vital for understanding the charge that free blacks also engaged in slave owning. It is true that some blacks were slave owners in the same sense that whites were, most notably in Louisiana. But many of the so-called black slave owners simply "owned" their wives and children.

Restrictions were not limited to the South:

In 1807 Ohio passed a law requiring that a Negro could not enter into the state unless he could furnish a bond of $500 as a guarantee of good conduct. Illinois required an incoming Negro to post a bond of $1,000; Indiana's constitution of 1851 outrightly prohibited Negroes from coming in the state to reside. In Oregon's territorial elections of November 9, 1857, the vote to deny admission to Negroes was carried by a one-sided majority, 8,640 to 1,081.[4]

Even when the legal restrictions did not exist, subtle forces were at work. In the North, blacks were systematically excluded from the trades. Domestic work was their major occupation, but even this proved increasingly difficult to obtain as the large migration from Europe began to arrive in the northern cities.

Despite everything, some blacks did acquire considerable wealth and others managed to live in comfortable circumstances. These blacks could not be ignored by the defenders of slavery, and thus, as Sterling Brown pointed out, "as a foil to the contented slave, pro-slavery authors set up another puppet: the wretched free Negro."[5]

In children's books, portraying the free black as an undesirable condition took two forms. The first was a matter of phraseology. One slave in *Diddie, Dumps, and Tot*, for example, uses the expression "mizer'bul as er free nigger."[6]

In *King Tom and the Runaways* Mrs. Carroll begins the conversation with Jim, the slave who has expressed a wish to be free, with: "I am unable to see how it could benefit you, Jim. The few free negroes are like lost sheep, and they have a hard time." Jim has learned that lesson and answers, "I year 'em say de free niggers ain't nigh ez well off ez we is."[7]

In *A Boy's Town* Howells speaks of "an impassable gulf" existing between the boys and freed blacks. He mentions a wide range of heroes the boys worship in varying degrees, including the town drunkards, dandies, and genteel loafers: "Far below these the boys had yet other heroes, such as the Dumb Negro and his family. Between these and white people, among whom the boys knew no distinctions, they were aware that there was an impassable gulf; and it would not be easy to give a notion of just the sort of consideration in which they held them."[8]

FREE BLACKS BEFORE 1865

The second method of dealing with free blacks was to present them as occupying lower positions in society than white people. Such depiction certainly represents a level of reality—being black in white America has never been easy or pleasant—but by stressing their lowly status without presenting at least some exceptions, the white authors reinforced the idea that free blacks were not much better off than the enslaved blacks. Only Arna Bontemps, a black author, drew a portrait of a well-to-do free black family, and his book, *Chariot in the Sky*, was not published until 1951.

Chronologically, the first free black actually presented in one of the books studied is Dinah, a washerwoman, in *Queechy*, and she is simply a convenience to the story. Fleda, the heroine, needs a place to talk with Mr. Rossitur, who has been caught in an illegal action and is preparing to flee the country. Dinah's living quarters are chosen as the setting for the talk, since the "obscure little tenement out towards Chelsea" in which she lives will keep the two whites from encountering people they know.

All we learn about Dinah is her occupation, that her living conditions border on squalor, and that she never questions her duty to the white folks who take over her small room, leaving her to stand guard outside the door. We do learn about the self-centeredness of that prototype Christian,

Fleda, who in her preoccupation with her own errand can ignore "all the varieties of dinginess and misery in her way."[9]

There are two freedmen in *Cudjo's Cave*: Toby and Barber Jim. The latter, while not appearing often in the book, is important to its plot. Trowbridge describes him thusly:

Barber Jim was a colored man, who had demonstrated the ability of the African to take care of himself, by purchasing first his own freedom of his mistress, buying his wife and children afterwards, and then accumulating a property as much more valuable than all the Silas Ropes and his poor white minions possessed, as his mind was superior to their combined intelligence.

Jim had accomplished this by uniting with industrious habits a natural shrewdness, which enabled him to make the most flourishing barbership in the place, and kept in connection with it (I am sorry to say) a bar, at which he dealt out to his customers some very bad liquors at very good prices. Had Jim been a white man, he would not, of course, have stooped to make money by any such low business as rum-selling—O, no! but being only a "nigger," what else could you expect of him?[10]

Unquestionably, Trowbridge meant well in pointing out the difference in the standards applied to black and white. However, sarcasm is a dangerous literary technique, particularly for use with children who do not bring to books the necessary experience to distinguish it from direct statement. How many youthful readers got Trowbridge's point and how many took him literally would be impossible to say, but the latter is far more likely than the former.

It develops that Jim's barbershop has a secret basement where the pro-Union white men of the area hold secret meetings in an attempt to hold Tennessee true to the Union cause. Jim is also one of the free blacks who will eventually be driven out of the state by Silas Ropes and his pro-Confederate companions.

Toby is the faithful family servant of Mr. Villars, one of the few white men in *Cudjo's Cave* who is both pro-Union and antislavery. Toby's place in the Villars household is made clear early in the book:

For Toby, though only a servant (indeed, he had formerly been a slave in the family), had had his own way so long in every thing that concerned the management of the household, that he had come to believe himself the proprietor, not only of the house and the land, and poultry and pigs, but of the family itself. He owned "ol' Mass Villars," and an exceedingly precious piece of property he considered him, especially since he had become blind. He was likewise (in his own exulted imagination) sole inheritor and guardian-in-chief of "Miss Jinny," Mr. Villars's youngest daughter, child of his old age, of whom Mrs. Villars said, on her deathbed, "Take always good care of my darling, dear Toby!"—an injunction which the negro regarded as a sort of last will and testament bequeathing the girl to him beyond mortal question.[11]

Here again, although Trowbridge really wants the reader to like Toby, he cannot resist poking fun at Toby. Moreover, while elsewhere in the book Trowbridge has Pomp destroy the concept of the slave as property, he indicates that Toby was able to think of inheriting people without questioning the idea.

As a faithful family servant, Toby demonstrates the major characteristics attributed to the happy slaves: he is loyal, hardworking, and dedicated to the family. He is also occasionally seen as a superstitious nitwit; as an egocentric old man who fails to see his limitations and who inflates his strengths, and as a person rightfully frightened when threatened with physical punishment by the villains of the book.

At the end of the book it is Toby and Barber Jim who together provide the money the white people need as they prepare to flee north for their lives. Mr. Villars is discussing the situation and the desperate need for money with his daughter when Toby comes "trotting in, jubilant and breathless," and lays a "dirty bag" on Villars' lap:

"I's fotched 'em! dar ye get 'em, massa!" And the old negro wiped the sweat from his shining face.

"What, Toby! Money!" (for the little bag was heavy). "Where did you get it?"

"Gold, sar! Gold, Miss Jinny! Needn't look 'spicious! I neber got 'em by no underground means! (He meant to say *underhand.*) "I'll jes' 'splain 'bout dat."[12]

Toby goes on to explain that since he has been free, Mr. Villars has been paying him seven dollars a month, and he has followed Mr. Villars' suggestion that he hire the money out to an honest man so it can earn "inference." The honest man proves to be Barber Jim who has invested it wisely, and there is enough money to finance the family's trip north.

As the faithful family servant, there is no question about Toby accompanying the Villars family north. To tidy matters up, Trowbridge has Mr. Villars take Jim's wife and children along as his servants while Jim makes his way alone to Cincinnati where the family is reunited and all ends happily. Just why Jim could not accompany the group is not made clear by Trowbridge, but as a fairly wealthy, free black, both his fortune and his life were in danger. The Confederates would not have felt the same degree of antagonism toward the elderly, kindly Mr. Villars, a respected man in the community.

Sam, the free black in Sophie May's *Little Prudy* (1864), appears only briefly. He is more than a plot convenience, as Dinah is in *Queechy*, but less than an integral part of the book. The scene occurs when the children are off on a picnic without adult supervision and Prudy's dress catches fire. The older children are in another area, having left Prudy and the two little boys alone.

Whether the boys would have known what to do, I can't say; but just then Sam Walker, a good-natured colored man, came up and put out the flames before Prudy fairly knew there were any. Then he brought water from a spring and drowned the bonfire, and gave the boys "a piece of his mind."

All the while poor Prudy was running off into the thickest part of the wood, crying bitterly. Sam ran after her, and caught her up, as if she had been a stray lamb; and though she struggled hard, he carried her to the picnic ground, where the large girls were spreading the table for supper.

"You'd better look out for these here young ones," said Sam. "This one would have been roasted sure, if I hadn't a-happened along in the nick of time."[13]

Prudy's tears are not because she has been harmed by the fire, but because she has discovered "*there—is—black folks!* O, he was just as— black!*" That evening, as she is being put to bed, Prudy asks her Aunt Madge:

"Where do they grow, auntie?" said she, "them black folks. Be they jispies?"

"O, they grow any where," replied Aunt Madge, laughing; "just like any body. They are not gypsies, but negroes."

"I should think they'd wash their faces."

"O, they do, but our Heavenly Father made them black."

"Did he?" cried Prudy, raising her head from the pillow. "And did he know how they was goin' to look when he made 'em? That man that catched me up, why, how he must feel."

"He was very kind," said Aunt Madge, trembling as she thought of the child's danger. "O Prudy, did you thank him?"

"No, I didn't," replied Prudy. "I didn't know as he could hear any thing. O, mayn't I go up to the jispy Pines tomorrow and thank him?"

"We'll see; but now it's time you went to sleep."

"Well, I will," said Prudy, "I'll go in a minute; but, auntie, he's good, ain't he? He ain't black all through?"

"He's quite a good man," answered Aunt Madge, trying not to smile, "and has had a great deal of trouble. I can't stop to tell you, and you wouldn't understand; but I dare say he has cried ever so much, Prudy, and felt worse than you can think, all because he is black; and some people don't like black men."

"I should think they'd be ashamed," cried the child. "Why I love him, 'cause he can't wash it off! Mayn't I put him in my prayer?"

Then Prudy had to get out of bed and kneel down and say her prayer over again. It followed the Lord's Prayer, and was in her own words:—

"O God, please bless every body. Bless all the big children, and the little children, and the little mites o' babies. And bless all the men and ladies that live in the whole o' the houses."

And now she added:—

"And won't you please to bless that black man that catched me up, and bless all the black folks, forever, amen."[14]

The scene can be read as the author's attempt to show white children who are afraid of blacks that their fear is groundless—that blacks are really white underneath the surface. It also intimates that pity is the emotion one feels for black people who have the misfortune of not being white. Whatever its effect upon white readers, the black child encountering it would find little to instill self-pride in his or her racial heritage, despite Sam's heroic role.

In *Little Women* (1868), the free black is "Hannah, who had lived with the family since Meg was born, and was considered by them all more as a friend than a servant." Hannah is present at all important events from birth to death in the March family. When Meg marries John, Hannah gets to kiss the bride, albeit "in the hall." True to the image of cooks, black or white, Hannah is boss of the kitchen, and when Amy plans a weekday party without consulting her, "Hannah was out of humor because her week's work was deranged." As a consequence, "Hannah's cooking didn't turn out well," a sign of independence displayed in literature, as in life, by more than one cook.

From 1868 until publication of *Journey Cake* in 1942, there is not another pre–Civil War freedman in the sample of books. Juba, the "free woman of color," in *Journey Cake* is the feminine counterpart of Toby in *Cudjo's Cave*. Just as Toby had been a slave to the Villars family and been set free by Mr. Villars, so Juba had once been a slave to the Shadrow family. Juba was set free when she saved the baby Rodney from a wildcat years before the book begins.

On the surface, freeing Juba might seem a fine gesture by Master Shadrow. But what good is being free to Juba while her husband Eli remains a slave? She is left with two choices: remain as a "servant" to the family—the choice she makes; or desert her husband—as Thomas Nelson Page tells us Uncle Balla's wife did in the *Two Little Confederates*.

As discussed in chapter 3, Juba's husband Eli has let it be known that Juba plans to take the Shadrow children to Kentucky to meet their father. The justice of the peace, technically in charge of the children, has other plans, not only for the children, but for Eli and Juba:

Rodney blurted out then a secret he had been trying to keep to himself. "He says he can sell Eli and Juba. She ain't got no papers to prove Pa gave her her freedom. He says we're big enough to fend fer ourselves. That Brother and I are to help Jim out in the store. That Kate can manage for us here and that his wife will take Dulcy in her cabin as a bound girl. He says he'll buy Juba and Eli his very ownself."

. . . Juba stood there, square and staunch, her head held high, her proud black eyes gleaming angrily. "Iffen I said what I'se got on my mind," she said fiercely, "dat fire would leap up in de fi'place. Dat onery Justice of the Peace been tryin' to git me an' Eli eber since he come to dis settlement. Us gwine trick dat man. Us gwine git shet o' dis place dis very night."[15]

The family does undertake the journey to Kentucky, and the first land-mark on the way is a small settlement where they hope to trade the ox and cart for packhorses. When they reach it, they are taken in by the Seth Tomkins family. At mealtime, Eli is relegated to the porch, but Juba, whether because she is free, a woman, or needed to care for the baby, is allowed inside, although not at the dinner table. While the Shadrow children sit at the table:

Juba with Bunny in her lap, was seated in Mary's own rocking chair in front of the fire. A three-legged stool stood close beside her, holding a horn of sweet sassafras tea and a big bowl brimming over with the best tidbits of the feast.[16]

After leaving the settlement, the party is attacked by Indians. True to children's books, Master Gordon and Long Knife, a scout, arrive in time to help beat off the Indians.

Juba, by that point, has risked the wrath of the justice of the peace in leaving without his permission. Along the road she has served as cook, mother, decision-maker, and she has eased the children's fears. When one of the oxen dies, Eli takes its place in the harness to pull the wagon. Juba and Eli have been towers of strength, yet in the joyous scene of reunion that ends the book, there is not one word of praise or thanks offered to either Juba or Eli. They have done nothing that one did not expect, apparently, of a faithful family servant and a loyal slave.

"Status" is a word that has many meanings, both by definition and in common usage. When applied to free blacks, status meant only that they had money, for there was no such thing as social status for a pre–Civil War freedman. The only book to depict free blacks as having money and living well and being educated was *Chariot in the Sky*, in which the Sazon family was described.

Caleb is sent by the white tailor he works for to deliver a suit to the Sazon home. He is jolted when he discovers they are "free Negroes."

Caleb had heard about free Negroes; Charleston was said to have a good many of them, but he had seen none before—none that he could recognize as free colored people at any rate. And here he was in this well-kept kitchen with his eyes popping out of his head, trying to take everything in as he drank the lemonade.[17]

Although it is a dangerous and illegal act, Phillip Sazon, the son, lends Caleb a book to aid him in learning to read. Caleb's father, Moses, works on the Charleston docks, and when the war breaks out, Phillip comes to Caleb and Moses for help in fleeing Charleston, because, as he explains:

"They want to make slaves out of us. I can't go on the street without running into trouble."
"You got free papers to show, ain't you?" Moses asked.
Phillip ran his hand inside his slipover. "They're right here, but that doesn't stop some of the bullies. They pretend there's something wrong with the papers, arrest me, take me to jail, hold me for several days and then discover that it was all a mistake. The papers are all right. Sometimes they do it just for fun; sometimes for meanness. I was born free right here in Charleston; my father and mother were both born free. I've had all I'm going to take."[18]

Moses smuggles Phillip aboard a ship due to leave Charleston in the morning. Both Phillip and Caleb survive the war, and their lives as postwar freedman are recounted in the next chapter.

There are two other free blacks in *Chariot in the Sky:* Precious Jewel Thomas and her mother. Caleb meets Precious Jewel when she comes to the store he is taking care of for his master, Mr. Coleman. There is no problem about being friends with Precious Jewel until Caleb betrays to Mrs. Thomas that he admires Precious Jewel very much. Then there is a change in her attitude: a freeborn girl is too good for a boy born in slavery, even though the war is over and all blacks are free.

Finally, in *Brady* (1960) there is the freedman Tar Adams, a barber who pretends he is a cripple as a means of self-protection. Tar's alibi is dramatized when a slave catcher comes to town. Slave catchers could count on being able to harass free blacks into helping them locate runaway slaves, or the freedman might find him- or herself "on the southern side of the border being sold as a slave again." The slave catcher sees Tar sitting on the hotel steps where Tar has his barber shop. When the slave catcher threatens Tar, Tar reaches for his crutches and rises:

Brady watched the slave catcher's scar turn red as he looked at the crutches and realized for the first time they belonged to Tar. The men began to snicker and pass jokes back and forth. Brady hadn't thought of it, but, after all, being a cripple made Tar pretty safe. You couldn't sell a cripple as a slave nor expect much help from one.[19]

Because everything in the book is seen through Brady's eyes, the author misses the opportunity to point out the tragedy of a healthy man having to spend his life pretending to be a cripple in order to be safe. Instead, the situation is seen only as a bit of cleverness on Tar's part.

THE FREEDMAN DURING THE CIVIL WAR

Because they learn their history from textbooks that simplify complex issues, too many Americans grow up with the belief that the Civil War was fought to free the slaves. The issue of states' rights versus federal control went way beyond the issue of slavery and many men fought for the Union who could not have cared less about whether the slaves were free or not. Conversely, not every member of the Confederate forces was an ardent defender of slavery.

One of the characters in *Cudjo's Cave*, Deslow, the man who engaged Pomp in the argument over slavery, is depicted in the beginning of the book as being pro-Union and proslavery. Eventually Deslow turns traitor and goes over to the Confederate forces, and Stackridge, the leader of the pro-Union forces, describes Deslow thusly:

"Well, I've watched him right close, and I've seen a good deal of what's been working in his mind. He's one o' them fools that believes slavery is God; and he can't get over it. Pomp, here, saved our lives in the fire the other night; and Deslow couldn't stand it. To owe his life to a runaway slave—that was too dreadful!" said Stackridge with savage sarcasm. "He's a man that would rather be roasted alive, and see his country ruined, I suppose, than do anything that might damage to the least degree his divine institution! Sence slavery had made war agin' the Union, and turned us out of our homes, I say, by the Lord! let it go down to hell, as it deserves."[20]

In contrast to the directness of the author's explanation of Deslow's behavior is the oblique statement found in Fosdick's *Frank on the Lower Mississippi* (1867) and the attitudes expressed in that book toward blacks. Frank is a naval lieutenant on a ship patrolling the Mississippi River for the Union forces, and he is planning to attack a nearby plantation. The action is justified by the observation that the owner:

and his family had taken part with the rebellion, not to secure any rights which they imagined had been denied them, but to assist in "establishing a confederacy of their own, whose cornerstone would be slavery," and to destroy "every vestige of the old Union."[21]

While the statement may appear to place the clergyman author firmly on the side of the Union and against slavery, the overall tone of the book is antiblack. The few occasions on which the blacks are mentioned, are denigrating. For example, the only freedman to appear in the book is an unnamed soldier who Frank meets when he is on a self-propelled spying mission. When Frank enters a store:

A negro was leaning against the counter, and of him Frank inquired—
"Boy, do you belong here?"
"No, sar," he answered indignantly; "I 'longs nowhar. I's a free man, I is. I'se a soger."[22]

Minor as the scene is, it contains a subtle implication that if a black man does not "belong to" someone, he belongs nowhere.

Fosdick does not tell us whether the unnamed soldier is a northern black or a runaway slave who has joined the local Union forces. Once Lincoln decided to let blacks fight for the Union, there were many from both sections of the country who did so. In some eyes slaves who deserted their masters to help the Union army were the equivalent of traitors. While not putting it quite that strongly, one children's book editor, Jean Poindexter Colby, wrote in the April 1965 issue of *Top of the News* that a manuscript (the work of an eighty-year-old southern lady) was giving her an editing problem because it "presents the Negro as a slave and a deserter." Then Colby opined parenthetically:

(Most of the Negroes in the book are fine people, but it is true that many slaves who perhaps were not so admirable deserted to the northern forces during the last months of the war.)[23]

By "fine people," Colby means they stayed on the plantation and went on being happy slaves. The black who would help the army trying to free him was a deserter. It is an astounding opinion to find expressed one hundred years after the end of the Civil War.

Any discussion of the role of blacks during the Civil War must stress the fact that the Emancipation Proclamation did not free *all* the slaves. It freed only those slaves within states in rebellion against the federal government. Four slave states, Delaware, Maryland, Kentucky, and Missouri were still in the Union and no slave within their borders was freed by the Proclamation. A book that has never been written might explore the feelings of a Maryland slave on January 1, 1863, when he learned that the slaves in neighboring Virginia were technically free while he remained enslaved.

While the Emancipation Proclamation technically freed some slaves, it was obviously impossible to enforce. Other slaves had already been freed under the Confiscation Act of August 6, 1861. As John Hope Franklin wrote:

The act provided that any property used by the owner's consent and with his knowledge in aiding or abetting insurrection against the United States was lawful subject of prize and capture wherever found. When the property consisted of slaves, they were to be forever free.[24]

One of the problems facing the slaves who were freed by Union occupation of a territory was the tenuous nature of that freedom. This fear is spelled out clearly in the opening chapter of Mimi Cooper Levy's *Corrie and the Yankee* (1959), the only book in the sample that explores the dilemma and the problems facing slaves who had been freed and then left behind when the Union forces left the territory.

Corrie is out picking strawberries and daydreaming a bit. Then:

> She started once again to fill her skirt. "Now that's plenty. Got to get to the hollow fast. What with the Confederate soldiers so close by—oh! If they'd catch you, they'd send you back quick as a wink to be a slave again."
> In spite of the heat, Corrie shivered. She knew that she was taking a chance being out here so far from the cabin. She remembered tales that Aunt Netha had told her about some of their neighbors in the slave quarters: of Thomas, and Ettie Mae and her husband, Charlie, and others—all stolen away by armed bands from the Rebel camp. The story was that they were sent to work in the turpentine camps far, far from their homes here in South Carolina. She thought the place was called Louisiana.[25]

The plantation on which Corrie lives had belonged to a Mr. Whitfield, but he had fled to Texas and left it in the care of a less-than-trustworthy overseer who had raided the house of its belongings and gone off with a pack of slave traders. The blacks (whom logic would dictate would be sold by the overseer) are allowed to remain behind. They have picked the cotton and tended the vegetable gardens. They think of it as their home and expect to remain when the war is over.

This explanation is undoubtedly designed to demonstrate the loyalty the blacks felt toward their home—even when it was a slave plantation— and the disloyalty of the overseer. Perhaps it does not bother young readers, but why did the villainous overseer go in search of blacks to trade when he had a homegrown crop at hand?

The book's plot has to do with the black inhabitants' caring for a wounded Union soldier, Andy, whom Corrie had found and brought to the plantation. Andy's presence places the blacks in a very dangerous position, for should the Confederate soldiers find them harboring a Union soldier, the result would be disastrous. Since not all of the blacks can be trusted, when Andy is well enough to travel, he plans to leave. But fighting conditions have become difficult, and Corrie is assigned to take Andy to meet her father who will help him return to the Union forces. Having been reunited with her father, Corrie wants to stay with him. She asks him if she couldn't be of help to him. He replies:

"Yes, Corrie, it's be a big help—for now. But after, when the war's over, are we goin' to need scouts then? It's folks who can read an' write, folks who can talk good—for their people—we goin' to need them much more. Corrie, they tell me you real smart with the readin'—tain't right you stop now. If you keep on learnin' maybe, someday, you even be a teacher, an' really help your folks."[26]

Corrie agrees to return to her studies, and her father says to Andy, "I got me a powerful beatin' once for tryin' to figure out the letters in the master's Bible, an' now my daughter, she's goin' to teach me how to read."

In real life, this dream of freedom and education was not fulfilled for most of the freedmen. As we have seen earlier, Pyrnelle, Page, and Pendleton ended their books with the free blacks either creeping back to the plantation or being busy getting drunk and voting. As we shall see, the end of the Civil War produced no panacea for the black man, either in real life or in children's books.

6

AFTER THE CIVIL WAR

Having freed and then left homeless four million, illiterate, untrained blacks, the nation turned its back on the problems created by emancipation.

The attitude of northerners toward the freed blacks during Reconstruction is often a mystery to those who do not realize that the war was fought not to free the slaves, but to save the Union. Most northerners were not Abolitionists. When the unity of the states was assured, there were other tasks awaiting: the Indians to be subdued, a vast continent to be conquered, railroads to be built. They could turn to the task of making money and living their own lives.

Some northerners, of course, were deeply concerned with the plight of the freed blacks. They founded Hampton and Fisk, they supported Tuskegee. They sent money, teachers, and old clothes to support the schools and the students of the South. But a national commitment was lacking.

The South was defeated, but far from penitent, and it set about putting the freed blacks in their place almost before the last gun was fired. In the early days of Reconstruction the attack upon freedmen came primarily from secret societies. As Franklin says:

The Camelias and the Klan were the most powerful of the secret orders. Armed with guns, swords, or other weapons, their members patrolled some parts of the South day and night. Scattered Union troops proved wholly ineffectual in coping with them, for they were sworn to secrecy, and had the respect and support of the white community. They used force, ostracism in business and society, bribery at the polls, arson, and even murder to accomplish their deeds. Depriving the Negro of political equality became, to them, a holy crusade in which a noble end justified any means. Negroes were run out of communities if they disobeyed orders to desist from voting; and the more resolute and therefore insubordinate blacks were whipped, maimed, and hanged. In 1871 several Negro officials in South Carolina were given fifteen days to resign and they were warned that if they failed, "then retributive justice will as surely be used as night follows day."[1]

Such intimidation meant that it was only a matter of time before the white southerners regained control of the state legislatures. With the legal apparatus of the states in their hands, the whites began to pass a series of laws that proscribed the life of the black. The United States Supreme Court did nothing to hinder this approach, which culminated in the *Plessy v. Ferguson* decision of 1896. The effect of this "separate but equal" doctrine was to bar the blacks from having recourse to the law in their fight for a fair place in American society. That, in actuality, the emphasis was upon the "separate," with little attention paid to the "equal," was of little interest to anyone except the blacks.

Without the protection of the courts and with the constant fear of Klan-like organizations threatening their life and limb, the only force blacks had on their side was public opinion—white public opinion. This point should be kept strongly in mind, most particularly by those whites who, having never lived in a community with black residents, are inclined to feel that blacks have no right to hold *them* responsible for the black condition in American society. The white whose self-pity leads him to cry, "But, I never did anything *to* them," ought better to ask himself, "What did I do *for* them?"

The authors and publishers who originated the books in this study as appropriate material for children, and the other adults who subsequently selected the books for their schools and libraries and individual children, can hardly have helped to create a climate of opinion that would actively support the blacks in their search for equal rights and opportunities. If the analysis of the books does not prove the point, the conditions of society should.

THE POST–CIVIL WAR FREEDMAN

Before looking at the portrait of the post–Civil War freedman we must note that all blacks born after the end of the war were born as American citizens. The term "freedman" does not apply to them, it is restricted either to those who were free blacks before the war or to those freed because of the war.

The distinction is raised here because it was impossible in many of the books to determine whether the black character was a freedman or a citizen. In order to keep the situation as uncomplicated as possible, the term "freedman" was applied to all characters in the books coming from the Jacob Blanck bibliography and to the characters in the *Children's Catalog* books that contained evidence of the status of the character. So many of the Blanck titles offered no internal clues to time or even setting that the decision had to be arbitrary.

Faithful Family Servants

According to children's books the occupation the freed slave chose most often was faithful family servant to the family that had formerly "owned" him or her. Epaminondas' auntie is a typical depiction of the faithful family servant even though she is not a servant in a white household. (See Figure 3.) The most famous of these servants is rarely thought of as free, even by so perceptive a critic as Charlemae Rollins who, in her introduction to *We Build Together*, refers to Uncle Remus as a slave.[2]

There is good reason for thinking of Uncle Remus as a slave: obviously, that is how Joel Chandler Harris thought of him, despite the Introduction to the first edition of *Uncle Remus: His Songs and His Sayings*, in which Harris wrote:

If the reader not familiar with plantation life will imagine that the myth-stories of Uncle Remus are told night after night to a little boy by an old Negro who appears to be venerable enough to have lived during the period he describes— who has nothing but pleasant memories of the discipline of slavery—and who has all the prejudices of caste and pride of family that were the natural results of the system; if the reader can imagine all this, he will have little difficulty in appreciating and sympathizing with the air of affectionate superiority which Uncle Remus assumes.[3]

There can be no question from the tone of the above that Uncle Remus is no longer under "the discipline of slavery."

Yet, in the *Nights with Uncle Remus* volume, after Uncle Remus has been away for a few days, he is greeted by the little boy who says that his mother—Miss Sally—had told him Uncle Remus probably had gone off to town to work. Uncle Remus replies:

Figure 3. A kindly auntie, but another "mammy" image nevertheless. From
Epaminondas and His Auntie, by Sara Cone Bryant; illustrated by Inez Hogan, Houghton
Mifflin Co., 1907.

"Is Miss Sally tell you dat, honey? Well, ef she ain't de beatenes' white 'oman
dis side er kingdom come, you kin des shoot me. Miss Sally tuck'n writ me a
pass wid her own han's fer ter go see some er my kin down dar in be Ashbank
settlement. Yo' mammy quare 'oman, honey, sho!"[4]

Earlier in the same volume there is the line, "the lady to whom Uncle
Remus belonged had been thoughtful of the old man."[5]

No slave owner would be so casual about a slave's disappearance as Miss Sally appears above. On the other hand, no freedman needed a pass to travel, and he certainly did not "belong to" anyone.

As for "the prejudices of caste," the attitude is very similar to that held by the loyal slave who lectured the master's children. When the little boy to whom Uncle Remus tells his stories is found playing with the Favers children, Uncle Remus tells him:

"Dem Favers's wa'n't no 'count 'fo' de war, end dey wa'n't no 'count endurin' er de war, an dey ain't no 'count attereards 'en w'iles my hear's hot you ain' gwine ter go mixin' up yo'se'f wid de riff-raff er creashun."[6]

The phrase "before the war," no matter how badly spelled, when appearing in a book by a southerner always refers to the Civil War. The preceding passage, coupled with Harris' introductory remarks, makes it clear that Uncle Remus is a member of the group of freedmen so approved of by Page and Pendleton.* He recognized his life should end where it began— on the plantation.

Mom Beck, in *The Little Colonel* (1896), is another freed black who must have been a happy slave before the war since she, too, becomes a faithful servant to her former mistress. Mom Beck washes, irons, cooks, looks after "the Little Colonel," and nurses both Mrs. Sherman while she is pining away for her absent husband and Mr. Sherman when he returns home ill from seeking his fortune in the West. Her value to the family is summed up by Mrs. Sherman who thinks, "dear, faithful old Becky! What a comfort she has been all my life, first as my nurse, and now as Lloyd's."

Mrs. Sherman at least appreciated Mom Beck, but Aunt Chloe, "the old colored servant" in *Mrs. Wiggs of the Cabbage Patch* (1901), is the stereotype of the faithful black protecting her white mistress, but without receiving any real appreciation for her concern. At one point in the book Miss Lucy announces that she is going to visit Mrs. Wiggs instead of resting up for a party she is going to that evening:

Aunt Chloe stuck out her lip and rolled her eyes in deprecation.

"Don't you do it, honey. What you wanter be foolin' 'round wif dat po' white trash fer? Why don't you set heah by de fiah an' bleach yer han's fer de party to-night?"

---

* See in chapter 3, "The Happy Slaves" and "The Postwar Fate of the Happy Slaves"; see also chapter 4.

"Bother the old party!" said Lucy, impatiently. She had begun disobeying Aunt Chloe when she was a very little girl.[7]

The comment about "disobeying Aunt Chloe" is one of the truest statements made concerning the basic disrespect young white children showed blacks, whether the blacks were slaves or freedmen. The attitude is found in all the children's books set in the South and is related in the writings of blacks, and on occasion in the adult writings by whites who did not seem to grasp the significance of what they were relating.

Esmeralda, the faithful servant of Jane Porter in *Tarzan of the Apes* (1914), is the most hysterical black in the entire sample. And in the portrait drawn of her relationship with Jane we will see used some of the most racist language in the entire sample of books. It will also stand as a prime example of an author's tendency to attribute to free blacks the same characteristics as were applied to slaves: dumb, superstitious, illiterate, but, oh, so loyal.

Readers first meet Esmeralda as the Porter group is being put ashore by the pirates who have taken over their ship. Esmeralda is described as "rolling her eyes in evident terror." When she and Jane enter the house in which lie the skeletons of Tarzan's mother and father, the scene "brought a shriek of terror to her lips, and like a frightened child the huge black ran to bury her face on her mistress' shoulder." While waiting in the cabin for the three male members of the abandoned party to return, Jane and Esmeralda lock themselves in, but Sabor, the lioness, attacks, and:

> Esmeralda, cowering still closer to her mistress, took one affrighted glance toward the little square of moonlight, just as the lioness emitted a low, savage growl.
> The sight that met the poor black's eyes was too much for the already overstrung nerves.
> "Oh, Gaberelle!" she shrieked, and slid to the floor an inert and senseless mass.[8]

This is, indeed, a "mass," for Esmeralda is described as weighing "some two hundred and eighty pounds."

Despite having been wounded by Jane's pistol shot, the lioness pries the bars of the windows apart. It seems that Jane and Esmeralda will be eaten alive. Jane's only thought is to kill herself; she turns the gun on herself, then, looking at Esmeralda, she thinks:

How could she leave the poor, faithful thing to those merciless, yellow fangs? No, she must use one cartridge on the senseless woman ere she turned the cold muzzle toward herself again.

How she shrank from the ordeal! But it had been cruelty a thousand times less justifiable to have left the loving black woman who had reared her from infancy to regain consciousness beneath the rending claws of the great cat.[9]

Needless to add, such heroics are not required of Jane, for Tarzan arrives in time to save them.

When Esmeralda regains consciousness, she asks:

"Fo' de good Lawd's sake, ain' Ah daid?"
The two [Clayton and Jane] turned to see Esmeralda sitting upright upon the floor, her great eyes rolling from side to side as though she could not believe their testimony as to her whereabouts.[10]

Later in the book, Jane is wondering who this new suitor is who signs his notes "Tarzan of the Apes," and worrying about her relationship with Mr. Clayton and the "forest God," not knowing that the latter is Tarzan.

"Esmeralda! Wake up," she cried.
"You make me so irritable, sleeping there peacefully when you know perfectly well that the world is filled with sorrow."
"Gaberelle!" screamed Esmeralda, sitting up. "What am it now? A hippo-nocerous? Where am he, Miss Jane?"
"Nonsense, Esmeralda, there is nothing. Go back to sleep. You are bad enough asleep, but you are infinitely worse awake."
"Yasm, honey; now you-all go right to sleep. Yo' nerves am all on aidge. What wif all dese riptamuses an' man eaten geniuses dat Marse Philander been a tellin' about—laws, it ain't no wonder we all get nervous prosecution."
Jane Porter crossed the little room, laughing, and kissing the faithful black cheek, bid Esmeralda good night.[11]

Uncle Remus has his troubles with Miss Sally; Miss Lucy talks back to Aunt Chloe; Mom Beck works hard, and Miss Jane and Esmeralda have, at best, an ambivalent relationship. None of these servants have to cope, however, with the outrages that beset Sarah Jane in *Miss Minerva and William Green Hill* (1909).*

* As this study progressed, I had minor reservations about certain titles in the Blanck bibliography as validly reflecting children's reading tastes. *Miss Minerva and William Green Hill* by Frances Calhoun is the book most open to question, in my opinion. It is

Sarah Jane works for the Garner family which lives next door to Miss Minerva. She lives in a little cottage on the back of the lot, without husband, with her son Benny Dick. When there is nothing else to do, Billy—William Green Hill—and Jimmy Garner feel free to play in Sarah Jane's cabin, even though they have been told to stay away from it. There is one incident in which they manage to tie themselves up in Sarah Jane's corset, an incident that is no more or less amusing (depending upon one's sense of humor) than most of the situations into which the boys get themselves. The worst of their pranks involving Sarah Jane is recounted in chapter 9, "Black Is Not Beautiful."

There are other faithful family servants briefly described in these books. In *Little Men* (1871), there is "Asia, the black cook," who runs the kitchen as any good cook would. She is mentioned only once as black. After that, while she appears at regular intervals, her identity is that of a cook.

Snow Baby (1901) by Josephine Peary, published in *St. Nicholas* magazine as "Ahnighito," is set in Alaska. It contains "the good colored nurse Laura," who is as upset with the Eskimos as they are entranced by her:

The nurse Laura was the first colored woman these natives had ever seen, and they thought her a great curiosity. She was invited everywhere with Ahnighito; but Laura was afraid to accept anything from these queer-looking people until Ahnighito and her mother went with her, and she found how kind every one was and anxious to please her.[12]

There is a level of irony in attributing to Laura reactions toward the Eskimos that parallel the reactions many white people had toward blacks.

The Local-Color Negro and Other Caricatures

One of the seven categories developed by Sterling Brown was "the local color Negro," a category "which stresses the quaint, the odd, the picturesque, the different." Brown also pointed out that the categories were not

still in print. Chapter one is entitled "The Reluctant Virgin"; the last chapter is entitled "Total Surrender," and that about sums up Miss Minerva's progress within the book. The whole tone of the book is similar to Art Linkletter's *Kids Say the Darndest Things*. That is, adult laughs based upon innuendo—primarily sexual, but not exclusively. But *Miss Minerva* is listed in Blanck and had to be treated within the study. Readers are alerted that it is doubtful that many children read the book; even more doubtful that many librarians recommended it to them.

discrete, with considerable overlapping. So, while much of what has been said here and what will be discussed in future chapters contains a strong flavor of these characteristics, there are three books that are particularly illustrative and contain black characters who fit Brown's category without question.

The first "local color" black is found in *What Katy Did* (1873) by Susan Coolidge. The book is a series of anecdotes about Katy's adventures, and the incident with the black is sandwiched in between her relationships with an Irish child and the daughter of a German jeweler. All incidents are designed to show what queer (Coolidge's word) friends Katy makes. Following the encounter with the Irish child:

The next was even funnier. There was a queer old black woman who lived all alone by herself in a small house near the school. This old woman had a very bad temper. The neighbors told horrible stories about her, so that the children were afraid to pass her house. They used to turn always just before they reached it, and cross to the other side of the street. This they did so regularly, that their feet had worn a path in the grass. But for some reason Katy found a great fascination in the little house. She liked to dodge about the door, always holding herself ready to turn and run in case the old woman rushed out upon her with a broomstick. One day she begged a large cabbage of Alexander, and rolled it in the door of the house. The old woman seemed to like it, and after this Katy always stopped to speak when she went by. She even got so far as to sit on the step and watch the old woman at work. There was a sort of perilous pleasure in doing this. It was like sitting at the entrance of a lion's cage, uncertain at what moment his Majesty might take it into his head to give a spring and eat you up.[13]

Before moving on, a word about the kind of bias demonstrated in *What Katy Did* and so many other books read from the Blanck bibliography, including those that did not pertain to this study. Only the white, Anglo-Saxon Protestant was excluded from ridicule or prejudice. Being poor was the ultimate crime, and it unites all the groups ridiculed in children's books. The blacks, it must be stressed, could not change their color or their names or their religion and thus blend into the established hierarchy.

Very similar to *What Katy Did* in terms of caricaturing many groups in society is *The Hole Book* (1908) by Peter Newell. No one comes off very well in this book in which a bullet travels through town creating havoc as it goes. The gimmick is that each page of the book has a hole in it, made by the bullet on its journey. And in keeping with the "humor" of the book, the bullet is finally stopped by a newlywed's first cake.

The picture showing the blacks (see Figure 4), and subsequently dropped from later editions of the book, is accompanied by the following text:

> A watermelon, large and fine,
> Was in the kitchen shed;
> The bullet drilled a hole through it
> As on its way it sped.
>
> "Who plugged dat melop?" mammy cried,
> As through the door she came.
> "I'd spank de chile dat done dat trick,
> Ef I could learn his name."[14]

Another black qualifying as a local-color character is Ebenezer, the ship's cook, in *Fur-Seal's Tooth* (1894). This is another of the pell-mell adventure stories in which the youthful hero, Phil, skips from one situation to another when, had he stayed put, his troubles would have ended on page two or three.

Phil is on board a ship, working off his passage, and the encounter with Ebenezer begins at breakfast:

> Just then the form of the schooner's black cook, Ebenezer by name, who was called "Ebb" for short, and sometimes, "Slack Ebb" or "Low Ebb," as the nautical fancy of the crew suggested, appeared at the entrance of the narrow passage leading from the gallery.
>
> Snatching a plate from the table, and flinging it at the cook's head to emphasize his remarks, the captain roared out a query as to why breakfast was not ready.
>
> Adroitly ducking like one well accustomed to such greetings, and thereby allowing the flying missle to crash against the side of Phil's bunk, Ebenezer grinned to show his appreciation of the captain's playfulness, and answered: "Yes, sah. Drackly, in free minute, sah."
>
> "Three minutes, ye black swab! See that it's on the table inside of one minute, or I'll have ye cut into fish-chum and make halibut bait of your heart."
>
> "Berry good, sah," responded Ebenezer, still grinning, though his eyes rolled wildly at this horrible threat, as he hastily shuffled from the cabin backward like a crab.[15]

Figure 4. "Who plugged dat melop?" Mammy cried. From *The Hole Book*, by Peter
Newell. Copyright © 1908 by Harper & Bros. Copyright © 1936 by Peter Newell.
Reprinted by permission of Harper & Row Publishers, Inc.

When Phil makes the mistake of complaining about the quality of the ship's food, the captain sends him to bail the trailer boat and leaves him there all afternoon.

> It was not until nearly sunset that the welcome sound of a voice came to his ears. Looking up, he saw Ebenezer's black face peering over the rail, and heard him announce, "Suppah, sah!"
>
> "Haul in on the painter, you grinning idiot!" shouted Phil, whereupon the negro placed his hand to his ear and called back: "Yes, sah. Suppah!"
>
> "Oh, what an old stupid!" groaned Phil, sinking back despairingly in the stern of the boat. "I may stay here until I starve or drown for all the help he'll give me."[16]

Phil neither starves nor drowns, but when he does get his supper that evening the taste of the food has improved considerably. Since Phil leaves the ship shortly after this incident, Ebenezer is not encountered again.

Full-Length Portraits

With the exception of the "mammy" in *The Hole Book*, who is not really a character in literary terms, all the blacks discussed so far in this chapter and most in the preceding chapters exist only in relationship to the whites who are in authority in their world. For the whites within the books, the blacks exist to make them more comfortable; for the white authors, the blacks exist as objects one can poke fun at, to make ridiculous, to draw a laugh from a bigoted reading audience.

Although some of these black characters, most notably Uncle Remus, are major characters in the books, they have no real life. No book from the Blanck sample offers a portrait of black family life. It was a welcome change, therefore, to find three books from the *Children's Catalog* that actually developed reasonable portraits of the freedman as a person with hopes and dreams and tragedies filling his life: *Shuttered Windows*; *Melindy's Medal*, and *Chariot in the Sky*. That the first two can be credited only with good intentions because they never got to the heart of the matter is unfortunate.

Shuttered Windows (1938) by Means takes place on Gentlemen's Island off the coast of South Carolina. It had a contemporary setting at its time of publication, but since the heroine, Harriet Freeman, is new to the area she must have the family and island history filled in for her.

Harriet's great-grandmother is a freedman, having been born in 1858. While she cannot read or write, she is, in Richie Corwin's words, "the most mannersable woman!" As Richie explains to Harriet, "Granny's folk was house servants. Mine was field hands. Make a difference, that did."[17]

A brief history of the island is related to Harriet:

At the close of the Civil War the land had been sold to the freed slaves at a nominal price—about a dollar an acre—in small farm tracts. In many cases their descendants still held the same ground, growing garden truck, cane, a little cotton, a little rice. But many of them had fallen behind with their taxes, and much of the land had been sold from under them by Northerners who used it for winter homes and hunting perserves. Of late it has also been in demand for truck gardening.[18]

The hurricane of 1893 that struck Gentlemen's Island took the lives of all of Granny's family with the exception of her grandson Thomas, Harriet's father, whom Granny saved.

With Tommy to live for, Granny had worked like a man. Neighbors had helped her raise a new cabin—this cabin.

"An' I root aroun' an' I root aroun' an' what y'all think I finds, all bruck up amongst de trash? Disyeah bed and deseyeah stools. Dat why I hope de good Lawd leeme keep'm twell I die."[19]

This last comment is directed most particularly to Mrs. Trindle, a black bourgeoisie from the North, who sees in Granny's bed an antique, worth money.

What is not explained in the book is the intriguing statement that white folks took Tommy north with them when he was seven years old. Certainly interracial adoption was not involved, but since he grew up to be an educated man, we can assume the whites were thoughtful of his well-being.

In *Melindy's Medal* (1945) by Faulkner and Becker, Melindy and Mo have a son, William, born during the Civil War while Mo is off fighting and winning his medal. When William is ten years old, his mother dies, leaving him and Mo to fend for themselves. William helps his father sell newspapers. He works very hard, taking time out only to go dancing. As grandmother says to Melindy, "Your grandfather William couldn't help going to wherever there was a dance because he was the best man dancer there ever was in Boston."

William is enamored of military life, and he drills every week with the company of blacks in Massachusetts. This was undoubtedly the famed Company "L" of the Sixth Massachusetts Infantry that had been formed during the American Revolution as the "Bucks of America," and that claimed to be the oldest black military group in America. However, the reader would not know that from the book.

With the advent of the Spanish-American War, William's company is made part of the state militia. This was the only black group of soldiers integrated into a white regiment—but the authors of *Melindy's Medal* did not point that out either.

William is sent to Cuba as a sergeant in charge of the horses. (His father Mo had been in charge of the mules during the Civil War.) It is a bad trip on ship, but William manages to keep the horses alive and to deliver them to Theodore Roosevelt for the famous charge at San Juan Hill. William dies and his medal, for "fortitude in the line of duty," is awarded posthumously.

In both *Shuttered Windows* and *Melindy's Medal* the information given the reader is retrospective. This is all right as far as it goes, and it is better than most of the books in terms of filling in the gaps. But it is information and does not engage the reader's emotions.

Arna Bontemps' *Chariot in the Sky* (1951) is the one book in the study that presents a realistic, complete, picture of the freedman, Caleb, in the South during Reconstruction.

Caleb hears the news that the war is over:

"I'M FREE. I'm free," he repeated as he walked back to the dry-goods store. "I'm not a slave no more. I'm what they call a freedman. Caleb Willows, freedman. That sounds good to me."[20]

As soon as he is relieved of the duty of caring for Mr. Coleman's store, Caleb journeys back to Charleston to see if he can locate his parents. He goes where they had been living, but the loft is deserted. Caleb goes to his old employer, Mr. Harvey, who tells him that Colonel Willows had sold all his slaves and there is no way of knowing where Sarah and Moses might be.

After wandering the streets of Charleston, Caleb returns to Chattanooga, and he begins to teach freedmen how to read and write in exchange for a little food and a roof over his head. He stays with Mr. and Mrs. Joel Burton. Mr. Burton is a barber and he tells Caleb:

"This freedom ain't working out so good, Caleb. All of us is free now—like we wanted to be—but most of us is walking the streets hungry. Free but hungry. That don't make sense. What you say about traveling is all right, but you need to know where you going. And you need to know how come. What the freedmen need now is somebody to show them how to get out of this fix they're in. They ain't slaves no more. But nobody has learned them how to walk like men and look after themselves and make a living."[21]

It is Caleb's need to learn to walk like a man that takes him to Nashville and the Fisk School for freedmen. He is also motivated by the knowledge that Precious Jewel Thomas is attending the school.

Caleb is accepted at Fisk, and from the first day, he is embroiled in the controversy that is a major part of the remainder of the book: the question of whether blacks should sing the slave songs and the spirituals. Mr. White, the school treasurer, is also a devotee of music, and in the evening he gathers a group of the young people to sing. He explains to Caleb that there is a difference of opinion concerning the singing of slave songs. One group of blacks feels that the singing of the songs only perpetuates the memories of slavery. The second group, to which Mr. White belongs, believes that the songs are wonderful music and should be sung.

Combined with the conflict concerning the blacks' attitude toward spirituals are Caleb's experiences as a teacher at a backcountry school—a job he takes to earn his fees at Fisk. All goes well at the school for several weeks; Caleb likes the people, they like him. But the Ku Klux Klan is in the area. At first there is only the menace of galloping horses in the distance; then the horses come closer; finally, there is musket fire.

After a weekend in Nashville, during which he reports the incident to the Fisk faculty, Caleb returns to the country, refusing to take the masked riders seriously. He is forced to reevaluate the situation when no one shows up for lessons. He learns that the masked riders have burned two houses and tarred and feathered the men and horsewhipped a woman. There is nothing for Caleb to do but return to Nashville.

Back at Fisk, Caleb becomes a member of the Jubilee Singers, and Mr. White takes the group off on a fund-raising tour. The initial results are disastrous. Newspaper reviews are excellent, but few people attend the concerts. The singers are refused decent accommodations, and their money runs out. When they sing for a Synod of Presbyterian ministers they are praised highly and a collection is taken up. Then they arrive in Oberlin, Ohio, to sing at a meeting of Congregational ministers. They are seated in the back of the auditorium (where else?). The meeting drones on, and it seems as if the chairman has forgotten his promise to let them sing.

Up to this point the group that demands the singers do traditional operatic concerts has carried the day. But Mr. White has had enough. He tells the group that they will sing "Steal Away," without invitation from the chairman. Bontemps brings alive the picture of the row of blacks suddenly starting in to sing from the back of the auditorium, and the song is, of course, the perfect selection. The effect is magical, in the book as it must have been in life, but the conflict between the two groups of singers must now be faced squarely.

The crisis is quite simple: sing the white man's music and receive rave notices but no money. Sing your own music and earn money, too.

Since the future of Fisk depends upon raising money, it is decided that from this point on the group will sing the slave sings and abandon the concert pieces. This decision causes several members of the group to leave, and the female chaperone must be replaced. The decision is a wise one, however; the Jubilee Singers earn a great deal of money during the remainder of the tour, and they return to Fisk triumphant. The school is saved, and there will be money for buildings and other needed equipment.[22]

Upon returning to Fisk, Caleb is delighted to find his old friend Phillip Sazon enrolled as a student. Phillip wants to be a doctor, but when Uncle Eph, from the country, asks Caleb to return and open the school, a conflict arises. The Jubilee Singers have offers from all over the world—they will eventually sing for Queen Victoria—and they will soon be departing on another tour. Caleb is torn between his duty to the Singers and his desire to return to the country people and help them learn to read and write.

The ideal solution would be for Phillip to teach the school and Caleb to go on tour. Toward that end, Caleb lures Phillip out to the country in the hope that once Phillip has seen the need and the enthusiasm of the people to learn, he will find it impossible to refuse. What challenges Phillip is not altruism, but being threatened by two blacks employed by whites who try to scare them off. Phillip decides he can delay his pursuit of a medical career, but his decision brings disaster: the school is burned and he is murdered.

Caleb feels that he cannot go on the tour after Phillip's death. He will go teach in the country for the three months of the contract offered. The Jubilee Singers will miss him, but he is determined to carry through in place of Phillip.

After school is out for the summer, Caleb journeys to Boston to rejoin the group for its European tour. Among the admirers on the dock, gathered to see the troupe off, are Caleb's mother and father. There is time for a brief but tender and joyful reunion. Then Caleb's mother asks him what songs they are going to sing for the Europeans. He tells her "slave songs" and goes on to explain:

"A heap of people don't want to sing slave songs nowadays. . . . They're the ones that's getting educated, mostly. They talk about forgetting what's past and gone, and they think slave songs remind them of slavery. They don't want to sing them themselves and they don't want nobody else to sing them." Caleb could see that the old folks were baffled, so he added lightly, "It's kind of funny when you think of it."

But Moses did not smile. He asked seriously, "Did you ever think anything like that, son?"

"No, Pa," Caleb answered honestly. "Of course, I didn't have any reason except that I always liked to sing the songs that I knew best, but here lately— well, I think I'm beginning to know how come."

"I'd hate to see you get so educated you couldn't enjoy good singing," Moses smiled.[23]

The Jubilee Singers carried the day in their own time, but the controversy over the role of black heritage in the lives of black people was to be a never-ending one. The antislave-song group wanted to erase all vestiges of black history before freedom, and eventually it dominated the black image projected to white society. Thus, part of the problem came from blacks themselves. But the blame for the "think white" group's success in suppressing black history must lie primarily with the whites, who wrote most of the books.

Not until the black-power movement in the 1960s did black culture regain any sizable following among black people and acceptance as existing by the dominant whites. Until then, a large segment of the black community lived by the Kelly Miller aphorism: "The Negro must get along, get white, or get out."[24]

7

THE LIFE OF THE FREEBORN BLACK

It is understandable that the freed slave might do no better than subsist and that he or she would exchange the role of slave for that of faithful family servant. But what of the blacks born to citizenship? What did life hold for them according to juvenile authors? Did any author offer a hope to Malcolm X, for example, that being a carpenter was not what he had to settle for in life?

Concisely put, the free black was told to keep in his "place," work hard, help elevate his race, but not to expect to enter white society. Much of this philosophy is the direct result of the work and writing of Booker T. Washington, and no one can understand the status of blacks in American society without reading *Up from Slavery*.

WASHINGTON VERSUS DUBOIS

Booker T. Washington lived less than sixty years, but during that time he was hero to the black race and the white man's ideal of what a "good" black should be. His influence was without equal during his lifetime, and for decades afterward, thanks to the popularity of *Up from Slavery*, his was the best-known name among both black and white populations.

What accounted for this popularity? Undoubtedly, Washington had charisma—all reports of the day speak glowingly of his sense of presence, good humor, and charm. More vital, however, is that Washington expressed ideas that met with the approval of whites. When Washington established Tuskegee, he rejected from the start the "New England" type of education that stressed a classical background as represented by Fisk and Atlanta. In writing about the objections white people raised to the founding of Tuskegee, Washington said:

These people feared the result of education would be that the Negroes would leave the farms, and that it would be difficult to secure them for domestic service.

The white people who questioned the wisdom of starting this new school had in their minds pictures of what was called an educated Negro, with a high hat, imitation gold eye-glasses, a showy walkingstick, kid gloves, fancy boots, and what not—in a word, a man who was determined to live by his wits. It was difficult for these people to see how education would produce any other kind of a coloured man.[1]

Tuskegee would produce blacks who could make bricks, plant crops, build houses, and use a toothbrush. Washington's philosophy can best be summed up in his own words:

I explained that my theory of education for the Negro would not, for example, confine him for all time to farm life—to the production of the best and the most sweet potatoes—but that, if he succeeded in this line of industry, he could lay the foundation upon which his children and grandchildren could grow to higher and more important things in life.[2]

While Washington may well have believed such progress would occur, the fact is it did not. At least not in children's books, even when, as time went on, more and more farmers were being forced off their lands by economic conditions during the 1930s and by the need for factory workers during the war years of the 1940s. Of the books listed in the *Children's Catalog*, the following titles show either the fathers or the father-substitutes as farmers or field hands: *Frawg* (1930), *Zeke* (1931), *Across the Cotton Patch* (1934), *Araminta* (1935), *Little Jeemes Henry* (1936), *Sad-Faced Boy* (1937), *Flop-Eared Hound* (1938), *Tobe* (1939), *On the Dark of the Moon* (1943), *Great Day in the Morning* (1946), *River Treasure* (1947), *Ladycake Farm* (1952), and *The Empty Schoolhouse* (1965). Adding *Roosevelt Grady* (1963), in which the father is a migrant worker, makes a total of fourteen books emphasizing farm work.

The bright spot in the picture, if one may put it that way, is that only Ezekiel Lee in *Zeke* is shown wanting to be a farmer. The following conversation between Scipio, Zeke's older brother, and Hazel might well have taken place between Booker T. Washington and W. E. B. DuBois.

"What are your plans for Zeke?" Hazel asked Scipio one day.
"Same as yours be, I reckon. Keep him in school."

"College even?"

"Maybe a work school."

"But why a work school, Scip?"

Scip found it difficult to explain. "Tom an' Julius," he said meditatively, "dey weren' much account here. Neber liked ter work. Dey's runnin' elevators now in Mon'gomery. Dat's der business, but I ain't hankerin' to see Zeke goin' up an' down all day in a box."

"Of course not. But if Zeke goes to college he can learn to be a doctor or a lawyer."

"I know. But doctors an' lawyers, an' preachers, dey can get mighty po' cause folks can't pay de bills. Den dat kind drops inter elevators. Seems if Zeke get a good trade, he safe. Tolliver Institute, dat's de best school."[3]

It is natural that Hazel would think of the possibility of Zeke becoming a lawyer, for we know from the first book, *Hazel*, that her father was a lawyer, even though he is dead when the book opens. It is not until the publication of *Mary Jane* in 1959 that another black lawyer appears in any of the books, and very little is made of the fact that Mr. Douglass is a lawyer.

As will be seen in chapter 10, "Religion and Superstition," there were a number of black "preachers" depicted in the books. None of them, however, are relatives of the central characters. And most resemble the preacher described by Washington when discussing black people who did not want to work with their hands:

This is illustrated by a story told of a coloured man in Alabama, who, one hot day in July, while he was at work in a cotton-field, suddenly stopped, and, looking toward the skies, said: "O Lawd, de cotton am so grassy, de work am so hard, and the sun am so hot dat I b'lieve dis darky am called to preach!"[4]

The speech that brought Washington to national and international fame was delivered at the Atlanta Exposition in 1895. Speaking directly to the white southerners present, Washington said:

You can be sure in the future, as in the past, that you and your families will be surrounded by the most patient, faithful, law-abiding, and unresentful people that the world has seen. As we have proved our loyalty to you in the past, in nursing your children, watching by the sick-bed of your mothers and fathers, and often following them with tear-dimmed eyes to their graves, so in the future, in our humble way, we shall stand by you with a devotion that no foreigner can approach, ready to lay down our lives, if need be, in defence of yours, interlacing our industrial, commercial, civil, and religious life with yours in a way that shall make the interests of both races one. In all things purely social we can be as separate as the fingers, yet one as the hand in all things essential to mutual progress.

. . . .

The wisest among my race understand that the agitation of questions of social equality is the extremest folly, and that progress in the enjoyment of all the privileges that will come to us must be the result of severe and constant struggle rather than of artificial forcing. No race that has anything to contribute to the markets of the world is long in any degree ostracized.[5]

Was it a mere accident that in the following year the United States Supreme Court in *Plessy* v. *Ferguson* made the "separate but equal" doctrine the law of the land?

One black man who understood Washington's assumptions, but refused to accept them was W. E. B. DuBois. In 1903, two years after the publication of *Up from Slavery*, DuBois wrote in *The Souls of Black Folk:*

Easily the most striking thing in the history of the American Negro since 1876 is the ascendancy of Mr. Booker T. Washington. It began at the time when war memories and ideals were rapidly passing; a day of astonishing commercial development was dawning; a sense of doubt and hesitation overtook the freedman's sons,—then it was that his leading began. Mr. Washington came, with a single definite programme, at the psychological moment when the nation was a little ashamed of having bestowed so much sentiment on Negroes, and was concentrating its energies on Dollars. His programme of industrial education, conciliation of the South, and submission and silence as to civil and political rights, was not wholly original; the Free Negroes from 1830 up to war-time had striven to build industrial schools, and the American Missionary Association had from the first taught various trades; and Price and others had sought a way of honorable alliance with the best of the Southerners. But Mr. Washington first indissolubly linked these things; he put enthusiasm, unlimited energy, and perfect faith into this programme, and changed it from a bypath into a veritable Way of Life. And the tale of the methods by which he did this is a fascinating study of human life.[6]

DuBois was certainly the man to challenge Washington. After graduation from Fisk University, he spent four years at Harvard, later spent two years at the University of Berlin, and was a recognized scholar. By speaking as forthrightly as he did—when he did—against the most honored and famed black man in the United States, he paved the way for the founding of the NAACP. But it was another six decades before DuBois was to become a hero to young blacks struggling in the civil rights movement.

Booker T. Washington, however, was demonstrating that most American of qualities: pragmatic consideration of the possible, or at least the acceptable. Myrdal sums up the argument this way:

Almost as soon as the movement for the education of Negro youth began, the quarrel started as to whether Negro education should be "classical" or "industrial." If the white Southerners had to permit the Negroes to get any education at all, they wanted it to be of the sort which would make the Negro a better servant and laborer, not that which would teach him to rise out of his "place." The New England school teachers—who did most of the teaching at first—wanted to train the Negroes as they themselves had been trained in the North: the "three R's" at the elementary level, with such subjects as Latin, Greek, geometry, rhetoric coming in at the secondary and college levels. But General S. C. Armstrong, a Union officer during the Civil War, had established Hampton Institute in the tidewater region of Virginia as an "agricultural institution." He wanted to see continued the skilled artisan tradition that existed among Negroes before the War. His most famous pupil, Booker T. Washington, founded the Tuskegee Institute in Alabama and became the apostle of industrial education for Negroes. There is no doubt that—quite apart from the pedagogical merits of this type of education—his message was extremely timely in the actual power situation of the Restoration. It reconciled many Southern white men to the idea of Negro education, and Washington has probably no small share in the salvaging of Negro education from the great danger of its being entirely destroyed. Meanwhile, the New England advocates of a classical education and their Negro followers carried on at Atlanta, Fisk, and at a few other Southern centers of Negro college education.[7]

Although the average man of any race may rarely participate in intellectual philosophical discussions, he does, in fact, make life decisions that parallel such discussions. Fundamentally, Booker T. Washington was trying to protect his students. However badly they must live, he wanted them to survive, not to die as victims of lynch mobs. In learning to read and write and do simple arithmetic, the black men and women could better protect themselves from fraudulent contracts. Washington, in retrospect, closely resembles the black mother described by psychiatrists Grier and Cobbs in *Black Rage:*

The black mother shares a burden with her soul sisters of three centuries ago. She must produce and shape and mold a unique type of man. She must intuitively cut off and blunt his masculine assertiveness and aggression lest these put the boy's life in jeopardy.

During slavery the danger was real. . . .

The black mother continues this heritage from slavery and simultaneously reflects the world she now knows. Even today, the black man cannot become too aggressive without hazard to himself. To do so is to challenge the delicate balance of a complex social system. . . . What at first seemed a random pattern of mothering has gradually assumed a definite and deliberate, if unconscious, method of preparing a black boy for his subordinate place in the world.[8]

Considering the circumstances of his own life, the time in which he lived and the place in which he chose to work, there is little question that Washington was right. What went wrong was that whites took his statements about the then-present condition of the blacks and ignored his long-range goals. The sweet-potato-growing farmer, however well he farmed, did not pave the way for his children or grandchildren to go on to higher things. The humility and docility preached by Washington came to be expected behavior, and any deviation from these norms led to a black man being termed "an uppity nigger."

Two books that reflect the Booker T. Washington philosophy throughout are *Shuttered Windows* (1938) and *Great Day in the Morning* (1946), both by Florence Crannell Means. A characteristic both books have in common is the author's refusal to allow either central character to achieve her stated goals.

If Washington's long-range goals had succeeded, Means would not have been able to write *Shuttered Windows*. Harriet Freeman's father had been a school principal, her mother a highly trained secretary. Harriet's initial goal is to be a concert pianist. But Means is determined that black people must choose occupations that will help their race "rise." Toward that goal, she creates situations that pressure Harriet into accepting the idea of being a teacher.

One of the first contrived situations has Harriet being lured into taking a trip into the backcountry with Miss Francis, the white head of Landers School, and Miss Joan, a white teacher. In trying to tell the little black children a story, Harriet discovers that they cannot even locate their own state on a map. After each sentence she utters, the children go "Mmmmmm!" She struggles through the story, but is obviously upset. Then, on the ride home:

"You know," she exploded at last, "I wouldn't have believed there were such schools in the United States."

"This particular school has one unusual feature," Miss Francis said mildly. "Some of the children have never seen white people before."

Miss Joan gasped and sputtered. "But Miss Francis—! Will you say that again? You don't mean—? Why, how many miles is it from the highway?"

"I know; but I do mean it. It's true, isn't it, Mossie?"

"Yes, m'm. Dey plenty dem chillen ain' saw no whi' folks twell dis very day."

"But—how could that *be?*" Harriet demanded.

"Mostly lack of roads, I suppose. No roads to bring the white people in and nothing to take the colored people out,—I know it's almost unbelievable. But the school situation is pretty hard to believe. The last statistics I've seen showed that our state spent an average of $7.84 per colored child per year for education. Some counties spend less than that."[9]

Deplorable as conditions are, Harriet is still going on with her music. Then Granny not only becomes seriously ill, but her house is to be sold for unpaid taxes. Harriet relents. She tells Richie, the young man she loves:

"I—I want to finish at Landers. Afterward I'll go somewhere not too far away—maybe Spelman, in Atlanta—where I can learn lots more about Home Ec—nursing, cooking, diet, babies. And then"—her voice thickened with earnestness—"I'm coming back to Gentlemen's and help my people *live.*"[10]

Not only may Harriet not become a pianist, but in becoming a "teacher," she must be a teacher of very practical subjects. By identifying Spelman, as opposed to Atlanta University, Means tells us where she stands. But then, since Richie's goal is to help the black farmers raise better crops and produce healthier cattle, together Richie and Harriet will turn Gentlemen's Island into a veritable paradise.

By 1946, Means had sharpened her pen and was ready to really zero in on blacks who thought they could decide for themselves what to do with their lives. Almost from the very beginning of *Great Day in the Morning,* Lilybelle Lawrence is being nagged by the head mistress at Penn to reconsider wanting to teach:

"But there was never a time when nurses were so needed. And you showed such a knack for it. When girls have been sick here. And in First Aid." Miss Land laughed irrepressibly. "I shan't forget the time when you were bandaging Callie St. Francis and picked her up bodily to do it. And Callie's no featherweight."[11]

While Lilybelle "secretly enjoyed planning diets, reading thermometers, even making hot sick bodies cool and clean," she is determined to be a teacher. This is a matter of pride, or perhaps even vanity, for what Lilybelle wants is to be called "Miss Lilybelle, m'm," and she believes that teaching is the quickest route to that kind of respectability. She can see herself living in Harlem and far removed from the sweat and toil of her grandfather's field work.[12]

Or, as Booker T. Washington said of his students, "The chief ambition among a large proportion of them was to get an education so that they would not have to work any longer with their hands."[13] For Washington, that was not an approved reason, and Means obviously agreed. No black character was going to be allowed to take an easy way out. Good blacks did what was needed for their race, not what might lead to an easy life for themselves. Just why teaching was no longer an acceptable vocation to Means is not answerable.

Lilybelle goes off to Tuskegee where she encounters George Washington Carver. She speaks to him of her conflict. Hesitantly, she tells him of the pressure from her teachers to be a nurse while she wants to be a teacher. Should she give up her dream and yield to the wishes of others? Dr. Carver answers:

"But you feel that this is a time when nurses are needed even more than teachers?" he asked, his dark face glowing. "Hard to know which is the greater call. But it is true that sick bodies make sick minds, and teaching is of little use to the sick mind."

He sat easy and relaxed, his kind eyes upon her. "I know. You want to put your life where it will count the most. Once I knew a boy who studied to be a painter. Never was he so happy as when he was making flowers grow under his brush, or beautiful trees and rivers. But it was brought to him that he was needed for something different. So he laid aside his brushes and set out on the new road that was pointed out to him."

"And he's been happy?" Lilybelle murmured rebelliously. "When he could have been a great artist?"

Doctor Carver beamed at her below the horizontal furrows of his brow, "Of course he is happy, doing what his Father told him to do," said the caressingly gentle voice.

. . . .

Doctor Carver studied her happily. "You were made to do the big things, the hard things," he said as if congratulating her. "Few young women have your look of vibrant strength."[14]

But Lilybelle is tired of doing the hard things in life. She has planted and harvested potatoes and washed and ironed white folks' clothes to come to Tuskegee. She resents the thought of more physical labor. But the author will have her way, even if it means magically turning her paragon of physical strength into a weakling.

Lilybelle must leave Tuskegee for a drier climate. The family she has been baby-sitting for is transferred to Denver—and, of course, Lilybelle is taken along. Within a short time three accidents involving friends and family occur, and Lilybelle says, "Three times God had to speak to me."[15] Her decision is made: she will become a nurse.

The first book in the *Children's Catalog* to mention a life goal for a black is *Hazel* (1913) by Mary Ovington. In this exchange with two white southern ladies about her college aspirations, Hazel, a northern-born-and-raised black, is still learning how to talk to southern White Folks:

"What will you do with all your learning?" Miss Jane asked.
"I'll teach."
"Niggers?"
Hazel did not want to answer; but sitting very erect, with a precision that would have done any teacher credit, she replied: "Everybody goes to school in Boston, every single child. And the teachers don't ask whether they are black or white, or rich or poor."[16]

Teaching, of course, was one of the respectable vocations open to black people, although it is doubtful that in 1913 black teachers taught white children as Hazel is implying in her answer. And, if it were true in 1913, one can only observe that conditions deteriorated in the following decades, for Boston is no utopia for black children, as Kozol detailed in *Death at an Early Age*.[17]

The motivation for black children to want to become teachers is lacking in most of the children's books. While Means does shift Harriet Freeman toward that goal, she discourages Lilybelle Lawrence from pursuing it. A few of the teachers in Means's two books are black, but only in *Zeke* is the head of the school a black. No living relative of a central character is a black teacher. Harriet Freeman's father had been a teacher, but he is dead when the book opens.

Both of Ovington's books, *Hazel* and *Zeke*, were very good for their dates of publication. A major characteristic of both is the author's concern with the individual happiness of her characters; she did not preach to them about helping serve their race.

What other occupations did juvenile book authors hold up before black people as possibilities? We know that Malcolm X's teacher urged him to be a carpenter. There is one carpenter in the sample: Mr. Robinson in Lattimore's *Junior, A Colored Boy of Charleston.* Mr. Robinson is also the only unemployed male parent in the books analyzed. The author has very precise views on what black children can aspire to in the adult work world:

> Everybody had to go to work some day. Junior and Rosalie would have to go to work as soon as they were through school. Maybe before.
> "I am going to be a nurse," said Rosalie, "and roll babies down on the Battery. I want to roll a baby in one of those big black carriages, and all dressed in pink."
> Junior didn't know which he wanted to be, though: a shine boy, or a mailman, or a carpenter like his father.[18]

Rosalie obviously is not talking about being a nurse, but a nursemaid. As for Junior, as was noted in chapter 1, the last words in the book show him still concerned about earning a living and still not knowing "what he wanted to be."

When Junior thinks about being a mailman he is dealing with reality. There is one mailman in the books: Mr. Bright in *Bright April,* but being black prevents him from becoming the postmaster. In fact, except for April's older sister who is in nursing school—and apparently wants to be a nurse—the Bright family does not fare too well when it comes to aspirations. April's brother, Ken, has dreams of being either an architect or an engineer (from the context, it is not quite clear which), but in the Army he is "working in the laundry!"

A discussion about what they want to be when they grow up takes place among the girls in April's Brownie troop. (See Figure 5.) April says:

> "I thought I'd like to be nurse like Sis, but now I think I'll be a hat designer and be boss of a big store on Chestnut Street." She airily sat up and tossed her head.
> One of the girls laughed and said, "You? Why they never let—" But she got no farther, for Mrs. Cole quickly slipped her hand over the child's mouth and, while she smoothed her cheeks and kept her from talking, went on to speak herself. She looked kind, but very grave.

Figure 5. The Brownie troop meeting at which April learns that being black places limitations on her life goals. From *Bright April*, by Marguerite DeAngeli; illustrated by the author. Copyright © 1946 by Marguerite DeAngeli. Reprinted by permission of Doubleday & Company, Inc.

"Suppose all of you learn to do the things you have to do *now* as well as you possibly can, then you will be ready to do whatever comes along. It is all very well to be at the head of things, but homely work is important too. Don't think you are too good to do any kind of work that seems necessary. You are respected for *the way* you do your work, any work. Remember many people cannot do the things they want to do." The girls looked at one another, but they did not laugh.

When it was time to stop work and put the things away and the girls had left one by one, April was the last to go. She helped Mrs. Cole put the things in the large box in the shed and was putting on her coat when Mrs. Cole drew her close and said:

"April, dear, you are very good at planning things and clever with your hands. There are many things you will be able to do when you are grown. Be sure you choose well. Then be sure you are so well trained that you will be able to take your place in the world. You may find you will have to go somewhere you don't want to go in order to be of the greatest service. Perhaps by the time you are grown up you can go anywhere you want to go." Then she added slowly, "I hope so."[19]

It is heartbreaking to think of the number of blacks in real life who were given this lecture about "serving your race." However, the lectures in life and in books did reflect the way things were, which is more than can be said for the presentations in Doris Gate's *Little Vic*[20] and Don Lang's *Strawberry Roan*.[21]

The male parental occupations in the two books are, respectively, jockey and horse trainer. In *Little Vic* Gates does admit that Pony Rivers' father had not been a very successful jockey, but in *Strawberry Roan*, Lang makes Roscoe Stewart's father a very successful horse trainer at the beginning and the end of the book (in between he has a run of hard luck to facilitate the plot). Gates ignores reality, however, when she has Pony Rivers ride in and win the Santa Anita Handicap, an event which simply could not have happened at the time the book was written. According to the *American Negro Reference Book* (1966):

Out of 1,500 jockeys and 4,000 trainers in racing today, only a mere handful are Negro; and none of these has an outstanding record. This is the way it has been for fifty years or more.[22]

An even more fundamental objection to the Gates book is that she depicts a black man's success as being made possible by the good will of one white man. When dealing with institutional racism—and becoming a licensed jockey was not a matter of the whim of an individual owner—the problem must be attacked and the system changed. The idea that the good intentions of nice white individuals could solve a black man's fight with society's restrictions is one of the most erroneous concepts found in children's books.

Gates did, at least, confront Pony with prejudice, if only in the presence of one bigot. In *Strawberry Roan*, Lang avoids the entire question of bigotry. His youthful character, Roscoe Stewart, travels from New England through small towns of the Midwest, and nothing is made of his race. The only time the subject is a problem, and then it is handled so obliquely that young readers may not know what is going on, is when money is missing from the store where Roscoe is working. The black cook of the store's owner is very angry with Roscoe for letting down his race. But none of this has anything to do with what starts out to be the problem of the book— the boy's determination to be with his beloved horse. Why Lang felt it necessary to make the Stewart family black is a question only he can answer.

Before leaving the subject of unrealistic situations, a small word about May Justus' *New Boy in School*.[23] Justus makes Lennie Lane's father a construction worker—one so highly thought of that he is moved by his company to Nashville. However, in the early 1970s the blacks are still trying to win entry into the construction trades.

As an indication of how little progress children's books make, a brief look at the two books with the latest publication dates in the original study will serve. Both *The Empty Schoolhouse* by Natalie Savage Carlson and *Who's in Charge of Lincoln?* by Dale Fife were published in 1965. In the latter, Lincoln's father is a railroad porter; in the former, the father is a field hand.

Not everyone, of course, can be a professional or a white-collar worker. Pride in one's work is important, regardless of the job level. Such pride is expressed by Emma Royall, the narrator in *The Empty Schoolhouse*:

"Emma Royall," I often tell myself, "if you were a teacher or stenographer, you'd want to be the best. So since you can't be them, you'll just have to try to be the best scrub girl there is."[24]

Emma can't be a schoolteacher or stenographer because she has no head for books—or so she says.

The limited horizons of Emma Royall is the subject of a lengthy discussion in "Black Perspective in Books for Children."[25] The authors, Judith Thompson and Gloria Woodard, object primarily to the fact that there is a relationship between Emma's self-concept and her having dark skin. The younger sister, Lullah, is light in color—and bright. The subtleties may not be as obvious to readers who have not pursued the subject at length, but anyone who delves into the relationship between light skin and success will agree with Thompson and Woodard.

THE BLACK AS PERFORMING ARTIST

Although there were distinct limitations placed upon what a black could expect to be allowed to do within the area known as the performing arts—Paul Robeson could play Othello, but he could not play Hamlet—it was a field open to blacks of superior talent. Three books, Hope Newell's *Steppin and Family*, Margaret Taylor's *Jasper, the Drummin' Boy*, and Florence Hayes's *Skid* depict young blacks as wanting to be in some form of show business.

Of the three, only *Steppin and Family** actually offers a look at the reality of being a performer. The major adult character, Bob Williams, is a thinly disguised Bill Robinson, a dancer of fantastic grace and skill. Steppin meets Bob Williams who arranges for him to have dancing lessons, to see a dance performance, and eventually to join the chorus of a show Williams is taking on the road.

The focus of the book is upon the discipline and hard work involved in being a quality dancer. In 1953, Newell wrote again about the Stebbins family in *A Cap for Mary Ellis*. By that time, Steppin was a star, able to provide his mother and sister with a nice apartment and pay for Mary Ellis' nursing education at Woodycrest.

Jasper, the Drummin' Boy† is a slight book dealing with a familiar situation: Jasper's drumming is an annoyance to everyone until an outsider proclaims him talented. The very first words in the book are future-oriented:

"When our children grow up I want them to be somebody," Mrs. Anderson said to Mr. Anderson. "So, I think Donna Jean should take dancing, and Jasper should take piano lessons."

"That's right," said Mr. Anderson. "But I don't know about Jasper playing the piano."

"Someday he will be a great concert pianist," Mrs. Anderson said with a dreamy look in her eyes.[26]

Jasper has his own ideas about success, and his idol is Stomp King, a black bandleader. After a series of annoying incidents, Jasper borrows his mother's new cake tin, a washtub, a scrubpail, and a broom handle. When

---

* See also chapter 11, "The Musical Black."

† A completely revised edition of *Jasper, the Drummin' Boy* was published by Follett in 1970. Analysis here applies to the original, 1947, title.

his mother discovers what Jasper has done, she leads a parade of neighbors to the corner where Jasper has set up his street band. Stomp King, who just happens to be among the people in the audience listening to the band, tells Mrs. Anderson that Jasper has the makings of a great drummer. Mrs. Anderson relents: Jasper can forget piano lessons and concentrate on drumming.

As with so many books in the study, *Jasper* is nothing more than a pleasant little story. It's only real value is the insertion of a successful black man, Stomp King, into the plot.

Both Steppin and Jasper have prominent black performers as idols; both are depicted as wanting nothing more than to be, respectively, a dancer and a drummer. Such is not the case with Skid Parker in *Skid*.

As the only black child in the Connecticut school he attends, Skid has been uncomfortable and unhappy. Then the boy who is to play the butler in the class play becomes ill, and Skid asks for the part. Miss Lewis, his teacher, tells him he can have the part, "But—I believe your parents and Aunt Alice may not want you to have such a part, and I understand their feelings." Miss Lewis is right. Aunt Alice, in particular, thinks Skid is stereotyping himself by playing a servant.

The night of the play's performance, Allyn, the bigot whom Skid has nicknamed "Flour Face," almost ruins the play. Skid saves it. The local newspaper gives him a great write-up; everybody in school talks to him; the teachers are nicer to him, and so, even Aunt Alice feels better.

Alice's eyes were like stars as she turned around to Skid. He thought for a minute she was going to kiss him. He ducked and started for his room. "Hot dog!" he shouted. "I'm going to be an actor!" In the doorway he stopped. "Mom," he called out, "you reckon old Flour Face will ask can he be my publicity agent?"[27]

Skid's proclamation that he is going to be an actor is very true to childhood. Doubtless the boy who wins the championship game for his Little League team thinks for a time that he will be a superstar in the big leagues. But the idea that a black's success will turn a bigot into a fan is highly questionable.

PROFESSIONAL ASPIRATIONS

Not much space is needed to discuss blacks who want to be professionals, there being only two. Charley Moss of Jesse Jackson's *Call Me*

Charley wants to be an engineer, and the title character in Dorothy Sterling's *Mary Jane* wants to be a biologist.

Charley has shown himself talented in the building of an airplane model, and Mr. Hamilton asks him:

> "What do you aim to be when you grow up? You want to be a mechanic?"
> "Yes, sir."
> "Aw, Charley, Why don't you tell him what you really want to be?" Tom said.
> George joined in. "Yes, Charley, go ahead and tell it all. . . . Charley wants to be an engineer!"
> "Well, what's wrong with that?" Mr. Hamilton asked.
> The boys looked at George.
> "Whoever heard of a colored engineer. My father's an engineer, and he says there just aren't any," George said.
> Mr. Hamilton worked on with the plane. The boys looked at him.
> "Maybe your father just hasn't seen any colored engineers," Mr. Hamilton said.[28]

Charley's mother approves of his dream of an education and a profession, but no encouragement at all comes from his father.

> Charley's father got up and yawned. "Like I said—it's all a lot of foolishness. Charley ought to be thinking about a job instead of keeping his head in a book all the time. When I was his age—"
> A shadow passed over Mrs. Moss's face as she raised her hand to tuck a braid of hair under her cap. "That's why I hope the good Lord will let me live long enough to see Charley get through school. He sure would have a tough row to hoe expecting anything from you."[29]

Charley's father is a handyman and his mother a combination cook-housekeeper. Charley is fortunate in having one of his parents encourage his dream, but then, Mrs. Moss is shown throughout the book as an intelligent, dedicated woman. Mr. Moss, on the other hand, is a chronic complainer, dissatisfied with his life, but unable to help his son aspire to a better one.

Mary Jane's desire to be a biologist does not create a family conflict since she comes from an educated family. Her grandfather is a George Washington Carver prototype; her father is a lawyer, and her older brother and sister are both away at school. What does create a problem is her desire to go to the white school, a topic covered in chapter 13 "Black-White Relationships." When Grampa asks her why she wants to go to Wilson Mary Jane explains in terms of her long-range goal:

"Because it's better than Douglass, that's why. Douglass has French, but Wilson has French and Latin. Douglass has just plain science—stuff I mostly know already. Wilson has physics and chemistry and biology. How'm I going to be a biologist if I don't go to Wilson?"

Grampa took the pipe out of his mouth and studied its bowl. "Some people," he observed, "seem to think I'm a biologist and I never went to Wilson."[30]

There is an answer to Grampa's statement, but Sterling does not give it. In an era of increasing specialization and the knowledge explosion, there is no room in the technological world for a self-educated, self-made man. Degrees are important, indeed vital, and the person with the best background stands the best chance of being able to move to the next step on the ladder.

A SPECIAL BOOK

The only book in the study to deal with the day-to-day existence of a poor black family is *Roosevelt Grady* by Louisa Shotwell. It is the only book that stood up under constant rereading. It is the only book to look at a black family's goals in a total context of life and not just the question of how to earn a living.

Shotwell zeroes in on the need to belong, the need to have a place of one's own, even if a humble one. This goal is shared by Mrs. Grady and Roosevelt; but Mrs. Grady's ambitions for her children go beyond just providing them with a settled home. At one point, she and her husband have an argument about the children picking beans and she says:

"You just put this in your pipe and smoke it, Mister Henry Grady. My children are going to grow up to be something else besides stooping, crawling bean-pickers. They're going to get educated. Never you mind how. They're going to train for jobs where they stand up straight or sit down in back of a desk. They're going to be somebody." All of sudden Mamma choked. A tear rolled down her cheek. A real tear.

"Hey, there," said Papa, and he wasn't teasing any more. "I didn't know you felt all that bad about it."

For a minute he didn't say anything at all, and then he went on, "They're my kids too, you know. Suppose they grew up to pick beans and the beans grew all in one place so they wouldn't have to go trucking around the country looking for them? Maybe even they'd be their own beans? Would you mind if they stooped over and crawled along after their very own beans?"

"Well," said Mamma, "well, I don't know. Maybe I wouldn't. But—oh, all right, you're so crazy to have them pick, let them pick. Only just so long as there isn't any school around for them to go to. When we come to a camp where there's a school, they're going to school. Understand? No more picking then."

"Okay," said Papa, "it's a deal. We get to a camp where there's a school, and we'll have no more picking. But tomorrow, everybody gets up early. Tomorrow everybody picks."[31]

In "Black Perspective in Books for Children," Thompson and Woodard set forth a criticism of the Grady family's goals similar to their objection to Emma Royall's limited goals in *The Empty Schoolhouse*, namely that the characters' goals seem tied to the color of their skin. They also make the point that the characters' responses are entirely too cheerful, considering the circumstances of their lives.[32]

While the objection to the Grady family being too cheerful appears logical, the social psychiatrist, Dr. Robert Coles, on the other hand, confirms Shotwell's portrait. In *Uprooted Children: The Early Lives of Migrant Farm Workers*, Coles discusses the ability of the parents to maintain hope, most particularly in relationship to their children's futures.[33] Moreover, at least for this reader, at no point did the Grady family demonstrate brainless cheerfulness. The ability to hope and dream, even under the most horrendous circumstances, is one of the continuing miracles of mankind.

As for being black, actually it is irrelevant to the book. Being a migrant worker is burden enough, a point Shotwell makes by never identifying the family as black. Were it not for the illustrations, *Roosevelt Grady* could not be identified as a black book. On the surface this may seem to run contrary to the statement made in chapter 1 that a writer cannot ignore a black's color since it is all-important. That holds true only at a certain level of existence. Unhappily, in our society, migrant workers are all equal in terms of deprivation, of treatment by the communities whose crops they pick, and of being trapped in a dead-end situation.

8
THE PRIMITIVE

The word "primitive" has many definitions and is, on all-too-many occasions, used quite loosely. Two of the definitions proved applicable to the children's books under discussion. The first is the anthropological definition: "Of, or pertaining to a race, groups, etc., having cultural or physical similarities with their early ancestors."[1] In anthropological terms the word "primitive" is not an antonym of "civilized," but rather a matter of degree. The anthropologist sees civilization as a scale, and some groups are merely at different points on the scale. Insofar as possible, value judgments are not made concerning the mores of a group, but rather the culture is described within the value system of the society being analyzed.

However, cultural anthropology is one of the youngest of the social sciences, and until the twentieth century, most information imparted to children about people living in other lands and in other societies was contained in exotic adventure stories or in travel books that recounted the author's adventures in a faraway land. How much of the purported true adventures were, in fact, true is questionable.

For example, in the 1830 publication *The Tales of Peter Parley About Africa*—a book not analyzed in the original study, but of prime interest— Goodrich was to come to the fore as a strong defender of the African and as an antislavery man. He wrote:

Formerly, the accounts given us of the people of Africa, represented the negro race, as a stupid, debased portion of the human family, only fit to be the slaves and servants of the rest of mankind.

But modern travellers, more worthy of credit, give more favorable representations. Both Denham and Clapperton found the Negroes of Central Africa more intelligent, and more civilized, than the world had been led to believe them. The Caffrees and Hottentots are now known to be superior in every respect, to what their Dutch neighbours, used to say they were.

There is in truth little reason to doubt, that for the purpose of providing some excuse, for the barbarous and cruel treatment of the Negroes, the Europeans have been accustomed to misrepresent their character. How much more delightful would it be, to see all christian people uniting with heart and hand, to spread the light of education, and religious knowledge, among the unfortunate millions of Africa, rather than to send people to force away the inhabitants, by violence and treachery, and then to excuse this mean and dastardly conduct by representing them as brutes, rather than men.[2]

The tone of the book makes it possible to believe that Goodrich had, indeed, traveled in Africa. Were it not for the detailed description of that legendary, nonexistent animal, the cameleopard, this reader might never have questioned Goodrich's observations. Obviously, he was a voracious armchair traveler who absorbed his information from books.

The trouble with the early books and many books today that are written by nonanthropologists is that, with the best intentions in the world, the authors do make value judgments. By modern standards, Goodrich's overall favorable tone is marred by the assumption that the education and religion of the Western Christian world are necessary additions to the African's life. There is a similar attitude in Paul DuChaillu's *Stories of the Gorilla Country*. In *Tarzan of the Apes* it is seen that when the fiction writer is convinced that white, Western society alone contains the truth, he depicts less-developed cultures in unrelentingly negative terms. For authors like Burroughs, "different" automatically meant "inferior."

The second definition is of the "cultural" primitive, and as used here this means: "unaffected or little affected by civilizing influences."[3] This definition presupposes some kind of innate characteristic that resists cultural change and that will surface whenever individuals or members of a race in general, are faced with situations stressful enough to make them "revert" to ancestral patterns. Booth Tarkington is a devotee of this attitude, and he represents a shift in emphasis from the idea that God intended the black to be inferior to the simplified Darwinian idea that the black has simply not made his way up the evolutionary scale.

Theoretically the books set in Africa ought to have presented a portrait of the anthropological primitive—and on the whole they do—while books set in the United States should have produced a portrait of the cultural primitive—but they do not. The books with American settings emphasize the innate characteristics of Africans and considerably blur the dividing line. Therefore, for practical purposes the nine books that contain images of the black as a primitive are treated together.

CRUELTY AND SUPERSTITION

Considered within the context of its time of publication, 1864, *Stories of the Gorilla Country* by Paul DuChaillu is a good book. DuChaillu is meticulous in detailing the differences among the numerous African tribes he encounters. Some tribes are man-eating, others are not; some are very black, some are brown; some are tall, others are short of stature.

Unhappily, the differences are presented in less-dramatic terms than the similarities. Being a good Christian, DuChaillu was shocked and appalled by the idolatry and belief in witchcraft that he found common to all tribes. DuChaillu was first and foremost a good storyteller, and he knew that the vividness with which he described the beliefs in witchcraft and idolatry would capture his youthful audience. Thus, early in the book, he describes his first night in Africa:

After my meal, I walked through the streets of the village and came to a house, in the recess of which I saw an enormous idol. I had never in all my life seen such an ugly thing. It was a rude representation of some human being, of the size of life, and was made of wood. It had large copper eyes, and a tongue of iron which shot out from its mouth to show that it could sting. The lips were painted red. It wore large iron earrings. Its head was ornamented with a feather cap. Most of the feathers were red, and came from the tails of gray parrots, while the body and face were painted red, white, and yellow. It was dressed in the skins of wild animals. Around it were scattered skins of tigers and serpents, and the bones and skulls of animals. Some food also was placed near, so that it might eat if it chose.[4]

Later that night he watches the natives dance and sing wildly around the idol and discovers that they are going on a hunt and are asking it to bring them luck.

After relating in detail how an elderly king attempts to keep from dying by worshiping his idol devoutly and by employing witch doctors, Du-Chaillu defines what the natives think a witch is, as well as the penalty for being adjudged a witch:

You would like to know, I dare say, what these Africans mean by a wizard or a witch? They believe that people have within themselves the power of killing any one who displeases them. They believe that no one dies unless some one has bewitched him. Have you ever heard of such a horrible superstition? Hence those who are condemned for witchcraft are sometimes subjected to a very painful death; they are burnt by slow fire, and their bodies are given to the Bashikouay ant to be devoured. I shall have something to tell you about ants by-and-by. The poor wretches are cut into pieces; gashes are made over their bodies, and Cayenne pepper is put in the wounds. Indeed, it makes me shudder to think of it, for I have witnessed such dreadful deaths, and seen many of the mutilated corpses.[5]

In the primitive world it is not only people who have evil powers. There are inanimate objects that can be used against one's enemies, such as the gall of a leopard. And there are evil spirits that live in or near graveyards and that, when angered, can cause illness or death.

One of the more intriguing beliefs recorded had to do with a group of natives who could not eat the meat of the hippopotamus because it was "roonda" for them. "Some of their ancestry had a long time ago given birth to a hippopotamus, and if they were to eat any, more births of hippopotami would come to them, or they would die."[6]

At one point, DuChaillu sums up this emphasis upon witchcraft by saying, "Of course the Commi people, like all other negroes, are firm believers in witchcraft."[7]

So firm is the African's belief in witchcraft as presented in the books that it rises to the fore when the African is under stress, even after he has been exposed to the supposedly civilizing influences of Christianity. In *Cudjo's Cave*, Trowbridge describes Cudjo as a fire-idolator:

Penn shuddered with awe. For the first time in his life he found himself in the presence of an idolator. Cudjo belonged to a tribe of African fire-worshippers, from whom he had been stolen in his youth; and, although the sentiment of the old barbarous religion had smouldered for years forgotten in his breast, this night it had burst forth again, kindled by the terrible splendors of the burning mountain.[8]

Cudjo's frenzy at seeing the fire is such that, even though Cudjo is leading the trapped people to safety, Penn experiences doubts about him: "A horrible suspicion crossed Penn's mind; the fanatical fire-worshipper had brought them there to destroy them—to sacrifice them to his god."[9]

While DuChaillu and Trowbridge's prose is vivid enough, it pales when compared to Burroughs' descriptions in *Tarzan of the Apes*. When Tarzan first sees the African natives, they are described as:

armed with slender wooden spears with ends hard baked over slow fires, and long bows and poisoned arrows. On their backs were oval shields, in their noses huge rings, while from the kinky wool of their heads protruded tufts of gay feathers.

Across their foreheads were tattooed three parallel lines of color, and on each breast three concentric circles. Their yellow teeth were filed to sharp points, and their great protruding lips added still further to the low and bestial brutishness of their appearance.[10]

The tribe builds homes, plants crops, and settles down to lead a life of freedom and happiness. It is when Kulonga, son of the chief, kills Tarzan's ape-mother Kala, that trouble begins. Tarzan avenges Kala's death by killing Kulonga.

Seeing his prey dead, Tarzan, hungry, prepares to eat him, but doubts seep into his head, and finally:

All he knew was that he could not eat the flesh of this black man, and thus hereditary instinct, ages old, usurped the functions of his untaught mind and saved him from transgressing a world-wide law of whose very existence he was ignorant.[11]

The killing of Kulonga begins Tarzan's harassment of the tribe. He establishes a position in a tree near the village so he can observe the behavior of the natives. While the tribe is off bringing home Kulonga's body, Tarzan enters a hut (as fate would have it, Kulonga's) and, after examining the contents, places a headdress of the dead Kulonga upon a skull.

When Mbonga, the chief, described as wearing a necklace "of dried human hands depending upon his chest," enters his son's hut and sees the results of Tarzan's work, he emerges with:

a look of mingled wrath and superstitious fear writ upon his hideous countenance. . . .

Mbonga could explain nothing of the strange events that had taken place. The finding of the still warm body of Kulonga—on the very verge of their fields and within easy earshot of the village—knifed and stripped at the door of his father's home, was in itself sufficiently mysterious, but these last awesome discoveries within the village, within the dead Kulonga's own hut, filled their hearts with dismay and conjured in their poor brains only the most frightful of superstitious explanations.[12]

Continuing to observe the tribe, Tarzan "saw that these people were more wicked than his own apes and as savage and cruel as Sabor herself." This comment immediately precedes a description of the tribe's treatment of a captive who is tied to a stake around which the natives dance "in wild and savage abandon to the maddening music of the drums." The captive is then pierced by innumerable spears throughout "every inch of the poor writhing body that did not cover a vital organ." The effect of this torture upon the tribe is described:

> The women and children shrieked their delight.
> The warriors licked their hideous lips in anticipation of the feast to come, and vied with one another in the savagery and loathsomeness of the cruel indignities with which they tortured the still conscious prisoner.[13]

While the natives are thus occupied, Tarzan steals their supply of poisoned arrows, and then "he looked about for some hint of a wild prank to play upon these strange, grotesque creatures that they might be again aware of his presence among them." Tarzan's prank consists of stealing a human skull and throwing it amongst them, thus playing upon "their superstitious fears."[14]

Burroughs' thesis, that a white man of noble blood, reared among the apes, is superior in all ways to black men, is omnipresent. Black men eat other men, but ape-reared Tarzan balks at such behavior. But the theory reaches the ludicrous point when Tarzan kills a black man in order to steal his breechcloth. Tarzan has discovered he is a man, and modesty is more important a virtue than refraining from murder.

The Africans are not encountered again for many pages as the castaway Porter family occupies Tarzan's attention. When Jane Porter is stolen by Terkoz, the ape, a party of French sailors goes in search of her. The central figure is D'Arnot, the Frenchman who will eventually teach Tarzan to be a cultured gentleman. The column is attacked by a native tribe and D'Arnot is captured:

And then began for the French officer the most terrifying experience which man can encounter upon earth—the reception of a white prisoner into a village of African cannibals.

To add to the fiendishness of their cruel savagery was the poignant memory of still crueler barbarities practiced upon them and theirs by the white officers of that arch hypocrite, Leopold II of Belgium.[15]

The scene is a repeat of the earlier torture of the black prisoner. As D'Arnot is clawed, beaten, and stoned he begins to feel that he is in a horrid nightmare from which he will awake:

The bestial faces, daubed with color—the huge mouths and flabby hanging lips—the yellow teeth, sharp filed—the rolling, demon eyes—the shining naked bodies—the cruel spears. Surely no such creatures really existed upon earth—he must indeed be dreaming.[16]

They begin to pierce him with spears, but D'Arnot will not cry out. "He was a soldier of France, and he would teach these beasts how an officer and a gentleman died."

From the first mention of the Africans to the last in *Tarzan of the Apes* the emphasis is on bestiality and cruelty. DuChaillu, on balance, was much fairer to the African, but even he could not resist making the connection between blacks and animals. At one point in *Stories of the Gorilla Country* he relates how he mistook a chimpanzee for his fellow hunter, Aboko.

VIOLENT AND ANIMALLIKE NATURES

Not only do blacks look like chimpanzees, according to Thomas Nelson Page in *Two Little Confederates,* they can traverse paths through the woods that "were generally useful only to a race, such as the negroes, which had an instinct for direction like that shown by some animals."[17] Louis Pendleton, author of *King Tom and the Runaways,* obviously agreed in this assessment of the black's ability. The two white boys are hopelessly lost in the wood, "But, Jim never faltered, apparently as sure of his direction as any bird or animal would have been."[18]

In *Journey Cake,* Isabel McMeekin attributes Juba's ability to move in the dark to her racial ancestry when she notes that "Juba's mother had been born in the jungles of a hot far country and she was gifted with that unerring sense of direction and crafty carefulness which is as much an inheritance as the ability to see like a cat in the dark."[19]

The most subtle comment—subtle for children, not for adults—linking blacks and animals is found in Annie Vaughan Weaver's *Frawg*. Not only is "Frawg" an animal name, but after giving the names of Frawg's brothers and sisters, the author says, "The rest of the family lived out in the yard."[20] The "rest" consists of the cow, the mule, the pig, and the poultry.

According to Booth Tarkington's portraits of Herman and Verman in *Penrod* and in *Penrod and Sam*, acculturation does not lessen either the violent or the animal nature of the black man. Tarkington's depictions of Herman and Verman are among the most unrelentingly negative within the books analyzed. Tarkington's bias was ingrained, as can be seen in the portrait of the black man in *Seventeen*, a book not analyzed because it did not appear in the Blanck bibliography.

In *Penrod* (1914) there is a scene in which Herman and Verman fight the bully Rupe Collins. It begins when Rupe calls Herman "you ole black nigger" and discovers, much to his regret, that Herman will not stand for being called "nigger." This leads to a confrontation. Herman and Rupe stand nose-to-nose, as described by Tarkington:

Penrod's familiar nose had been as close with only a ticklish spinal effect upon the not very remote descendant of Congo man-eaters. The result produced by the glare of Rupe's unfamiliar eyes, and by the dreadfully suggestive proximity of Rupe's unfamiliar nose, was altogether different. Herman's and Verman's great-grandfathers never considered people of their own jungle neighbourhood proper material for a meal, but they looked upon strangers—especially truculent strangers—as distinctly edible.[21]

The fight is on, and Verman strikes Rupe from behind with the tines of the pitchfork down, because "in his simple, direct African way he wished to kill his enemy."

Rupe's problem, according to Tarkington, was that:

he had not learned that an habitually aggressive person runs the danger of colliding with beings in one of those lower stages of evolution wherein theories about "hitting below the belt" have not yet made their appearance.[22]

After Rupe is routed, Penrod asks Herman if he would have really cut out Rupe's gizzard, as threatened in the heat of the fight. Herman replies:

"Sho! I guess I us dess *talkin'* whens I said 'at! Reckon he thought I meant it, f'm de way he tuck an' run. Hiyi! No, suh, I uz dess talkin', cause I ney' would cut *no*body! I ain't tryin' git in no jail—no suh!"[23]

There is an echo in these last words of the phrase, "like father, like son," for the first introduction of Herman and Verman contains the information that their father is in jail for having cut up a man with a pitchfork. When Penrod plans his circus, Herman and Verman are important attractions. In shrilling for the show, Penrod shouts:

"*Next*, let me kindly interodoos Herman and Verman. Their father got mad and stuck his pitchfork right inside of another man, exactly as promised upon the advertisements outside the big tent, and got put in jail. Look at them well, gen-til-mun and lay-deeze, there is no extra charge, and *re-mem-bur* you are each and all now looking at two wild, tattooed men which the father of is in jail."[24]

In *Penrod and Sam* the scene in which Herman and Verman attack Georgie Bassett for calling Verman "a nigger," is not described, but the results are. Georgie is to be initiated into "The Order of the In-Or-In" Club at the insistence of the mothers, not the boys. When Georgie calls Verman "a nigger," the paddling administered is severe enough to cause Georgie's mother to complain and Penrod and Sam to be chastised. However, the real complaint has more to do with the boys' association with blacks than with Georgie's paddling.

While a tendency toward violence is the outstanding characteristic of the blacks in Tarkington's books, it is not the only negative trait, although it is the most dramatic. Equally important is the assumption of stupidity, or subservience. Difficult to determine is just what Tarkington was driving at in the many scenes of Penrod manipulating Herman and Verman. Herman and Verman's initial reactions to Penrod's propositions are usually negative—the two have, in fact, a great deal more common sense than Penrod—yet they do end up participating in Penrod's wild ventures.

One such episode is in *Penrod and Sam*. The two white boys are harassing a cat, and the cat escapes into a cistern. But the cistern is a temporary haven, since the cat needs help to get out. Penrod and Sam decide that the ideal ladder for the cat will be Herman's trousers. It is November and being without trousers is no joke. Herman resists, but as in all encounters with the whites, he ends up surrendering his trousers. The cat escapes, the trousers end up in the cistern, and Herman is left shivering.

As a follow-up to the rescue of the cat (not for humanitarian reasons) Penrod and Sam induce Herman and Verman to play "Fortygraphing Wild Animals in the Jungle." The game demands that Verman also remove his trousers so he and Herman will look like native "beaters." This episode offers a hint as to the source of the race pride that makes Herman and Verman refuse to let anyone call them "niggers." Their mother arrives in the midst of the scene and says, "My goo'ness, if you' Pappy don' lam you tonight! Ain' you got no mo' sense 'an to let white boys 'suade you play you Affikin heathums?"[25]

The violent nature of the black man is noted in *Miss Minerva and William Green Hill* in a scene in which the children are playing at being members of a prison chain gang. The first order of business is to decide what the criminals are guilty of. Jimmy is told he "done got 'rested fer 'sturbin' public worship." He replies:

"Naw I ain't neither . . . ; I done cut my woman with a razor 'cause I see her racking down the street like a proud coon with another gent, like what Sarah Jane's brother told me he done at the picnic."[26]

Thus we see that young readers are told that if the black man lives in Africa, he is brutally torturing his captives. If he has been transported to the United States, he uses a pitchfork or razor much as he used his spear in the jungle. A not-so-subtle implication of this portrait is that a tendency toward violence is a racial characteristic of beings who are, in Tarkington's words, "in one of the lower stages of evolution." How one progresses up the evolutionary ladder is never discussed.

9

BLACK IS
NOT BEAUTIFUL

For many whites the enthusiasm with which black people embraced the phrase "black is beautiful" was seen as little more than a fad. The sentiment would lose popularity just as hoola hoops did. If one rarely hears the phrase now, that does not mean it was a fad, merely that it accomplished its purpose in helping blacks see themselves as beautiful people. The task needed accomplishing because white society had emphasized for years that: (1) black is ugly, (2) black men prefer white women or light blacks, and (3) blacks would really like to be white. The three categories are not separate and distinct; they interlock to produce a portrait of black self-denigration, a people without self-pride.

The best example of a black child's lack of pride in her color is found in Georgene Faulkner's *Melindy's Happy Summer* (1949), and the effect is heartbreaking. Throughout the book, on every occasion when Melindy meets a blond girl she is shown telling the blond how pretty she is. The climax to this envy, concern, self-disparagement—call it what you will—comes when the lead singer in the Music Camp's production of the opera *Hansel and Gretel* has to have an emergency operation. The camp director asks Melindy to take the part since she just happens to know the musical score. Her response is, "But look at me. . . . Look at my brown skin and black hair—Gretel is a beautiful little blond girl."[1]

Melindy is assured that makeup and a wig will turn her into a properly beautiful Gretel, and she begins a week of rehearsals. The night before the performance the wig has not arrived. Although she is told not to worry:

a thousand worries beset Melindy that night—chief of which was the wig. What if it didn't come? Then everyone in the audience would know that there was something strange and different about her.[2]

As is inevitable in the world of children's books, the wig does not arrive on the scheduled plane. A flurry of activity results in plans being made for the wig to be dropped from a private plane in a field and picked up by Bill and Bob, the two boys with whom Melindy has been staying that summer. The boys have a flat tire and the wig arrives just five minutes before curtain time. When it is put on Melindy, her braids make a bump, so she says, "Cut 'em off," and the makeup man does. When Melindy is finally transformed into the blond Gretel, the makeup man says to her, "I wish you could see yourself. . . . You look beautiful."[3]

It is important to bear in mind that the word "beautiful" as used here and in the phrase "black is beautiful" does not have anything to do with beauty-contest-type physical appearance. Within all races there are some individuals who are more attractive than others. What is at issue is that color alone determined that black characters were unattractive, and with exceptions that will be noted later, the majority of physical portraits within the children's books were in one way or another derogatory.

That color was a major factor in unattractiveness can be inferred from the fact that there is only one positive description in the sample of a really black person, and he is a native African. A sampling of phrases that authors used to get around describing the various individuals as black includes Lattimore's "skins as brown as copper pennies"—for Louis and Julie in *Bayou Boy*; Means's "a bronze maiden"—for Harriet Freeman in *Shuttered Windows*; Newell's "coffee-brown face"—for Steppin—and "golden taffy-brown"—for Mary Ellis in *Steppin and Family*, and Hunt's "pansy-velvet"—for the three children in *Ladycake Farm*.

As recently as 1967, Charlemae Rollins could say in the Introduction to *We Build Together* that among the words Negroes objected to was "black." The authors cited above were undoubtedly aware of this aversion to the word "black" and went to pains to avoid using it. That does not change the basic premise that black was, indeed, not beautiful to either blacks or whites.

BLACK IS UGLY

It was not always necessary to provide a description of the character to stress a particularly ugly feature of being black. In *The Young Marooners* (1852) Author Francis Goulding settles for "Ah! black and ugly as she was, that Judy was a jewel."[4] In the opening words of *Beautiful Joe* (1894) Marshall Saunders has the dog-narrator introduce himself by saying:

My name is Beautiful Joe, and I am a brown dog of medium size. I am not called Beautiful Joe because I am a beauty. Mr. Morris, the clergyman in whose family I have lived for the last twelve years, says that I must be called Beautiful Joe for the same reason that his grandfather, down South, called a very ugly colored slave-lad Cupid, and his mother Venus.[5]

The prototype of the ugly black is Cudjo in Trowbridge's *Cudjo's Cave* (1864). When the reader first meets him, Cudjo is described as "ugly, deformed with immensely long arms, short bow legs resembling a parenthesis, a body like a frog's and the countenance of an ape."[6] A short while later, Trowbridge again says "Cudjo was more like an ape."[7]

Trowbridge was reflecting a point of view that would later find its way into the famed Ninth Edition of the *Encyclopaedia Britannica*, which said of African aborigines: "By the nearly unanimous consent of anthropologists this type occupies at the same time the lowest position in the evolutionary scale, thus affording the best material for the comparative study of the highest anthropoids and the human species." The article pointed to "the abnormal length of the arm" and "weak lower limbs" of Africans. Other characteristics ascribed to the African by the *Britannica* author, A. H. Keane, and found in illustrations and textual comments throughout the children's books analyzed were: "prognathism" (jaw protection); "short flat snub nose," "thick protruding lips," and "distinctly woolly" hair.[8]

Of these characteristics, the one to receive the most attention, both in verbal description and in illustrations, was the hair, although all the other characteristics were represented consistently. The earliest verbal description of the African natives was found in *The Seven Little Sisters Who Live on the Round Ball That Floats in the Air* (1861) by Jane Andrews:

Their lips are thick, their noses broad, and instead of hair, their heads are covered with wool, such as you might see on a black sheep. This wool is braided and twisted into little knots and strings all over their heads, and bound with bits of red string, or any gay-looking thread. They think it looks beautiful, but I am afraid we should not agree with them.[9]

Eighty-five years later, Eleanor Lattimore described her characters in *Bayou Boy* (1946) in very similar terms:

Louis' hair, cut close to his head, was curly as a lamb's fleece. But Julie's hair was braided too tight to curl. It was braided in many little braids, each tied with a bright ribbon, green and red and pink and gold.[10]

Wool, whether from a full-grown sheep or a young lamb, is wool. If there are people who grew up without believing a black had wool instead of human hair that simply had a different texture, it was not because of children's authors, even black ones. Here is Arna Bontemps' description of Shine Boy (in *You Can't Pet a Possum*) getting ready for his ninth birthday party:

> He would need to comb his hair. He tried to bring the comb through his tightly knotted wool. There was no use trying that, he decided. The comb just would not go through. He remembered that sometimes folks made their hair look slick and fresh by greasing it. That *was* an idea. So away Shine Boy hurried to the lard barrel. He filled his hands and smeared them on his head. That did not make him look as well as he had expected, but it was better than doing nothing to his obstinate hair.[11]

In *Sad-Faced Boy*, another Bontemps title, the three runaways from Alabama knock on the door of their Uncle Tappin in Harlem, and when he looks out the door, Slumber sees "a tuft of gray wool on top of an old wrinkled head."[12]

Means presents a long scene in *Shuttered Windows* in which Harriet, her roommate Mossie, and her friend Johnnie are getting ready for a party:

> Mossie's dark little face was more somber than usual, with a stocking top pulled down to the brows. She had been using pomade on her hair and combing it with a heated iron comb set like a poker in a coiled handle.
>
> "Johnnie," she asked timidly, "how y'all keep yo' hair so straight an' shiny?"
>
> "It grew that way." Johnnie was almost regretful: Mossie had looked so hopeful.
>
> Mossie's lip sagged mournfully.
>
> "Why do you care?" Harriet asked. "I don't—much. I'll admit it's a nuisance to go to all the bother of straightening it and then have it wind itself up as tight as the dickens the minute a damp breeze hits it.—Especially here, where all the breezes are damp."
>
> "Oh, well"—Johnnie treated the matter lightly, not being personally annoyed by it—"did you ever see white girls with their hair all curled just so, and then after they'd been out in the rain and it looked like something the cat dragged in?—Of course not with permanent waves? They have their hair all twisted up tight and clamped to the electric light, and there they have to *sit*—anyway in the old-fashioned kind they do—looking like Medusa, for hours on

end, no matter how it pulls and burns. And then when the operator undoes it and combs it out, like enough they say, 'Horrors! it's just like *wool!*' "

Mossie cringed. Wool was a word she and her friends did not allow in their vocabulary.

Johnnie laughed at her discomfort. "Why on earth is it so much worse to have to *straighten* your hair than to have to *curl* it?" she demanded.

"Because it is," Harriet said flatly.

"A fellow's own handicaps are always worse than the other fellow's," Johnnie jeered.[13]

Mrs. Means understood that for many black girls the question of straightening their hair was of paramount importance, and in *Great Day in the Morning* she eventually examined why it was so much worse to have to straighten hair than to curl it. The subject first comes up early in the book when Lilybelle Lawrence is getting ready for her graduation day and is shown thinking:

The last day of school! She wanted to look her best. Lucky she'd had her hair pressed just before Grampa was taken so bad with rheumatism last week. The pressing had to be done about every two weeks, rain or shine. Even here on this island off the Southern coast very few of the women folks left their hair "natural" after they were twelve or fourteen; without hers pressed Lilybelle would have felt like a girl caught in her under-slip. She surveyed the lacquer blackness of her head with satisfaction as she took off her kerchief. Carefully she combed the sides into smooth wings and tied a ribbon around them.[14]

Later in the book, Lilybelle and the other girls at the YWCA in Denver are talking about what they are going to do with their lives. One of the girls mentions that she is going to be a beautician. This reminds Lilybelle of a black woman who had made a fortune by marketing a new hair pressing-oil, and she thinks of other possibilities:

Lilybelle sometimes dreamed what a person could do if she studied chemistry hard enough. Couldn't she work out a pressing-oil that would be permanent, or at least as permanent as a permanent wave? Couldn't she develop one that wouldn't soil collars? And why not a cream that would bleach dark skin?

There were plenty of Negroes today, she had heard, who wouldn't be white if they could choose. And Doctor Carver would have thought the idea trifling. Yet what a burden dark skin and tight-curled hair could be in a land where light skin and straight hair predominated.[15]

It is clear in so many ways throughout both the Means titles that she understood a great deal about the "Negro" condition. Time and again she comes close to the heart of the matter, but in the end, always backs off from facing the issue of white intolerance for difference. As we will see later, her message to black people was that they wait with patience, work hard, and someday the whites would admit them to society.

What is so depressing about children's books is the length of time it takes for a changing attitude to appear in them. The Means book was published in 1946; nineteen years later, in 1965, Natalie Carlson wrote in *The Empty Schoolhouse* the same kind of apologetic, forgive-me-for-being-dark nonsense. Emma, the narrator, describes the Royall family:

Lullah is the spittin' image of Mama and her kin. Her skin is like coffee and cream mixed together, and she has wavy hair to her shoulders. Me, I'm dark as Daddy Jobe and my hair never grew out much longer than he wears his. . . . Little Jobe looks like me and Daddy Jobe *but* [emphasis added] he's a handsome little boy all the same.[16]

An inference the reader might draw from this physical contrast is that intelligence can be equated with the lightness of skin color since Emma says she is dumb and Lullah is bright.* It would also have been a pleasant change to have the father be the lighter of the two parents.

A light mother and darker father are shown in a photograph in Stella Gentry Sharpe's *Tobe*. As in the Royall family, the father is dark, with tightly ridged hair; the mother is lighter and has longer, straighter hair.[17] In Ellis Credle's *Across the Cotton Patch*, one of the twins, Atlantic, who can't be more than five or six years old, complains that she cannot get exposed to the sun because, "Ah can get mo' blacker dan what Ah is, and de cullud boys lak yaller gals."[18]†

While "cullud boys" might prefer "yaller gals," Hugh Lofting makes it quite clear that white girls do not prefer black men. In the now infamous chapters involving Prince Bumpo in *The Story of Doctor Dolittle*, Lofting has the Prince relate how he went in search of the sleeping princess, found her, kissed her awake, only to be rejected with "Oh, he's black!" The

---

* See also the chapter 7 references to the relationship between light skin and success.
† It may appear to be quibbling, but putting this type of comment in a very young child's mouth is offensive and could not have occurred in a children's book with white characters saying something similar.

Prince says to Doctor Dolittle, "If you will turn me white, I will give you half my kingdom and anything else besides you ask."[19]

The good doctor suggests that Prince Bumpo settle for blond hair. Nothing will do, however, but that he become white. The doctor does turn Bumpo's face white and is freed from captivity. But when the doctor expresses doubt that the whiteness will last, Dab-Dab says, "Serve him right, if he does turn black again! I hope it's a dark black."[20] This type of comment shows Lofting's real attitudes, and it cannot be discounted. There is no reason for Dab-Dab's animosity toward Prince Bumpo—except that Bumpo is black. In keeping his part of the deal, Bumpo has shown himself an honorable man.

The two six-year-olds, Billy and Jimmy, in *Miss Minerva and William Green Hill* by Frances Calhoun are not as ambitious as Doctor Dolittle and settle for changing the color of a small black child's hair. The incident is entitled "Changing the Ethiopian."

While Sarah Jane, the Garner family's faithful family servant, is "in the kitchen cooking supper," the two white boys invade her cabin and cover her son Benny Dick's head with "Blondine" lotion three times:

The effect was ludicrous. The combination of coal black skin and red gold hair presented by the little negro exceeded the wildest expectations of Jimmy and Billy. They shrieked with laughter and rolled over and over on the floor in their unbounded delight.

Returning to her cabin, Sarah Jane sees "her baby with his glistening black face and golden hair":

She threw up her hands, closed her eyes, and uttered a terrified shriek. Presently she slowly opened her eyes and took a second peep at her curious-looking offspring. Sarah Jane screamed aloud:

"Hit'd de handiwork er de great Jehosphophat! Hit's de Marster's sign. Who turnt you' hair, Benny Dick?" she asked of the sticky little pickaninny sitting happily on the floor. "Is a angel been here?"

Benny Dick nodded his head with a delighted grin of comprehension.

"Hit's de doing er de Lord," cried his mother. "He gwine turn my chile white an' he done begunt on his head!"[21]

So we have Prince Bumpo, wanting to be white so he can marry the Sleeping Beauty, and we have the mother, joyfully thinking God is going to turn her son white. But God has washed his hands of the black man. According to the Pyrnelle story in *Diddie, Dumps, and Tot* (see chapter 2), the black man was too lazy to be finished up with the superior coating of white, and the Uncle Remus tale, "Why the Negro Is Black," has a similar flavor to it.

According to Uncle Remus, "Niggers is niggers now, but de time wuz w'en we 'us all niggers tergedder." Then came the word that there was a pond in the neighborhood "w'ich ef dey'd git inter dey'd be wash off nice en w'ite." The last people to get to the pond found only enough water "ter paddle about wid der foots en dabble in it wid der han's." That is why the black man is black except for the palms of his hands and the soles of his feet, all because he was too late to be washed white.[22]

BLACK IS OKAY—SEPIA IS BETTER

Not all black characters were depicted as unattractive (see Figures 6, 7, and 8), but favorable descriptions tend to fall into one of two categories. The first category is that of superspecimen; the second, that of the light brown, coffee-with-cream images mentioned earlier.

John Townsend Trowbridge, author of *Cudjo's Cave*, was clearly a man who disapproved of slavery and was, at the very least, sympathetic toward the black man's plight. But even he could not resist making a superman out of his central black character, Pomp, who was "a negro upwards of six feet in height, magnificently proportioned, straight as a pillar, and black as ebony."[23]

Penn Hapgood, who is being nursed back to health by Pomp, is fascinated by the man, whose:

demeanor was well calculated to inspire calmness and trust. There was something truly grand and majestic, not only in his person, but in his character also. He was a superb man. Penn never wearied of watching him. He thought him the most perfect specimen of a gentleman he had ever seen; always cheerful, always courteous, always comporting himself with the ease of an equal in the presence of his guest. His strength was enormous. He lifted Penn in his arms as if he had been an infant. But his grace was no less than his vigor. He was, in short, a lion of a man.[24]

Throughout the book Trowbridge consistently maintains this image of Pomp as perfect man.

Figure 6. Although the black male was the target of the worst antiblack sentiments, the three most attractive blacks depicted in the illustrations are male. See also Figures 7 and 8. Richie Corwin, from *Shuttered Windows* by Florence Crannell Means; illustrated by Armstrong Sperry. Copyright © 1938 by Florence Crannell Means. Reprinted by permission of Houghton Mifflin Co.

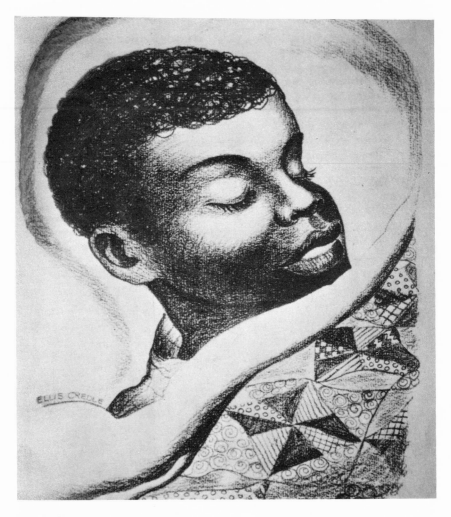

Figure 7. Little Jeemes Henry asleep is a tender portrait of a young black boy.
Ellis Credle, *Little Jeemes Henry*, illustrated by the author. Reprinted by permission
of the publisher, Thomas Nelson Inc. Copyright © 1936, 1964 by Ellis Credle.

Trowbridge at least made Pomp "black as ebony," which was more than
Howells did in his description of "the Dumb Negro's family" in *A Boy's
Town*. About the women of the family, there is not a word, but Howells
tells us that:

The men were swarthy, handsome fellows, not much darker than Spaniards,
and they were so little afraid of the chances which were often such fatal

Figure 8. Tobe is an engaging real-life child. From *Tobe*, by Stella Gentry Sharpe; photographs by Charles Farrell, University of North Carolina Press, 1939.

mischances to colored people in that day that one of them travelled through the South, and passed himself in very good company as a Cherokee Indian of rank and education.[25]

Howells' book was published in 1890, the same year that produced *King Tom and the Runaways* by Louis Pendleton. Pendleton's approach to describing his major black character was to couple physical statement with personality characteristics. Thus:

The negro Jim was what would have been described as a well-grown "young buck" of nineteen or twenty, above the average of his race in intelligence and sagacity, and endowed with good-nature and cheerfulness to an astonishing degree.[26] *

Aside from Pomp, the only other really black character is Natu, an African, who is Zeke's roommate in the book *Zeke* by Mary Ovington. In describing Natu as seen through Zeke's eyes, the author also manages to convey that Zeke is good looking, although lighter in color than Natu. Ovington also took the opportunity to point out the kinds of pictures of Africans that most people were exposed to.

Natu did not in the least resemble the African savages pictured in books. He had delicately shaped feet and hands that were as slim as a woman's. His ears were very small, his nose and mouth no flatter or broader than Zeke's own— and Zeke at church had often heard people tell his mother that he was a good-looking boy. Only his black skin and deep, coal-black eyes were different.[27]

In both Mrs. Means's books her black central characters are depicted with a great deal of dignity. The basic descriptions occur early in the books, and in both cases the female character is seen in contrast to a male progenitor. In *Shuttered Windows*, Harriet is described in relationship to her ancestor Black Moses: "Harriet was as handsome as he could have been: a bronze maiden, eyes straight-gazing under brows that frowned with thought; hair cloudy black; full lips well cut; smooth, brown skin stained

---

* Although Pendleton took great pride in being a member of the "New South," his style throughout the book indicates that while he had learned what he was supposed to say, his heart was not in it. In the above quotation, for example, he knows that the phrase "young buck" is not acceptable. Yet he uses it, but prefaces it with the qualifying words: "what would have been described as." His description of Mrs. Carroll's views on slavery (see chapter 2 of this study) is a similar example of his ambivalence.

with dusky red."[28] Armstrong Sperry's illustrations for the book capture Harriet's beauty and dignity very nicely.

Lilybelle Lawrence in *Great Day in the Morning* is seen compared to her grandfather:

He was a tall old man, prune-black, his close-cropped hair like a gray cap. His old eyes still showed something of the bold tilted oval of Lilybelle's young ones, an oval like that in Egyptian sculptures. Their faces were formed with the same strong, flat planes, as if carved from wood richly brown. Before toil and rheumatism had knotted his hands, they must have resembled hers—long and smooth-knuckled and square-tipped.[29]

In a scene on a bus at the very beginning of *Bright April* DeAngeli establishes that the Bright family is black. A small white girl in the seat in front of April and Mrs. Bright turns around and says to April:

"You're brown!"
The child's mother looked startled, but April's mamma just smiled and said:
"Yes, she's brown and you're pink. Isn't she a nice warm color?" But the little girl didn't answer, and she and her mother got off the car. April's smile faded, and she turned to ask:
"Am I brown, Mamma?"
"Yes, of course. You are just the color of coffee with good cream in it."[30]

Despite Mrs. Bright's warm, positive response, April will eventually have to learn that there are people who do not see brown as an attractive color.

The physical description of Kennie Willard, the black baseball player in *Hit and Run* (1949) is favorable, but the reader should be aware that the book did not win favor with the *Children's Catalog* until the 1966 edition (see chapter 12). Kennie, as seen through the eyes of Chip, the book's central character, is "a big guy":

About six-feet even, Chip guessed; with the wide shoulders and narrow hips and catlike stalk of the born athlete. But he wasn't so young—he'd been batting around those Negro leagues a long time before this Sox deal came along. Probably pushing thirty. He had a way of always looking cheerful, but not the fake, smily kind like somebody posing in an ad for breakfast food.[31]

While Decker gives Willard the physical appearance of the "natural" athlete, he does not make the mistake of having his black be a superstar.

The Mulatto

One of the interesting changes that occurred in the children's books in this study was the disappearance of the mulatto. After *Penrod* (1914) in which Tarkington has Penrod harassing an octoroon named Victorine Riodan[32]—thus taking a swipe at both black and Irish—there is only Lindy, the happy slave in the story-within-the-story in *Melindy's Medal* (1945) who is able to flee to freedom because, as her mistress put it, "You're so light-colored nobody's going to question you, anyway."[33]

It is true that in the earlier titles the comments about mulattoes, for the most part, were casual and played no real part in the story. For example, in Aldrich's *Story of a Bad Boy*, the bully Conway taunts Tom by calling him a "sneaking little mulatter."[34]

However, one author pursued the subject at length. In *Diddie, Dumps, and Tot,* Louise-Clarke Pyrnelle had a great deal to say on the subject. This is not surprising, since we know from the journals of the time that one of the major embarrassments the white mistress faced was seeing her husband's features in the offspring of the slave cabins.

A technique dear to the hearts of the most biased of the southern white writers—Pyrnelle, Thomas Nelson Page, and Joel Chandler Harris—was to put the most denigrating comments about blacks into the mouths of black characters. Thus, in *Diddie, Dumps, and Tot,* we have the elderly Uncle Bob saying, "Now I ain't 'er talkin' 'bout'n *murlatters*, case dey ain't white, an' dey ain't black, an' dey ain't nuffin; dey's des de same kin' er *folks* ez de muel is er *horse*."[35]

Pyrnelle devotes two chapters to the story of "Poor Ann," and thereby manages to have her say, not only about mulattoes, but about the features of slavery so often attacked by the Abolitionists. The story begins with the children begging to go to see the slaves for sale by the speculator who has arrived in the area. We are told that "the negroes were well clothed, well fed, and the great majority of them looked exceedingly happy." In fact, some are dancing and singing while awaiting a prospective buyer. There is, on occasion "a sad face and a tearful eye," but only occasionally.

Major Waldron, plantation owner and father to Diddie, Dumps, and Tot, is a very kindhearted man, and when he encounters the "almost white" Ann who is dying of consumption and thus not worth much on the auction block, he buys her and her small son who is "almost as white as Tot." Ann and her son are placed in quarters in the laundryroom that are very well furnished. Their meals come directly from the white folks' table. While the white folks are being so kind, neither Ann nor her son, "strange to say, . . . gained favor with the negroes on the place."

This rejection bothers Ann since her major goal is to have her son, Henry, accepted so that when she dies he will be well cared for. Toward that aim, she engages Uncle Bob in conversation. His first words to her make clear the source of the rejection: "I ain't no bort nigger myse'f." To which Ann replies, "You are certainly very fortunate, for the slave that has never been on the block can never know the full bitterness of slavery."

When Uncle Bob comments, "Wy, yer talkin' same ez wite folks," Ann tells him that she has had "the misfortune to have been educated." This exchange establishes the bond, and Ann proceeds to tell Uncle Bob her sad tale.

Ann's mother had been a favorite slave, and when she died giving birth to Ann, the white mistress, who just happened to have a baby a few days older than Ann, took Ann to her breast and nursed her. For seven happy years, Ann and the mistress's daughter shared life together. Then the daughter died and Ann was taken in as daughter of the house. A governess was brought from the North and Ann was taught as white children were. Eventually, the governess's brother came to visit from Vermont, fell in love with Ann, and they went to Pennsylvania to be married, it being illegal in Maryland for a slave to get married. While the good mistress always intended to free Ann, somehow she never got around to it. The husband dies in a train wreck, the mistress dies in debt, and Ann and Henry are sold as part of the estate. Ann goes into a decline and only the good fortune to be bought by kindly Major Waldron has kept her alive this long. What will happen to son Henry? She cannot bear the idea of his growing up a slave, but her relatives in Vermont are too poor to buy him.

This sad tale moves Uncle Bob to propose to Major Waldron that he, Uncle Bob, buy Henry and send him to his grandmother in Vermont. Upon hearing the whole story, Major Waldron frees Ann and Henry, matches Uncle Bob's three hundred dollars, buys the ship passage for Ann and Henry, and thus he "bade adieu to the only slaves he ever bought."[36]

A point of pride with Pyrnelle is that Waldron does not *buy* slaves, only *raises* them. This thoroughly romantic idea is nonsense: no Mississippi planter in the 1850s could run an estate the size of Waldron's on home-bred slaves. However, if we grant Pyrnelle her case, how then does she account for "Aunt Milly, a lame yellow woman," Candace, "a yaller nigger," and the mulatto children in the cabins? She doesn't account for them, of course, but had anyone asked, undoubtedly they were the products of overseers.

10
RELIGION
AND SUPERSTITION

Although the traits "religious" and "superstitious" appear separately on most lists of personality characteristics, there is no clear line dividing them. This ambivalence is true for most people, but for blacks in children's books it is intensified. Religion and superstition are so consistently interwoven in some books as to make separation of the two impossible. It is as if the blacks might acquire an overlay of religious beliefs, but their basically primitive nature would still have great control over their behavior and reactions.

For Christian slave owners—and all slave owners in children's books took pride in being good Christians—the question whether to expose the blacks to religion was a difficult one. Their Christian duty dictated that slave owners assume an obligation for their slaves' souls; but to admit that a slave had a soul was to undermine the argument that he was property. The dilemma did not last any longer than it took for the slave owners to recognize that the Christian religion offered an ideal form of control over the slaves. Rather than being a liberating force, religion became a tool of suppression. If the slave believed what he was taught, he would be docile on earth since his reward was to come in the life hereafter.

WHITE MAN'S RELIGION

Malcolm X summed up the consequences of the religious indoctrination of slaves as follows:

And while the religion of every other people on earth taught its believers of a God with whom they could identify, a God who at least looked like one of their own kind, the slavemaster injected his Christian religion into this "Negro." This "Negro" was taught to worship an alien God having the same blond hair, pale skin, and blue eyes as the slavemaster.

This religion taught the "Negro" that black was a curse. It taught him to hate everything black, including himself. It taught him that everything white was good, to be admired, respected, and loved. It brainwashed this "Negro" to think he was superior if his complexion showed more of the white pollution of the slavemaster. This white man's Christian religion further deceived and brainwashed this "Negro" to always turn the other cheek, and grin, and scrape, and bow, and be humble, and to sing, and to pray, and to take whatever was dished out by the devilish white man; and to look for his pie in the sky, and for his heaven in the here-after, while right here on earth the slavemaster white man enjoyed *his* heaven.[1]

Impressions gained from the children's books in this study support Malcolm X's interpretation. Aunt Chloe, for instance, whose cross on earth is the forever-weeping Elsie Dinsmore, replies, when talking about Jesus, "I's only a poor black sinner, but de good Jesus, He loves me jes the same as if I was white."

Martha Finley's *Elsie Dinsmore* was, and is, little more than a religious tract. Everyday Elsie reads from the Bible, and when things go wrong, Aunt Chloe quotes biblical passages back to Elsie. At one point, for example, Aunt Chloe says "earnestly":

"Darlin', . . . didn't you read to your ole mammy dis very morning dese bressed words: 'If any man sin, we have an advocate with the Father, Jesus Christ the righteous,' an' de other: 'If we confess our sins, He is faithful and just to forgive us our sins.' Go to de dear bressed Lord Jesus, darlin', an' ax Him to forgive you, an' I *knows* He will."[2]

What is so fantastic about the passage is the way Aunt Chloe suddenly speaks perfect English when quoting Scripture.

In *The Young Marooners* Goulding avoided this problem, of either quoting the Bible in outlandish dialect or making the character magically literate, simply by describing the scene in which Sam is allowed to select the passage for Bible reading:

The chapter selected at Sam's request was the third of John. With this he was so well acquainted as to be able to repeat verse after verse, while Mary was reading, and he seemed withal to have a very clear idea of its meaning. Mary was surprised. She knew that her father was in the habit of calling his plantation negroes together on Sabbath evenings, and instructing them from the

Scriptures, but she had no idea that the impressions made by his labour had been so deep.[3]

Twain's opening escapade in *The Adventures of Huckleberry Finn* begins when Huck has gone to his room after "they fetched the niggers in and had prayers." While Finley, Goulding, and Twain have little else in common, they agree that religion comes from the white masters.

The same cannot be said for Pyrnelle. In her Preface to *Diddie, Dumps, and Tot,* she wrote:

I hope that none of my readers will be shocked at the seeming irreverence of my book, for that *intimacy* with the "Lord" was characteristic of negroes. They believed implicitly in a Special Providence and direct punishment or reward, and that faith they religiously tried to impress upon their young charges, white or black; and "heavy, heavy hung over our heads" was the DEVIL!

The least little departure from a marked-out course of morals or manners was sure to be followed by, "Nem' min', de deb'l gwine git yer."

And what the Lord 'lowed and what he didn't 'low was perfectly well known to every darky. For instance, "he didn't 'low no singin' uv week-er-day chunes uv er Sunday," nor "no singin' uv reel chunes (dance music) at any time"; nor did he " 'low no sassin' uv ole pussons."[4]

Pyrnelle repeats this point of view later in the book when she has Uncle Snake-bit Bob set up a Sunday school for the children. After "all of the little darkies, with their heads combed and their Sunday clothes on, assembled for the Sunday-school," Uncle Bob explains to them why they are there:

"Chil'en," he began, "I fotch yer hyear dis ebenin fur ter raise yer like yer ought ter be riz. De folks deze days is er gwine ter struchshun er dancin' an' er pickin' uv banjers an' er singin' uv reel chunes an' er cuttin' up uv ev'y kin' er dev'lment. I ben er watchin' 'em; an' min' yer, when de horn hit soun' fur de jes' ter rise, half de niggers gwine ter wid de onjes!"[5]

Later, Uncle Daniel, the plantation black preacher, delivers a sermon about the sins that bring about man's damnation. Among them are the "sassin' uv white folks," and the "slightin' uv yer wuck!"

But the damning power of the Lord was not the same for blacks and whites. For while "sassin" a white or an old person was a sin, it was not a sin for a white child to talk back to a black adult. When black Mammy threatens Dumps with God's vengeance because she has been disrespectful, Dumps replies, "You ain't none o' my mother. You're mos' black ez my shoes' am' de Lord ain't er goin' ter pull all my hair off jes 'boutn you."

The counterpart of this double standard is that religion as practiced by whites is superior to religion as practiced by blacks. The point was made by Ovington in *Hazel*, a book that was predominately sympathetic to the black. Early in the book, Hazel and her mother, Mrs. Tyler, are seen attending a white church. Mrs. Tyler is a northern-born black who had married a southerner:

After her marriage with her southern husband she had gone a few times to listen to the big-hearted oratory at the colored church; but the service there did not touch her spirit, and she and her husband had agreed on Sunday mornings to worship in different places the same Heavenly Father. Hazel had always accompanied her mother, and she was quite at home among the white people.[6]

In contrast to the sedate, reserved service of the white church is the scene in the southern black church that dismays Hazel. As the time approaches for the service to begin, "the place grew crowded and the air became close and full of an uncleanly odor." The text for the sermon is "Ye serpents, ye generation of vipers, how can ye escape the damnation of Hell?"

The preacher describes the joys of heaven, but not for long. "He was concerned with showing his hearers the terrors of the underworld." As the congregation responds with such phrases as "Lord save us!" Hazel is aghast. "She was wholly unaccustomed to hearing the congregation take a spontaneous part in the service." Before the service is finished, Hazel slips out, upset by the emphasis on fire and brimstone. She cannot go to sleep until she equates God with her dead father: "My own father wouldn't have hurt anybody. Not even if they were wicked. And God is my Father in Heaven."[7]

The enthusiasm of black church services costs Little Jeemes Henry, in Ellis Credle's book of the same name, his hard-earned fifty cents. As the congregation sings, Jeemes Henry begins to feel very good; by the time the preacher is well into his sermon, Jeemes Henry is feeling not only good, but warm, so he takes off his shoes.

"Dare go Ole Man Sin!" shouted the preacher. "Done drove him clean away!"

"Yas Lawdy! Whoopee!" The colored folk shouted and clapped their hands. They stood up and threw their hats into the air. Little Jeemes Henry stood up and threw his shoes into the air.[8]

The shoes break a church window, the fifty cents goes to pay for it, and Jeemes Henry must begin again to earn the money to go to the circus.

Florence Crannell Means was certainly aware of the difference between "that old time religion" and the more sophisticated religion practiced by educated blacks. However, she was more sympathetic toward the values of the southern church service. In *Shuttered Windows* she describes her heroine's reaction to the service:

> Jericho Church had no hymnals, no organ, no piano, but it had music that swept its oblong whitewashed box like an ocean tide of splendid sound. Harriet had heard spirituals all her life, but never anything quite like the great ebb and flow of these. "Great Day, the righteous marchin', God gwine build up Zion's wall!"—"Oh, Lawd, come by here!"—"Let your light shine over!"
> Feet beat time, bodies swayed, the close, hot church throbbed with the rhythm like a pulsing heart.[9]

The only example in which religion is depicted as a genuine comfort to the black character occurs in Isabel McMeekin's *Journey Cake*. Juba is a tower of strength throughout the book, and as the journey becomes more dangerous, the author offers Juba's faith as the source of her strength:

> When they started off, her one idea had been to get away from the Justice. She hadn't thought beyond that. She hadn't dared to. Master Gordon Shadrow had gone over the great mountains, and he had said, "Follow me when summer comes." That had been enough for Juba to know. Those words had brought them this far, under the hand of God. And surely God would continue to temper the wind to his shorn lambs. The way ahead was dangerous and steep and sharp. But they were in God's hands. . . . Juba slept.[10]

The perils Juba faces are either natural dangers—a wild cat—or attacks from heathen Indians, both of which could be expected to yield before the power of prayer, and Juba's faith in God is rewarded. No amount of faith or praying is any help, however, when it comes to trying to enroll a black boy in an all-white school, as seen in Jesse Jackson's *Call Me Charley*. Mrs. Moss has been rebuffed by the school principal in her attempt to enroll

Charley in the white school. Charley describes the situation to his friend Tom:

> "When he said I couldn't go to his school Mom just looked at him and I could see her lips moving with a little prayer."
>
> "She wouldn't pray in school, would she?"
>
> "You don't know my mom. This was jus' a little prayer. I could see her lips moving slowly. Not like she prays in the morning or at night. You can hear her say the words then."
>
> "Did old Future hear her?"
>
> "He looked awful funny, but I don't think he knew what she was doing. Because the way she was prayin' wasn't loud like it is when she prays in church. Mom's a prayin' woman. Even when she whips me she prays."[11]

At the risk of appearing to carry on a vendetta against *Melindy's Happy Summer*, one incident involving church-going in that book needs particular attention.

Melindy, the little girl whose lack of race pride is presented in the preceding chapter, is depicted attending Sunday school while visiting the white Gray family:

> When the teacher was telling the story of the day, about Moses leading the Children of Israel out of bondage into the Promised Land, Melindy interrupted and said excitedly, "I know that story, Miss Lester. My Granny often tells me about it. She says it's just like Abraham Lincoln leading our people into the Promised Land of Freedom."
>
> Miss Lester answered quietly, although there was a little frown of annoyance on her forehead, "Yes, that's right, Melindy."
>
> Then Melindy realized that she had been up to her old tricks—"putting in her two cents' worth" as Tom called it. "Oh, why can't I learn to keep my big mouth shut?" she asked herself forlornly, as she noticed the other children staring at her.[12]

Melindy's comment seems reasonable enough, and just why Miss Lester should be annoyed by it escapes this reader's understanding. After all, Melindy has been taken from a Boston black ghetto to serve as a "good will ambassador" to the white rural town. What is wrong with pointing out parallels in man's struggles for freedom? Involving the other children in a discussion might have served to help all present learn something, but no, the item was not on the lesson plan for that day, and the bright child who sees connections is made to feel a fool.

The problem, of course, is that once an author has made up his or her mind to use a book to show that all children are alike, he or she eliminates the uniqueness of the black experience. Melindy cannot be an individual; she must, to serve the author's purpose, be beaten down at every point until she is just as docile as the white children. This type of situation serves to reinforce the white child's (and the black's) idea that the closer the blacks come to thinking and acting "white" the more acceptable they are.

Finally, it raises once again the question discussed in chapter 2, "Slavery." Does religion relate to man's social-economic-political world, or is it a thing apart?

It would be belaboring the point to discuss all the references to religion and church-going in the twenty-four other books in this sample where religion is mentioned.* It should be noted, however, that a similar sample of children's books about white children would be strikingly devoid of religious references of any type. It is the cumulative effect and the overall lack of balance that gives rise to stereotype, not the presentation within any particular book.

GHOSTS, WITCHES, EVIL OMENS, AND LUCKY CHARMS

To this day innumerable white people dread the sight of a black cat crossing their path, will not walk under a ladder, and toss spilled salt over their shoulders. Superstition obviously is not the exclusive property of the black and, as Stampp observed:

There is no need to trace back to Africa the slave's fear of beginning to plant a crop on Friday, his dread of witches, ghosts, and hobgoblins, his confidence in good-luck charms, his alarm at evil omens, his belief in dreams, and his reluc-

---

* For interested readers the titles are: *Across the Cotton Patch* (Credle); *Araminta* (Evans); *Bayou Boy* (Lattimore); *Bright April* (DeAngeli); *The Empty Schoolhouse* (Carlson); *Flop-Eared Hound* (Credle); *Frawg* (Weaver); *Gooseberry Jones* (Berger); *Great Day in the Morning* (Means); *Hezekiah Horton* (Tarry); *Jasper, the Drummin' Boy* (Taylor); *Junior, A Colored Boy of Charleston* (Lattimore); *Ladycake Farm* (Hunt); *The Little Colonel* (Johnston); *Mary Jane* (Sterling); *Miss Minerva and William Green Hill* (Calhoun); *Penrod* (Tarkington); *River Treasure* (Burgwyn); *Roosevelt Grady* (Shotwell); *Skid* (Hayes); *Steppin and Family* (Newell); *Tobe* (Sharpe); *You Can't Pet a Possum* (Bontemps), and *Zeke* (Ovington). Four of these titles involve superstition as well as religion and are taken up in the section that follows, on "Ghosts, Witches, Evil Omens, and Lucky Charms."

tance to visit burying grounds after dark. These superstitions were all firmly rooted in Anglo-Saxon folklore.[13]

Yet one would be hard pressed to show white people acting superstitiously in children's books. When a white person was shown as superstitious within this sample of titles, it was inevitably a child, not an adult.

Booth Tarkington took care of the question of superstition in a single phrase that is a master example of his ability to be doubly denigrating when he wrote, in *Penrod*: "Dogs are even more superstitious than boys and coloured people."[14] Whether Mark Twain would agree about the dogs is uncertain, but he did consistently demonstrate throughout *The Adventures of Huckleberry Finn* a belief in the idea that adult blacks and white boys are equally superstitious.

Almost the first fact the reader learns about Huck Finn is that terror strikes him when he accidentally kills a spider:

I didn't need anybody to tell me that that was an awful bad sign and would fetch me some bad luck, so I was scared and most shook the clothes off of me. I got up and turned around in my tracks three times and crossed my breast every time; and then I tied up a little lock of hair with a thread to keep the witches away.[15]

Following this incident, Huck sneaks out to join Tom Sawyer. They pass by the sleeping Jim, and Tom takes Jim's hat and hangs it on a tree limb. When Jim awakens, he "said the witches bewitched him and put him in a trance, and rode him all over the state, and then set him under the trees again, and hung his hat on a limb to show who done it." The publicity this event brings Jim with the black population makes Jim "most ruined for a servant."

Even though Huck knows how Jim's hat came to be hanging in the tree, this does not weaken his belief in Jim's hairball, which Jim claims is magical. When Huck's father arrives back in town, Huck goes to see Jim to find out if Pap is going to stay around long. After an elaborate ritual with the hairball, Jim tells Huck:

"Yo' ole father doan' know yit what he's a-gwyne to do. Sometimes he spec he'll go 'way, en den ag'in he spec he'll stay. De bes' way is to res' easy en let de ole man take his own way. Dey's two angels hoverin' round 'bout him. One uv 'em is white en shiny, en t'other one is black. De white one gits him to go right a little while, den de black one sail in en bust it all up."[16]

This is a good example of what Malcolm X meant when he said religion taught that white was "good" and black was "bad."

The belief in good and bad omens and the reliance on talismans is much a part of Huck and Jim's world. It is important, however, to point out a fundamental difference between Booth Tarkington and Mark Twain. Tarkington asks the reader to laugh *at*, not *with*, his characters, whether they be black or white. Twain inspires respect for his characters, and if Huck and Jim are superstitious, it is because they are innocents and not because they are ignorant.

Other writers' attitudes are not as easy to discern. For example, in *The Young Marooners* the happy slave, Sam, is shown being able to recite the third chapter of John by heart. Yet when the white boy, Robert, suggests naming their island "The Enchanted Island," Sam's response is:

"Please, Massa," Sam implored, "don't call um by dat name. I gegin to see ghosts now; and I 'fraid, if you call um so, I will see ghosts and sperits all de time."[17]

Goulding also says that "Sam was a firm believer in ghosts, both human and brute," and broadening the base, he tells us that "Negroes are almost universally superstitious about dead people."

While Goulding spreads his comments about superstition and religion throughout the book, in *The Little Colonel* Johnston blends Mom Beck's belief in religion and superstition and presents it in one chapter. Mom Beck takes Lloyd to church with her and the scene is fully described: the singing, the taking up of the collection, and the varieties of people attending service. On the way home, Mom Beck walks with "Brothah Foster" and they talk about Mr. Sherman's poor health. Mom Beck is sure he is going to die. When Brothah Foster tries to calm her down by telling her not to cross the bridge until she comes to it, she replies:

"I know that; but a lookin-glass broke yeste'day mawnin' when nobody had put fingah on it. An' his picture fell down off the wall while I was sweepin' the pa'lah. Pete said his dawg done howl all night last night, an' I've dremp three times hand runnin' 'bout muddy watah."[18]

However, Mom Beck's faith is such that even when the situation worsens, she can say:

"The good Lawd is goin' to pahvide fo' us same as Abraham. . . . If we can only hold out faithful, there's boun' to be a ram caught by the hawns some place, even if we haven't got eyes to see through the thickets. The Lawd will pahvide whethat it's a burnt offerin' or a meal's vittles. He sho'ly will."[19]

Just as McMeekin wrote the strongest statement depicting a black's faith, so too, she managed in one scene to depict Juba's Christian faith as being strongly mixed with primeval beliefs. When the baby of the Shadrow family comes down with a high fever, Juba waits until all have gone to bed. Then she instructs Eli to stand guard at the fire, and she goes off to settle herself beside a black spring. There:

> She prayed, both to the Christian God and to the half-remembered jungle deities whose names she had heard whispered as a child at her mother's knee. Old voo-doo names were patterned on her lips, thunder gods and water witches, the seven-headed Greatness that ruled over the dangers of the night-time jungle and the little land spirit who gave safety through the swamps.
>
> There was, at last, the lisp of sound in the water and Juba's quick hand darted downward swift as lightning, and closed on the cool smooth coils of a water snake. With a grunt of satisfaction she raised herself to her feet and the snake's body whistled through the air like a whip as she cracked off its head with an expert flick of her strong wrist.
>
> With care she cut a strip of skin from the white belly of the snake and rolled it in a sweet-smelling bay leaf drawn from her pocket. Muttering strange incantations, she dipped it in the water seven times.
>
> Back again at the fire she held the thing between sticks over the flames till the edges scorched and writhed.
>
> She (Dulcy) opened her long lashes a crack and watched Juba bending over the baby. She knew that that strange thing, whatever it was that Juba held in her hand, was a good-luck charm. She saw her secure it deftly in a strip of woolen cloth and tie it tenderly about Bunny's thin little neck.
>
> Next day Bunny was unaccountably better.[20]

Juba's "half-remembered jungle deities" serve a useful purpose, a positive result is attained. Not so in most instances of mentioning witches and ghosts. The overall effect is to produce fear, either of the devil or witches.

The only other example of any import in which a black character is shown relying on a good-luck charm occurs in *Steppin and Family*. Steppin wants to invest in a good-luck charm that will give him the courage to ask the man at the dancing school to let him take lessons on credit. He buys a white rat, assured by the store owner that white rats are known for bringing people good luck. The whole episode turns into chaos when Steppin discovers the class consists entirely of girls, and the white rat gets loose, and Steppin's dog chases after it amid the madly screaming females.[21]

In *Uncle Remus* the little boy argues with Uncle Remus about witches, saying that his father has told him witches do not exist. Uncle Remus replies:

"Mars John ain't live long ez I is. . . . He ain't bin broozin' 'round all hours er de night and day. I know'd a nigger w'ich his brer wuz a witch, kaze he up'n tole me how he tuck'n kyoy'd 'im; en he kyo'd 'im good, mon."

"How was that," inquired the little boy.

"Hit seem like," continued Uncle Remus, "dat witch folks is got a slit in de back er de neck, en w'en dey wanter change dese'f, dey des pull de hide over der head same ez if 'twuz a shut, en dar dey is."[22]

Over seventy-five years later the witches from Uncle Remus' days are still shedding their skins in Burgwyn's *River Treasure* (1947). Guy, the central character, has a friend Peter who tells him that the little old lady, Miss Ceeny, is a witch. Guy asks Peter how he knows, and Peter says:

"Well, about a week ago she was sick. She was so sick everybody thought she was going to die, and folks from all around was sitting up there waiting for her to die."

"Yeah, I remember, she had an attack of asthma."

"I don't know what she had, but they was all sitting there and I went in to look at her and all of a sudden she took a deep breath and then she didn't breathe no more. I was looking straight at her, and while I was looking she shriveled up and oozed right out of her skin. There was a rushing and a roaring sound beating around my ears and a big wind pushing past me. It whirled me all round and took me right out the door with it, and I couldn't stop until I got home."[23]

Peter has a vivid imagination that once set in motion seems to have no bounds. He tells Guy that Miss Ceeny has tried to capture him because he witnessed her leaving her skin, but he was saved because he had placed brooms under the front and back doorsteps, and she could not enter his house.

Miss Ceeny can also turn herself into a bug, according to Peter. But she can be caught by placing a sifter by the bed since in order to reach her victim she would have to count all the holes in the sifter, and it would make enough noise to wake Guy in time to capture her.

Guy listens to all this, believing it all when with Peter, but inclined to be skeptical when alone. The one thing he is sure of is that Miss Dolly, his adopted mother, would not approve of his believing in witches. He ponders the subject, holding the Bible in his hands. It is then that he remembers what his father told him the time he came home from the third-grade class frightened badly because some of the boys had been telling witches' tales:

"You don't need to be scared of any witches or spirits or ghosts, Guy. There's only one and that's the Holy Ghost or Holy Spirit. They're both the same and you don't have to be afraid of that one as long as you love Him. That's the spirit you call on when you get scared or when you need help. Just don't forget to thank him for being there to help you. If you believe in that Spirit, you don't have to worry about any others."[24]

Religious belief works for Guy in this example, but it usually doesn't where black characters are concerned. Among the things Harriet Freeman must learn in *Shuttered Windows* are that it is bad luck to put a hat on a bed, that sweeping under a sick person's bed will "kill 'em sho' " and that a three-corner tear in a dress means that an enemy has set a trap for you.

Harriet's most dramatic encounter with the superstitions of Gentlemen's Island occurs when her boyfriend's mother is terrorized at seeing a small bag lying in the yard. Richie tries to assure his mother that it is only the work of some "fool chile" trying to frighten them, but even as he copes with the situation, the author indicates Richie's uncertainty by describing his action as "attempted non-chalance." After Richie has carried the small bag off and drowned it, he explains to Harriet:

"Somebody puts roots and a lock of you' hair in a little small bag and puts it where you' bound to step over it. To put a charm on you; make you die or have bad luck."[25]

Other omens that can bring bad luck are related to nocturnal events. In *The Little Colonel*, Lloyd says to one of the black servants, "Oh, look at the new moon!" The answer is:

"I'se feared to, honey," answered Maria, "less I should see it through the trees. That 'ud bring me bad luck for a month, suah. I'll go out on the lawn where it's open, an' look at it ovah my right shouldah."[26]

The title *On the Dark of the Moon* by Don Lang comes from the superstitious belief that "you daresn't ever be caught out on the dark of the moon."[27] Later, Siddy, the book's child hero, finds himself staying the night with a friend of his uncle's who has buried his parents on his property. As the man points out the headstones, Siddy thinks to himself that he would never have come if he had known there were graves so nearby: "The sun was going down. And there's nothing so bad as being out after dark in the vicinity of a graveyard."[28]

One discernible trend concerning books about blacks was the elimination of superstition as a characteristic. Of the fourteen books published after 1947 that were analyzed, not one had an incident built upon superstition, although as observed earlier, blacks did continue to be characterized as religious.

11

THE

MUSICAL BLACK

Since slaves were forbidden to learn to read or write, and the educational opportunities for free blacks were almost nonexistent unless they could afford to travel or were fortunate enough to find a private tutor, there is little question but that music was a major avenue of personal expression among blacks.

Rarely did a contemporary write about slaves without mentioning their music, for this was their most splendid vehicle of self-expression. Slave music was a unique blend of "Africanisms," of Protestant hymns and revival songs, and of the feelings and emotions that were a part of the life of servitude. The Negroes had a repertory of songs for almost every occasion, and they not only sang them with innumerable variations but constantly improvised new ones besides.[1]

The question arises, then, what is so wrong about the emphasis upon musicality? Is it really a negative portrait?

The answer is, yes, and for a number of reasons. First, it leads authors to say, as Mebane Burgywn wrote in *River Treasure*, that black people "sing, and all of them learn to dance with the syncopated rhythm which is an inherent gift."[2] In order to counteract the view, it then leads authors like Dorothy Sterling to make their central characters completely nonmusical and to stress the point.

In *Mary Jane*, Sterling has the music teacher stop Mary Jane in the hall and ask why she has not come out for the choir. Mary Jane tries to explain to Miss Collins that she cannot carry a tune, but the explanation is rejected:

"I'm sure you're just being modest," Miss Collins shook her head. "All your people have such wonderful voices. I just love your spirituals. Now suppose you come to the music room at three and let me decide where to place you."[3]

133

The point, once made, is dropped by Sterling, but one can imagine what might happen if Mary Jane were to appear and exhibit her non-voice before the teacher. The well-meaning, but condescending Miss Collins might then complain to all who would listen that she had tried to be nice to "them," but Mary Jane had deliberately refused to sing well.

While the scenes stressing the blacks' musical talents are not offensive in the way scenes stressing their tendency toward violence are offensive, the cumulative impact of the books is to reinforce people like Burgywn and the Miss Collinses of the world in their belief in the inherent racial gift of rhythm possessed by *all* blacks. If only to save one real-life Mary Jane from experiencing the humiliation and frustration of dealing with one real-life Miss Collins, the myth should be laid to rest.

A second objection to the image projected is that only two books, *Shuttered Windows* and *Steppin and Family*, present truly talented black characters. And only in *Steppin and Family* is that talent allowed to bring the black wealth and fame, and most important of all, happiness. In *Shuttered Windows*, the author forces Harriet Freeman to give up her dream of becoming a concert pianist in exchange for helping "elevate" her race. If children's book authors had had their way, there would have been no Marian Anderson or Paul Robeson.

The absence of truly talented people in the books is, in many ways, worse than the presence of so many references to singing and dancing, and it overlooks an important point made by Imamu Amiri Baraka (LeRoi Jones) in *Blues People*. Baraka points out that in many areas of music the black man did the innovating and the white performer made the big money and earned the headlines.[4]

ENTERTAINING AND COMFORTING THE WHITE FOLKS

While historians like Stampp and music critics like Baraka stress the "self-expression" aspect of the black man's music, it would appear in children's books that the musicality of the blacks would not count for much if it did not comfort or entertain the white folks who listen to it.

The "vigorous and mellow" voice of the "gwine on eighty" Uncle Remus provides the solace for the little boy to whom he tells stories. As the little boy lies in bed, half-fearful after hearing a story about witches, "it soothed him, however, to hear the strong, musical voice of his sable patron, not very far away, tenderly contending with a lusty tune."[5]

In Pendleton's *King Tom and the Runaways* the ability to entertain his young white master earns Jim his job as court jester. The author spells out Jim's qualifications:

The young negro Jim had never attracted any especial attention on the plantation until Tom took a fancy to him and he was promoted from the position of a field hand to that of an attendant on his young master during the hours of recreation. It then came to light that he could not only sing songs of his own make and play on reed quills, but that he knew how to "pick" the banjo and dance with remarkable agility and originality—accomplishments viewed by Master Tom with great favor and admiration. It must also be added that he was a quick-witted negro of a fertile imagination and with a truly remarkable talent for lying—qualities fitting him so well for his position that he had acquired a strong hold on Tom's affections. Others had sung and danced for Master Tom and followed him on the chase, only to be sent back to the field after a short time, being like more illustrious favorites, subject to their master's caprice; but Jim's tenure of office promised to be lasting.[6]

During slavery, the ability to perform for the master could rescue a slave from the fields. Rosalie and Junior Robinson in Lattimore's *Junior, A Colored Boy of Charleston,* see singing and dancing in the streets of Charleston as a way to earn money:

Rosalie could sing as well as Junior, and they both danced as easily as they sang. People who came to Charleston from the North sometimes liked to see colored children dance and sing, and gave them pennies.[7]

The idea does not work out, however, since the children are frightened off when a policeman tells their friend, James, "Move on, there, boy! Run! No begging allowed!"

The idea that the black children of Charleston are quaint and curious beings to be displayed for the northern visitors has the same undertone of condescension found in stories of tourists to exotic lands who find the customs of the native peoples "charming." One hardly knows whether southern whites should be pleased or offended to have been excluded by Lattimore.

Another black with a "rich and beautiful" voice that helps comfort the white people is Juba in McMeekin's *Journey Cake.* At appropriate moments throughout the book, Juba sings. For example, she sings a lullaby to sooth the baby, and she sings hymns to raise the children's spirits when the trip is rough-going.

In *Ladycake Farm* Mabel Leigh Hunt has a black family's ability to make beautiful music save them from a confrontation with the sheriff. The Freed family have friends out to visit, and after supper they all gather under the big maple tree to have a songfest.

Oh, it was good, singing together in the May moonshine! They sang hymns, and spirituals. They sang sentimental old songs which gave all but the frogs, snakes, and rhinoceroses the most delightful heartaches.[8]

One who is not a frog, snake, or rhinoceros but who is also unmoved by the music is the Freeds' bigoted neighbor, Mr. Carle, who calls the sheriff to complain that the Freeds are "disturbing the peace." On the way to the Freed farm, the sheriff stops to listen and falls under the spell of the music. His only regret is that his wife isn't along with him to hear the singing.[9]

Street performances for the whites were not limited to the South. Bontemps, in *Sad-Faced Boy*, has the three brothers doing their band-playing in the streets of New York City to earn money to support their newly acquired addiction for water ices, popsicles, and Eskimo pies. Their knowledgeable friend, Daisy Bee, tells them about the Times Square theater crowds who like to be entertained while standing out on the sidewalks during intermission. The boys are a great success, but little Willie comes down sick, and that is the end of the steady supply of nickles.[10]

In *Diddie, Dumps, and Tot* Pyrnelle devotes a chapter to "Plantation Games." On Saturday night the young people gather to dance and sing, and Diddie persuades Mammy to take them to watch. Once they arrive a bench is brought from Aunt Nancy's cabin for "marster's chillen" to sit on. The black children "squatted around on the ground to look on."

The first dance game is entitled "Monkey Motions," and the first and last stanzas are:

"I ac' monkey moshuns, too-re-loo;
I ac' monkey moshuns, so I do;
I ac' 'em well, an' dat's er fac'—
I ac' jes like dem monkeys ac'.
. . . .

"I ac' nigger moshuns, too-re-loo;
I ac' nigger moshuns, so I do;
I ac' 'em well, an' dat's er fac'—
I ac' jes like dem niggers ac'."[11]

The author offers a description of the kind of motions that go with each verse. For the two quoted above:

While the dancers were singing the first verse, "I ac' monkey moshuns," the one in the middle would screw up his face and hump his shoulders in the most grotesque manner, to represent a monkey.

. . . .

"I ac' nigger moshuns" was represented by scratching his head, or by bending over and pretending to be picking cotton or hoeing.[12]

A more sedate form of entertainment is provided by the black band that plays for a formal dance aboard ship in *The Man Without a Country*. And in *The Bow of Orange Ribbon*, the author explains the background of the blacks playing at a party:

At that day there were but few families of any wealth who did not own one black man who could play well upon the violin. Joris possessed two; and they were both on hand, putting their own gay spirits into the fiddle and bow.[13]

After slavery ended, some of the fiddlers apparently earned money playing for street dances. In *Mrs. Wiggs of the Cabbage Patch* Hegan has the residents of the Cabbage Patch decide to hold a benefit dance to buy Chris Hazy a new wooden leg:

At one time there threatened to be trouble about the music; some wanted Uncle Tom, the old negro who usually fiddled at the dances, and others preferred to patronize home talent and have Jake Schultz, whose accordian could be heard at all hours in the Cabbage Patch.

Mrs. Wiggs effected a compromise. "They kin take turn about," she argued; "when one gits tired, the other kin pick up right where he left off, an' the young folks kin shake the'r feet till they shoes drop off. Uncle Tom an' Jake, too, is a head sight better than them mud-gutter bands that play 'round the streets."[14]

Whether it is the slave entertaining and comforting the master's children or the freedman playing for a street party, the major thrust of descriptions of the blacks' music ability has to do with performances before whites. From the scenes presented by Lattimore and Bontemps, it becomes clear that black children learn early that performing for whites is the way to earn money.

THE HARD WAY TO SUCCESS

The first of two authors to stress the idea that hard work is involved in being a successful musician was Mary Ovington in *Zeke*. Soon after Zeke's arrival at Tollivar Institute, there is a drill parade, and as Zeke stands in line, the band approaches. Zeke listens to the stirring music, admires the gleaming instruments, and imagines himself someday being able to play the cornet, the instrument that particularly attracts him. "He had always wanted to make music but he had never had anything but a whistle."

Zeke's desire to play the cornet is a thread running throughout the book. Finally, after a series of personal disasters have left Zeke feeling low, his friends Matt and Vesta persuade Jerry, the cornet player, to help Zeke learn to play. One evening after putting his chickens to bed, Zeke returns to his room and Jerry holds out the cornet to him. He asks Zeke if he wants to give it a try:

Zeke forgot he was tired, forgot everything but that he held the cornet in his hands. Here was the enchanted trumpet through which he would tell the world of his love and ambition, of the many things that he was too shy to talk about. Here was glorious, blaring expression. He put it to his lips, took an immense breath and blew.

Nothing happened.[15]

Zeke thinks he is being teased, and Jerry, knowing how very susceptible to teasing Zeke is, is hard put not to take advantage of the situation. However, he does explain to Zeke how one makes a lip, and just before the lights are scheduled to go out Zeke makes one "creditable blare," and goes to bed happy.

Unlike many children's book characters, Zeke does not become an instant star. The reader never knows whether Zeke will even become competent at playing the cornet.

Ovington's point in *Zeke*, that desire, or even talent, is not enough to produce a skilled performance, is also made by Newell in *Steppin and Family*. Like so many children who want to dance, Steppin equates ability with activity—and the more gyrations he does, the more he is sure he is performing well. When he is admitted to Dad Kirby's professional school, he learns the hard way about what it takes to become a professional dancer. Steppin wants to learn "dance steps," but Dad Kirby has the class doing a series of strenuous exercises. Steppin can hardly move after the first day, and he complains to his friend, who he knows only as The Wishing Tree Man.

The Wishing Tree Man gives Steppin three free passes to go see the great Bob Williams dance. Steppin, his mother, and his sister, Mary Ellis, go to the theater, and the first shock Steppin receives is the recognition that his friend The Wishing Tree Man is Bob Williams. Then Steppin finds out what dancing is all about:

> Not once did Bob drop into any of the grotesque postures or strenuous gymnastics that Steppin used. Bob's dance was like a duet in which Dandry carried the accompaniment and Bob played the melody with his feet.
>
> . . . .
>
> And although part of him went on enjoying every minute of the wonderful performance, another part of his mind went sick with humiliation as he realized how ridiculous his bragging and ham dancing must have seemed to Bob Williams.[16]

For Steppin this recognition that discipline is required for star performances marks the beginning of his upward climb. While Steppin will be an established star in his own right by the time Hope Newell writes A Cap for Mary Ellis some eleven years later, the first book ends with him a member of the chorus.

IRRELEVANT REFERENCES TO THE BLACKS' MUSICALITY

Equating black characteristics, musical or otherwise, with low levels of attainment, is one of the more insidious techniques that authors use to demean the blacks. In An Old-Fashioned Girl, for example, Alcott wants to make the point that her heroine Polly has higher standards than Polly's "society friends." Alcott has Polly attend a theater performance with her friend and relates that:

> at first, Polly thought she had got into fairyland, and saw only the sparkling creatures who danced and sang in a world of light and beauty; but, presently, she began to listen to the songs and conversation, and then the illusion vanished, for the lovely phantoms sang negro melodies, talked slang, and were a disgrace to the good old-fashioned elves whom she knew and loved so well.[17]

In *Betty Leicester*, Jewett observes that ladylike Aunt Barbara found "the droning of the violin over cheap music was more than she could bear"—the "cheap music" being "Golden Slippers" and "Sweet By-and-By."[18]

A favorite technique of authors to reinforce the blacks' basic musicality is to make numerous references to music, even when such references have nothing to do with the book as a whole. In *The Young Marooners*, Goulding just throws in "Sam's African voice, which was marked by indescribable mellowness."

In *Frawg* Weaver has everyone sing: Frawg himself sings on the way fishing; he sings on the way home; he sings when eating watermelons (see Figure 9); and he sings when he gets his long-coveted drum. Ma sings; Pa sings; the dog sings, and the chicken sings. This is in keeping with Weaver's basic premise that there is not much difference between black people and the animals.

As noted earlier, Junior, in Lattimore's *Junior, A Colored Boy of Charleston*, is not able to earn money by singing and dancing in the streets. He does, however, eventually earn a ten dollar prize while pushing the shrimp man's cart in the Azalea Festival. Lattimore sets the background for this eventual triumph by remarking on Junior's singing activities:

Junior liked to sing. He sang in school, and he sang in Sunday school, and he sang in church. He had never pushed a cart full of shrimp, though, and sung about them like the shrimp man.[19]

Bright April contains just enough brief references to musical talent to keep the image in mind without obviously belaboring it. April's brother Tom is crazy about drumming and is never without his drumsticks. When April's sister comes home from nursing school to spend the weekend, there is a jam session with Tom tapping and mother playing the piano. And there is a mention that Sis always sings in the church choir when she is at home.

For two little girls, going to church is characterized by the opportunity to sing. In Faulkner's *Melindy's Happy Summer*, the comment is made, "Melindy loved Sunday School. Best of all, as at home, she loved to sing the hymns." And in *Indigo Hill*, Lattimore tells us that:

Figure 9. Singing and eating watermelon are major activities for Frawg. From *Frawg*, by Annie Vaughan Weaver, illustrated by the author. Frederick A. Stokes, 1930.

Lydia liked to go to church. The Reverend Baxter's sermons sounded grand and solemn in her ears. Best of all, she liked the singing. When the whole congregation sang, the music carried her away.[20]

If May Justus' character Lennie Lane, of *New Boy in School,* had not been able to sing, he might never have made any friends in his new school. Only his ability to sing "The Wishing Song" that his father has taught him enables Lennie to overcome his shyness at being the only black child in an otherwise all-white class.[21]

When we combine all the references to music found in the church scenes with those found in other chapters throughout this study, the sum total of references is staggering. In no comparable collection of books about whites can there possibly be as many references to singing, dancing, and playing instruments.

12

SEGREGATION

One of the most famous sentences uttered by Booker T. Washington is: "In all things that are purely social we can be as separate as the fingers, yet one as the hand in all things essential to mutual progress."[1] As with so many of Washington's thought-patterns, he knew precisely what white people wanted to hear. And, as with the "separate but equal" doctrine, they latched onto one part without feeling any compulsion to take the other.

Segregation arose very early in the United States and occurred in all major areas of life: housing, travel, schools, churches, and social relationships. Examples of all of these types of segregation are found in children's books, and with notable exceptions, segregation was accepted without question by the authors.

There can be no argument about the reality of the picture presented by the authors. What is at issue is that by failing to question the validity of the arrangements made by society to keep black and white separated, the authors lent their support to the practice. The implication of that statement raises the issue of the responsibility of authors as social critics, which will be discussed in detail in chapter 14. For the present, it is simply an observation.

The first statement on segregation as a condition of the black man's life is by Trowbridge in *Cudjo's Cave*. The white pro-Union men are discussing the difference between black Toby's humanity and the lack of same in the villainous Lysander Sprowl. Mr. Villars observes that God will provide a higher seat in heaven for many a black man than for his haughty masters. This statement sums up the contamination attitude concisely, that is, whites would rather deprive themselves of experiences than allow blacks to be present in their company:

"According to that," replied Withers, "maybe some besides the haughty masters will be a little astonished if they ever git into heaven—nigger-haters that won't set in a car, or a meeting-house, or go see a theater-play, if there's a nigger allowed the same privilege."[2]

A *de facto* presentation of segregation took place between 1932 and 1950 when ten children's books about blacks were published without an identifiable white character. The ten books are: Hogan's *Nicodemus and His Little Sister* (1932) and *Nicodemus and the Little Black Pig* (1934); Evans' *Araminta* (1935) and *Jerome Anthony* (1936); Bryant's *Epaminondas and His Auntie* (1938); Faulkner's *Melindy's Medal* (1945); Burgwyn's *River Treasure* (1947); Gerber's *Gooseberry Jones* (1947); Taylor's *Jasper, the Drummin' Boy* (1947), and Lattimore's *Indigo Hill* (1950). Excluding the *Nicodemus* and *Epaminondas* titles, it seems reasonable to assume that the authors' intentions were to present black life as encompassing the same problems and hopes as those found in white life. It is difficult to evaluate what, if any, impact the books actually had upon youthful white or black readers.

SOCIAL SEGREGATION

Housing

Segregation in housing is both implied and stated clearly almost from the very beginning of the titles analyzed. In *Queechy*, Warner has the washerwoman Dinah's "dingy tenement" selected as a meeting place for Fleda and Mr. Rossitur. Dinah lives in an area where the two whites can meet without fear of encountering any of their friends, and the thrust of the scene indicates the Chelsea neighborhood in Boston is for blacks.

Three brief, but revealing, references to housing segregation are made in other early books. In *Jack Hall* (1888) by Robert Grant there is a reference to a snowball fight between the "Round-pointers and the Nigger-Hillers." In Owen Johnson's *The Varmint* (1910), the boys must pass through "the negro settlement" on their way to the canal to swim. Howells is even more specific in *A Boy's Town*, when he says of the boys, "one night, out of pure zeal for the common good, they wished to mob the negro quarter of the town." Just why violence directed against the black community can be described as "for the common good," is never explained. It is possible to believe that Howells was trying to be satirical along the lines of his idol, Mark Twain, but with Howells, it never quite comes off.

After these early pointed references no direct comments are made about housing segregation. However, the absence of white characters, as cited above, indicates a concept of black neighborhoods. Also, the problems encountered by the black characters in *Skid*, *Call Me Charley* and *Lady-cake Farm* occur because they are the first black families in their new neighborhoods. In *Skid* and *Call Me Charley* the question of integrating a neighborhood is ignored in favor of stressing the problem of school desegregation. The authors, Hayes and Jackson, are able to ignore the situation because the parents in both *Skid* and *Call Me Charley* are employees of white families, and it has always been more acceptable to have black servants living in a neighborhood than black professionals who want to buy a house. The former are "in their place" while the latter are being "uppity."

The absence of books about housing integration (Phyllis Whitney's *Willow Hill*, 1947, never did find its way into the *Children's Catalog's* list of recommended books about blacks) can be accounted for by the overall refusal to accept books that portrayed conflict between the races, a point pursued in the following chapter.

Churches

As with the subject of housing, there is more implied segregation than outright discussion when it comes to churches. All but one of the scenes in chapter 10, "Religion and Superstition," occur in all-black churches. (See Figure 10.)

Beyond the implied examples, there are only two forthright comments, and neither is pursued by the author. In *The Empty Schoolhouse*, the only title in which the church-going blacks are Catholics, Carlson has the narrator observe: "Since the colored folks sit in back of the church, they got out first."

The second instance occurs in *Skid* and is an example of self-imposed segregation, although it is questionable whether the Parker family would have been welcome in a white church. The scene occurs just after Skid and his parents have arrived in the small Connecticut town. Skid hears his mother ask:

Figure 10. The churchyard scene makes clear that the congregation is all black. Ellis Credle, *Little Jeemes Henry*, illustrated by the author. Reprinted by permission of the publisher, Thomas Nelson Inc. Copyright © 1936, 1964 by Ellis Credle.

"Where do you go to church, Alice?" . . .

Alice hesitated. "I don't go much. It's too far away. But if you want to go we can take a bus. It's about a half hour's ride."

. . . .

Skid got a surprise when the bus stopped to let him and the others off at the

Negro church. It was so big he could almost have pushed his mother's church inside it through one of its big front doors. He thought at first it might be a white church.[3]

As with so many scenes in children's books about blacks, the incident is simply dropped into the story. The point is made that the trip is expensive, but no discussion occurs concerning the possibility of attending a church nearer home. Since Aunt Alice, in particular, has no compunction about sending Skid to an all-white school, it is reasonable to wonder why she cannot bring herself to think about attending a white church.

Eating and Sleeping

Social segregation related to eating appeared in a previous chapter in respect to Eli not eating inside the house in McMeekin's *Journey Cake*. As was so often the case, it fell to Mark Twain to take a look at an attitude and show by understatement just how stupid it was. In *Tom Sawyer*, Huck Finn and Tom are planning to follow Injun Joe to find out where the treasure is hidden. When Tom asks Huck where Huck will be sleeping, Huck replies:

"In Ben Rogers' hayloft. He lets me, and so does his pap's niggerman, Uncle Jake. I tote water for Uncle Jake whenever he wants me to, and any time I ask him he gives me a little something to eat if he can spare it. That's a mighty good nigger, Tom. He likes me, becuz I don't ever act as if I was above him. Sometimes, I've set right down and et *with* him. But you needn't tell that. A body's got to do things when he's awful hungry he wouldn't want to do as a steady thing."[4]

The good white folks of the town may worry about civilizing Huck and giving him religion, but it is to a slave that he turns for food.

This question of black and white eating together—or even in the same room of a public facility—has been one of the emotional areas of black-white relations. While it has not provoked a similar cliché to "would you want your sister to marry one?" it has, nevertheless, been a potent issue. As DuBois observed in *The Souls of Black Folk*, one of the few times Booker T. Washington did not fare well in public opinion was when he dined with President Theodore Roosevelt.[5]

Louise-Clarke Pyrnelle went a step further in *Diddie, Dumps, and Tot* by reminding readers that not only did black and white not eat together, they did not eat the same food. Relating the preparations for the Fourth of July barbecue, she says:

Major and Mrs. Waldron were to go in the light carriage, but the little folks were to go with Mammy and Aunt Milly in the springwagon, along with the baskets of provisions for the "white folks' tables"; the bread and vegetables and cakes and pastry for the negroes' tables had been sent off in a large wagon."[6]

The problem of eating together in public is depicted by Hunt in *Ladycake Farm*. When Joe Freed wins second prize in the American Legion essay contest on American citizenship, the Freeds are denied permission to attend the luncheon where the prizes are to be given. The organizer of the luncheon tells the Freeds, "It is against the policy of this hotel to entertain colored people. Therefore we cannot hold the Legion luncheon here." With no advance planning or warning, the luncheon is moved across the street, and all ends happily—again! This is almost a classical example of wishful thinking. Anyone who has been involved in setting up a formal luncheon for a large group knows that it cannot be shifted to another place on ten-minutes notice. Only in children's books can such unreality solve serious social problems.

A far more realistic presentation (but one readers of the Scholastic Press Book Club edition will find deleted from their copy) is found in Sterling's *Mary Jane*. Mary Jane's mother has taken her shopping for an entirely new wardrobe in which to face the white students. They have spent a great deal of money, with mother constantly making comments about "they" and what "they think" and "they expect." Mary Jane wonders:

And was it also the same "they" who said that she and Mamma couldn't eat in any of the Main Street restaurants when they were hungry?
After "socks" and "pocketbook" and "dickies" and "petticoat" were crossed off the shopping list, Mary Jane and Mamma walked around the corner to the parking lot. It was too far to go home, so they ate a picnic lunch in the car.[7]

There is another scene in *Ladycake Farm* that concerns eating, but probably should be classified as overall exclusion, involving churches, eating, and public events. The Freed family are having their house moved from its town lot to the newly purchased farm. It is being pulled on rollers by mules and the progress is slow. The mover doesn't work after dark so, as evening approaches, he unhooks his mules and leaves the Freeds sitting in the middle of an elite white section of town:

On either side of the street, beautiful houses stood in wide, grassy lawns. Almost opposite the stranded cottage arose a massive stone church. It was Poppy who called the children's attention to the words chalked on the outside blackboard. ICE CREAM FESTIVAL. COME ONE. COME ALL. Bright paper lanterns were strung on wires from tree to tree. Suddenly it seemed altogether delightful that Temple should have left three little travelers at a place where there was going to be a big party.

"Shall we come one, come all, to the festibul?" asked Pearlie May.

"Course not, Honey," laughed Poppy, in his easy slow way. "This is white folks' festival. But there's not a minikin of harm if my young 'uns want to watch the goings-on."[8]

The white people are not happy at finding the cottage outside the church, but there is really nothing they can do about it except complain to each other. At the end of the festival, one lady (who doubtless also gave second-hand clothes to her cleaning woman) brings the Freed children "the leavings" of the festival—a bowl of ice cream and a package of cake. This, the author seems to say, makes the evening a joy for the children. The cake is "ladycake," and that is where the name of the farm comes from.

Sleeping accommodations also created problems and are implied in the problems a black man encountered when traveling. The most precise statement on the subject is made by Pendleton in *King Tom and the Runaways* (1890). For a second time, the slave Jim has rescued the two white boys, Tom and Albert, from the terrors of the Georgia swamp. Jim has been living on an island with his wife Venus and their baby. Jim has a cabin and as night falls the question of where the boys will sleep arises:

It was now late, and the question of accommodations for the two boys during the night presented itself. Jim retired and gravely discussed the matter with Venus. Of course white and black could not sleep in the same cabin, and what, then was to be done? For his part, Jim declared that he would willingly sleep by the fire outside, but this would be hard lines for Venus and the baby. On the other hand, he could not bring himself to suggest to the young masters that they sleep on the ground in the open air as long as there was a roof within reach.

Albert chanced to overhear a part of this anxious consultation and immediately conferred with Tom. Neither of the boys could have been induced to spend the night under a negro's roof in any case, and they settled the question at once by calling Jim and telling him that they intended to sleep outside by the fire.[9]

Pendleton really means it when he says nothing could have induced the boys to sleep under a "negro's roof." Later in the book the campsite is threatened by a bobcat, but the boys would rather be attacked by a wild animal than move inside.

Tarkington draws a fine line in social relationships between black and white. In both *Penrod* and *Penrod and Sam*, the two black boys, Herman and Verman, seem to be acceptable playmates as long as the adults are not involved. But the boys are never invited to a social function, and when they become members of the club created by Penrod, there is parental objection:

Roderick's punishment was administered less on the ground of Georgie's troubles and more on that of Roddy having affiliated with an order consisting so largely of Herman and Verman.[10]

One incident seems to reflect the essence of Tarkington's view of the black. Verman has been captured while playing a game with Penrod and Sam; the white boys place Verman in Penrod's sister's closet to keep him from being freed by his own side. In the darkness of the closet, Verman falls asleep. When he awakens, he realizes where he is:

White-Folks' House! The fact that Verman could not have pronounced these words rendered them no less clear in his mind; they began to stir his apprehension, and nothing becomes more rapidly tumultuous than apprehension once it is stirred. That he might possibly obtain his release by making a noise was too daring a thought and not even conceived, much less entertained by the little and humble Verman. For, with the bewildering gap of his slumber between him and previous events, he did not place the responsibility for his being in White-Folks' House upon the white folks who had put him there. His state of mind was that of the stable-puppy who knows he *must* not be found in the parlour. Not thrice in his life had Verman been within the doors of White-

Folks' House, and, above all things, he felt that it was in some undefined way vital to him to get out of White-Folks' House unobserved and unknown. It was in his very blood to be sure of that.[11]

This idea that it is in the blacks' blood to remain separate from whites reaches the ridiculous in Inez Hogan's *Nicodemus and the Little Black Pig*. The sow has given birth to nine white piglets and one black piglet:

"Lawdy Land!" said Nicodemus, "dat old sow done got herself a heap o' young 'uns.

"Lawdy, Lawdy! one em's black.

"Come here, little black fellow, you don't belong among all those white pigs.

"You is black like me, and I 'spec you b'long to me."[12]

Of course authors were prone to attribute similar ideas to white children. In *Miss Minerva and William Green Hill* Calhoun has six-year-old Jimmy shout at a passing black boy: "Me and Billy and Frances and Lina's got the mumps and you ain't got no business to have 'em' cause you're a nigger." Whether having the mumps can be considered a social relationship may be questioned, but it certainly seems the ultimate in discrimination not to be allowed to have mumps.

Unlike Pendleton's characters who could not be induced under any circumstances to socialize with blacks, Howells admits that when his boy "had to come home alone through the dark, [he] was so afraid of ghosts that he would have been glad of the company of the lowest-down black boy in town."

Finally, blacks and whites did not even have to meet for signs of social segregation to be projected. The children in Rossiter Johnson's *Phaeton Rogers* discuss shoe throwing in relation to an upcoming wedding:

"I'm afraid it won't do to have any throwing about it," said Holman. "Last week I read a paragraph about a negro wedding where they all threw their old shoes after the couple as they were riding away, and one of them knocked the bridegroom's five-dollar silk hat into the middle of next week, while another broke the wife's jaw."

"Was there a full account of the other ceremonies at that wedding?" asked Patsy Rafferty.

"I don't remember," said Holman. "Why?"

"Because," said Patsy, "whatever they did, we must do the very contrary."[13]

SEGREGATION OF PUBLIC FACILITIES

Considering the extent to which public facilities have been segregated in the United States, there is very little in children's books to reflect the truth of the conditions.

Recreational Facilities

There is an off-hand comment by Credle in *Flop-Eared Hound* when Boot-jack and his parents go to the circus. The statement is made that the clown "came over to the place where the coloured folks sat and shook hands with little Boot-jack."

In *Call Me Charley*, Jackson has Charley Moss win the contest that carries a free pass to the swimming pool as a prize. The judges, upon discovering he is black, offer him a ten dollar bill instead, and make it clear that whether he takes it or not, he will not be allowed to use the pool. Charley's friend, Tom Hamilton, is forced to learn about how white people treat black people as a result of this incident.

In a similar fashion, Mary Jane, in Sterling's book of the same name, is forced to teach her white classmates in the science club the facts of life as seen by a black. The group is talking about places to go on field trips. Mary Jane listens, and finally says: "The places you're talking about, I don't know if I can go. That museum has a special day for colored, and of course the park is out entirely. So you just go ahead and make your plans without me."[14] The group votes not to go anywhere unless Mary Jane is welcome, a decision that "was far and away the best thing that had happened to Mary Jane at Wilson High."

Medical Facilities

Sitting in a separate section at a circus, not being allowed in a swimming pool, or a museum, or the public park are degrading, insulting conditions. But they pale before the results of segregating hospital facilities, as Means shows in *Great Day in the Morning*. There is an automobile accident, and Lilybelle's friend Trudy is seriously injured. Major and Mrs. Tolliver, the people for whom Lilybelle works as a baby-sitter, are at the scene:

"Where's the nearest hospital?" Mrs. Tolliver was asking.

"Tuskegee . . ."

"But surely in a town this size . . ."

Lilybelle shook her head. "Nothing for colored. Oh, lay her flat, Major Tolliver . . ."

"We'll call the hospital ambulance," he gasped.

"No use," said Lilybelle. "I know this town. It won't take colored."[15]

Major Tolliver, a northern black, refuses to believe such a situation is possible. He calls the hospital and returns from the telephone shaken: "No accommodations for colored."

Trudy dies, and the doctors report that there would have been a 50–50 chance she could have lived with immediate care.

Travel Facilities

In *Hazel*, Ovington has a scene in which Hazel and her older companion are traveling by train after leaving the boat which brought them to Boston.

The landing was wearying, and the long journey to Alabama in a dirty, ill-ventilated car was inexpressibly tiring. The child grew wretchedly weary, and a big lump rose in her throat when night came on. She was homesick and uncomfortable. Instead of her pleasant bed at home, there was only a hard seat on which to rest. Mrs. Graham pillowed her as well as she could, but the sensitive child lay awake most of the night: for if she fell asleep from weariness, a vicious jolt of the train shook her awake again. Early in the evening their train stopped to wait until an express overtook it and passed on ahead. Hazel saw the Pullman with its comfortable beds and its brightly-lighted dining car where colored waiters were serving delicious looking food to white people.

"Why don't we ride in a car like that?" she asked Mrs. Graham.

But she knew the answer before she heard it. "Colored people are not allowed to in the South."[16]

When it is time for Hazel to return home to Boston, she travels with a white woman as her "serving maid" and is allowed a Pullman berth even though she may not eat in the dining car.

Ovington's second title in the sample, *Zeke*, reminds readers that blacks and whites may not share the same waiting-room facilities. She describes Zeke's departure:

Lots of the folks in the community saw him off. They filled the end of the platform by the colored waiting-room and screamed and wished him good luck as the train drew out. They cheered the first boy from their section of Callis County to enter Tolliver Institute.[17]

Harriet Freeman, the orphan in Means's *Shuttered Windows*, encounters segregation when she and the couple escorting her to her great-grandmother's, take the ferry that will carry them to Gentlemen's Island:

> "There's more room on top. Let's go up there," said Harriet, pushing toward another staircase.
> Mrs. Trindle laid a hand on her arm. "No, Harrie, That's the white people's deck. This. . . . Look, honey!"
> Harriet's frowning gaze followed Mrs. Trindle's pointing finger. Over the door of the enclosed deck was a large sign: COLORED. Over the staircase she had wished to climb stood a similar sign: WHITE.
> Harriet sat down, feeling sick. She had of course read of the "Jim Crow" trains and waiting-rooms, but it was the first time she had ever encountered them herself.[18]

The scene was designed for impact, not reality. It is impossible to believe that the Trindles and Harriet could have traveled from Minneapolis to New York City and then down the coast to Charleston, South Carolina, without encountering numerous examples of exclusion based on their race. Until the passage of the 1965 Civil Rights Act, the road from New York City to Washington, D.C. was a constant embarrassment to the government when nonwhite delegates to the United Nations were refused food. Conditions in the South might have been more obvious in Means's time, but to leave the impression that only in the South were the blacks faced with such degrading circumstances is to distort the truth.

In *Great Day in the Morning* (1946), Means makes her characters a bit sharper in their comments about segregation. Lilybelle Lawrence, with her friends Callie and Lonnie, are on their way to school at Tuskegee. It is Lilybelle's first trip.

> Even the shabby coach impressed Lilybelle, being the first time she had ever ridden.
> "White folks' car new and shiny," Callie grumbled. She had gone to the water tank and loitered there, peering into the next car as she drank. "Look how wore out these seats are. White folks' car got electric lights, too."

"Maybe this is one they fish out of their stockpile because the war use so many. These lights pretty nice, though," Lilybelle said, contentedly surveying the old oil lamps set along the ceiling. After all, the white folks always did get the best of things. You took it for granted. "We got just as good scenery as they got," she added.

"That must gripe 'em," Callie retorted.[19]

That travel was difficult for a black man was made obvious also in *Skid* (1948). "When the driver came out of the station, the bus began to fill, the white folks taking the front seats, the Negroes going to the back." Skid and his father and mother are on the back seat, which is less than comfortable. Even at rest stops, the black encountered problems.

At the end of two or three hours, the bus stopped for a short rest period. Skid watched the white folks leave the bus and go into the side of the station under the sign "White." Then he and his mother and father and the other Negroes who sat near them in the back section of the bus, got off and went into the side of the station for colored folks. There they found a small lunch counter, with no seats to sit on, and so far as Skid could see, nobody to wait on them either. He stood there awhile, then walked outside and past the white entrance. Folks were eating there, and sitting on seats, too. He told his mother and father about it.

"You stay here. You hear me?" Ed whispered. "But wait till we get to Washington! Alice says there'll be no having to sit on the back seat of the bus there, either."

Skid's mother shook her head. "I've been sitting on back seats so long, I've got to see that to believe it."[20]

By having big, strong Ed "whisper" to his son, the author effectively conveys the idea that in the world of whites, the black man loses something of his manhood.

Sports

Before the 1954 Supreme Court ruling directed at desegregating schools, the black-white situation to receive the most attention in the media and to engage people's emotions was the desegregation of professional baseball. Even people not involved with sports followed the trials and tribulations encountered by the late Jackie Robinson as he broke the color barrier in 1947.

In 1949 Duane Decker, one of the best of the sports-book authors, wrote *Hit and Run*. It was a very good book, and in historical terms is still a good book, although its subject matter has become obsolete. Yet, the book was not listed in the *Children's Catalog* until 1966—seventeen years later—when it was no longer relevant, the issues having become far more sophisticated, such as the absence of a black big league manager or social segregation that occurs on teams that do not allow black players and white players to room together.

The point to be kept in mind in reading the following passage—just one example of the strength of Decker's writing—is that the story would have been relevant and meaningful to readers in 1950, but by 1966 when it finally made its appearance in the *Children's Catalog* it could have no impact except in historical terms.

Kennie Willard, the black player trying to make the Blue Sox team, is assigned the lead-off position in an exhibition game being played in a small Florida town. As he stands swinging a couple of bats:

A policeman in uniform darted out on the field and grabbed Willard by the arm. The policeman barked, in a voice of authority, that carried far: "Git out'n the park. Git out'n the park else I'll put ya' in jail. Ah'm a tellin' ya!"

Willard stood there, motionless, looking down at the red-faced little cop. Jug Slavin had said, later: "I knew Kennie had majored in English at college so I thought maybe the cop's grammar was so bad, Kennie might not get it. Kennie could have picked the cop up by the seat of the pants and thrown him over the left-field fence but I guess it's just as well he did what he did."

What he did was nod and turn toward the Sox bench. The cop stayed on his heels, still shouting "git'n" and "out'n" every time he opened his mouth. Jug met them both, halfway.

"What gives here?" Jug demanded of the cop.

The cop pointed his club at Kennie. "He come out on this heah field, that's what gives," he roared. "This town ain't gonna stand for no Nigras playin' ball on the same field as white boys. This ain't the nawth and no nawth Nigras is comin' down heah and tell us how to run things. They think we're ignorant or what?"[21]

The one problem with *Hit and Run* is that Kennie Willard is not the central character. He is used as a foil to Chip, the bantam white player whose name comes from the fact that he has a "chip" on his shoulder. Willard is used to show that being black is far more serious a handicap than being short.

The only other book to treat the subject of sports segregation is Curtis

Bishop's *Little League Heroes.* The task of desegregating the West Austin (Texas) Little League falls to Joel Carroll. It is an easier job than Kennie Willard's was, and the basic conflict has very little to do with the baseball playing field. (Joel's major problem in *Little League Heroes* will be discussed in the following chapter under "Black-White Conflict.")

The important point to be made about *Little League Heroes* and *Hit and Run* is that neither author showed his character as a "natural" superstar athlete. The distinction to be made between the two authors is that Decker knows how to write while Bishop is never able to combine literary expression with his obvious knowledge of sports and social issues.

SCHOOLS: SEGREGATION AND DESEGREGATION

Three titles, *Zeke, Shuttered Windows,* and *Great Day in the Morning,* are set in all-black southern schools. Not one of the books questions the idea that blacks should go to school exclusively with other blacks. Two other books, *Gooseberry Jones* and *Melindy's Medal,* contain scenes set in schools that may be presumed to be all-black.

Seven books, ranging in publication dates from 1945 to 1965, treat problems of school desegregation. Three of the titles are set in the South: *Mary Jane* (1959), *New Boy in School* (1963), and *Empty Schoolhouse* (1965). All three take place after the 1954 Supreme Court ruling outlawing school segregation. Three of the titles take place in the North and all precede the court decision: *Call Me Charley* (1945), *Skid* (1948), and A *Cap for Mary Ellis* (1953).

The setting of the seventh title, *Ladycake Farm* (1952), cannot be determined from the text, except that it is rural. As seen in the preceding sections, the Freeds are not welcome at a church festival, and there is trouble about attending a luncheon at a local hotel, but neither of these situations is exclusively southern in nature. They could have happened in New York City or anywhere in the United States. In fact, they still could happen, although the hotel manager would have to be more subtle in excluding the Freeds.

Working against the idea that the setting is southern is the fact that the children attend the story hour at the local Hoytville Public Library. They are also admitted to the school system, which would have been impossible under southern law. Perhaps the author had a border state, such as Indiana or Maryland, in mind.

The Freeds are the first blacks to attend the New Hope Township School, and Mr. Freed (Poppy) gives Little Joe the following advice:

"Little Joe, . . . when you get on that bus next Monday morning, and all the time at school, you keep square an' steady on your feet. Keep your hands to yourself, forevermore. And no matter what, you keep your grin on your face. Maybe you'll get plum' tired o' that grin before the school boys quit their tormenting and take up with you. But don't you get tired of your grin 'til they get tired of their tormenting."22

In a much simpler form, May Justus has Mr. Lane give his son Lennie the same advice in *New Boy in School*. The way to make friends is to be friendly, is the essence of Mr. Lane's counsel.

For Charley Moss of *Call Me Charley*, the advice offered by his mother combines humility with pride. As Charley relates the situation to his friend Tom, he says:

"Well, Mom kept on talking. She said: 'Charley, I want you to behave yourself and don't pick any fights. 'Course if you have to take up for yourself, I want you to stand up like a man. You understand?' I said, 'Yes'm' "23

When the time comes for Charley to go to his school, his mother tells him:

"It's all up to you, Charley," she said. "Mr. Winter (the school principal) says here in this letter that you will only be allowed to attend their school for a three months trial. He says the school you used to go to in the Bottoms wasn't up to the standards of his school. I'll work and see you go to school clean, but you'll have to get the kind of grades it says here in the letter. You'll have to keep out of trouble. It ain't like you were one of the other boys. They'll have their eyes on you. First trouble you get into, Mr. Winter will say: 'See, I knew we shouldn't have let that colored boy come here.' "
"I'll study hard, Mom," Charley said.
"And watch your manners, boy. Good manners go a long way to help a colored boy get along in this world."
"And I'll watch my manners, Mom."24

However "good" or "bad" the advice given to Joe Freed, Lennie Lane, or Charley Moss may be, at least they receive the courtesy of a discussion from their parents. In *Skid* (1948), Edward "Skid" Parker only finds out he is going to an all-white school by overhearing a conversation. Skid's

Aunt Alice, who has provided the money for the trip north and has found the Parkers their jobs, is explaining to Skid's mother why it is essential for Skid to have a new suit:

"We've got to get him a good suit, Em. White children will judge him a great deal by the way he dresses."

"What do we care about the white boys as long as he looks as well as the other colored boys," Skid's mother asked.

Alice hesitated a moment before answering.

"Em, maybe I should have told you before you came up," she said. "There are no other Negro boys and girls in this town."[25]

In Hope Newell's *Cap for Mary Ellis* (1953), Mary Ellis Stebbins and Julie Saunders have no desire to go to an all-white nursing school. Both girls have their hearts set on Jefferson Nursing School in Harlem, New York. But the director of nursing, Miss Laurie, explains why she thinks it is important for Mary Ellis and Julie to go to Woodycrest.

"Quite recently, Woodycrest, a fine privately endowed nursing school in upper New York State has decided to admit Negro students. Its Board of Directors came to this decision so late that the school has not had time to look for suitable students to enter the June class.

. . . .

"Naturally, Miss MacKay's experience with her first two Negro students will be an important factor in Woodycrest's decision on admitting other colored girls."[26]

The idea that the entire black race must stand or fall on the individual performance of one or two members of the race is one of the most invidious forms of prejudice found in the children's books within this study—just as it is one of the worst forms of discrimination in life, whether directed at races, ethnic groups, or sexes.

The title character in *Mary Jane* is going to Wilson High School despite her parents' lack of encouragement. While her mother and her father do not actively discourage Mary Jane in her determination to break the color barrier, neither do they encourage her. At one point, just before school is to open, her father tells Mary Jane that she can still change her mind and go to Douglass without anyone thinking the worse of her. The suggestion does not make real sense to Mary Jane since she does not see herself as a social crusader. She is merely a girl with a burning desire to be a biologist, and one who knows that Wilson provides a better program than Douglass.

The Empty Schoolhouse is the story of the desegregation of a Catholic school in Louisiana. Thus, it is not primarily a matter of the legality of segregation, but the morality. Unhappily, Carlson gives the church fathers no role to play in the book: once the order is given, that is the end of church influence upon the community.

Lullah Royall, the little black girl who is the major character, does not expect any trouble, although her father has his doubts about the peacefulness that will attend desegregation. All begins well. A number of blacks choose to attend the school. Gradually, they drop out. Subtle threats are made and their families yield. For some time Lullah is the only child attending the school because the whites transfer to the white public school and the blacks transfer to the black public school. While other parents are yielding to the pressures that are being exerted, Lullah's parents remain stoic, refusing to pressure her one way or the other.

Technically speaking, Lennie Lane, the seven-year-old in *New Boy in School*, is not the first black to attend the Nashville school. The teacher tells him there are other blacks in the school, but not in his particular class. This knowledge doesn't change much for Lennie. As the only black face in the class, he feels as lonely as if he were the only black in the entire school. This is the only book in which there is absolutely no conflict about desegregation. Everyone is nice to Lennie, and he is treated exactly like the white children by both teacher and playmates. There is no end to the utopias of children's literature!

In *Call Me Charley, Skid,* and *A Cap for Mary Ellis* the central black characters must deal only with one white bigot, all other whites accept or are at least indifferent to their presence. *Call Me Charley* and *Skid* have a number of factors in common: the boys are in school because their parents are working for white people in the neighborhood; each has one loud-mouthed antagonist who is depicted as an insecure boy with parental problems; and each has a crisis over participation in the play being put on by his homeroom class.

When Mary Ellis and Julie arrive at Woodycrest, they find the way has been paved for them. The new administration is determined to see that the "experiment" is a success. Only one girl in the school, Ada Belle Briggs, objects to their presence, and she is eventually dismissed from school as a selfish neurotic. In fact, the one point *Call Me Charley, Skid* and *A Cap for Mary Ellis* emphasize is that bigots are mentally disturbed people—to some degree.

The three Freed children in *Ladycake Farm* have a minimum of trouble in their school situation. The two girls, India Rose and Pearlie May, have no trouble at all. Little Joe is forced to stand up on the school bus going to and from school for the first week, and the first day he is tripped while getting off the bus, but nothing really serious happens. The second Monday, the bus stops to pick up a new girl, and while everyone is staring at her, Little Joe sneaks into a seat, and that is the end of the hazing.

Mary Jane and *Empty Schoolhouse* both treat of the problems created by screaming mobs determined to keep the schools from integrating. In *Mary Jane*, the familiar chant of: "Two-four-six-eight / We ain't gonna integrate" and "We don't want her / You can have her / She's too black for me" are repeated. Unlike the books already discussed in which the black has only one enemy, the central character in *Mary Jane* has exactly one friend. Unfortunately, the friend is also an outcast, being too small for her age and sensitive to her childish appearance. It would almost seem that whether one is a bigot or a lone defender of a black, the end result is a neurotic personality. Eventually, through a science club, Mary Jane acquires a few in-school friends with whom she can be comfortable. Socializing is still not acceptable outside of school, however, and her friend Sally is not allowed to visit Mary Jane's grandfather's farm, nor can the girls visit with each other in their homes.

Mob rule does not prevail in *Mary Jane*, but for the greater part of *Empty Schoolhouse* it does carry the day. The first day of school a crowd gathers, but nothing serious happens. Then begins a series of threats: a rock is thrown through the window of the Royall family's neighbor, the Roches, and they remove their children from the school; the threat of losing a job forces one of the white men to withdraw his daughter. Finally, only Lullah is in attendance, and even she eventually withdraws, but for more personal reasons—it gets lonesome being the only student. In the end, she returns to the school and is shot by an "outside agitator." Although not seriously wounded, the shock of the attack brings the white people to their senses, and the school regains its students, the agitators are run out of town, and blacks and whites in rural Louisiana live happily ever after—together!

13

BLACK-WHITE
RELATIONSHIPS

While segregation of the races was a way of life in much of the United States, there were, of course, points of contact between blacks and whites. In this chapter we will look at the relative position of black to white, black-white conflict, and statements of black pride.

MR. CHARLEY RULES THE ROOST

The simplest way to make the point that the white was always in authority, the source from which all good things came, is to point out that in no book is a black depicted in a position of authority over a white. Even in a play situation, as found in *Across the Cotton Patch*, we find the sentence, "Atlantic felt very uneasy but she did not like to oppose the little white girl."

A more subtle presentation of this subordinate position of the black can be seen in *The Flop-Eared Hound*, where Boot-jack is seen as a very little black boy looking up at the white woman who sits astride a large horse. And in *Little Jeemes Henry* the boy is shown opening the gate for the white people sitting in the big automobile.

When a black needed money, it was always to a white that he turned. Throughout *Junior, A Colored Boy of Charleston*, the children turn to whites to earn pennies and nickles. Mrs. Robinson's washing-work comes from the whites, and in the end it is the white man, Mr. Clarkson, who finds Mr. Robinson a job. The all-black southern schools in *Zeke, Shuttered Windows*, and *Great Day in the Morning* owe their existence to northern white supporters.

Rather than detail all occasions in which white largesse is bestowed upon blacks, let us look at a scene in *Call Me Charley* that summarizes the entire problem. Tom Hamilton is angry with Charley for withdrawing from school and life, and he accuses Charley of being a crybaby. Tom's mother takes the occasion to set Tom straight.

"Look here, Tom," Mrs. Hamilton said. "It seems to me that all you have against Charley is that he does not speak up. Now stop and think a minute— you remember when Charley came here first and wanted to get into your school?"

"Yes, Mom."

"Well, Mrs. Moss went to Mr. Winter, and she certainly did speak up. But did it help her? No. Mr. Winter turned the boy down. But then Doctor Cunningham talked to Mr. Winter—and that helped instantly."

"Yes, Mom."

"Well, that's the way it is, even though it shouldn't be that way. Some people don't like colored people and don't want to give them a chance. And that's where their friends have to stand up for them. I know it wouldn't have done Charley one bit of good to speak up to the manager. But I certainly think *you* might have said a word for him or some of the other boys. You should have been ashamed not to."

"Yes, Tom," Mr. Hamilton said. "Your mother is right. And I think we should all try now to do something for the boy."[1]

Mrs. Hamilton uses her influence at the P.T.A. meeting to see that Charley is given a part in the class play. This stand by Mrs. Hamilton serves the second purpose of helping neutralize the bigot, George Reed. George's mother is present at the meeting, and being very concerned with what Mrs. Hamilton thinks of her, she backs off. Mrs. Reed is by no means converted to the brotherhood of man, nor is son George, but the social-pressure approach is sound psychology for dealing with prejudiced people.

BLACK-WHITE CONFLICT

One of the most interesting facts to emerge from this study is that prior to the publication of *Call Me Charley* in 1945 no book in the sample contained a black-white-conflict situation. With the exception of a few "poor white trash" types, all white people were depicted as benevolent, if not downright patronizing, toward blacks. And while some blacks in the books did express antiwhite opinions, they did it to each other and not to the whites.

The predominant attitude in most of the books is that "quality white folks" are not mean to black people. The attitude is best summed up in a scene from *Hazel*. Having learned that Hazel is going to Alabama, her friend Charity offers the following advice:

"But don't you have nothing to do with white folks. There's two kinds of white folks down there: those that hates you and those that calls you 'a cute little nigger.' My mother says that ain't so, for she knows the first families of Virginia, but I ain't acquainted with 'em."

"My father used to tell about white people near his home who were nice," said Hazel reflectively.

"Poor white trash, I guess. There ain't any first families in Alabama."

That night, before going to bed, Hazel questioned her mother about the white folks.

"Won't they like me?" she said. "Will they call out 'Nigger,' the way the boys on Shawmut Avenue do to Charity?"

"I don't know, dear, I don't know. Granny can help you about that, not I. But I would not bother with them, Hazel. They go their way and you go yours. On the steamer, in the train, at the church and at school—everywhere you will be separated. Their world will not be your world. Leave them alone."[2]

It is not always possible to keep entirely to oneself, and Hazel has a painful encounter with two maiden white ladies. Hazel becomes lost and stops at a house to ask her way. The first mistake Hazel makes is in going to the front door. Miss Jane calls to her sister, "Here's Aunt Ellen's child come to ask the way, and if the little nigger didn't knock at the front door!" Hazel is hurt at the word "nigger," but the ladies do know where Granny lives, so she says in a most dignified manner, "If you will please explain to me how to get to Granny's, I will go."

The ladies are gossips and are not willing to let Hazel go quite so easily. She is taken to the kitchen to warm herself by the fire. There she is questioned about the excellent quality of her coat, and Hazel must explain that it was a gift from a friend of her father's.

"You know my father is dead," Hazel added.

"Yes, I know, honey," Miss Jane said sympathetically. "He was a right nice boy. He used to come here to sell my mother vegetables. He'd fix everything to sell as neat and nice, and he'd tell about the doings around his way until we'd almost die laughing. I've often wondered if he took to gardening up North."

"We had a tiny garden where we lived," Hazel answered eagerly, "and father worked in it in the early morning before he went to business. He was a lawyer, you know."

"A lawyer?"

"Yes, ma'am, a lawyer."

"A nigger lawyer! That beats all."

After coffee and biscuits, the ladies send Hazel home in the care of their cook, Marty. However, before departing, Hazel makes the mistake of calling Miss Jane by her surname, "Miss Fairmount," and is told that she is impertinent. At home, Hazel tries to explain to Granny how hurt she was by the entire encounter. Granny's advice is:

"Watch *how* folks says things, and not *what* they says. Now, Miss Jane, she didn't do that to-day, and she hurt my baby girl. She ain't quality and that's a fact."[3]

However painful the scene is to Hazel, it does not qualify as a conflict situation since the "ladies" obviously have no intention of offering offense. Neither in the book nor in life would they be capable of understanding the hurt their words inflicted; it is beyond their training and experience.

Thus, what is being analyzed in this section are those incidents where the white bigot shows *some* understanding of what he is doing. The word "conflict" in this section can be applied only to children's books; by adult standards, there is very little real conflict in the sense that both parties fight openly. The black here, as elsewhere in the books, is at best a "passive resister" of the white person's taunts.

When whites are not depicted as being benevolent toward blacks, there are three forms their antiblack conduct take: name-calling, avoidance, and the invoking of double standards. The first two are directly connected since one does not associate with people toward whom one directs epithets. Double standards, on the other hand, are usually the weapon of people who think of themselves as well-meaning.

As observed earlier, *Call Me Charley* was the first book to present anything resembling a genuine black-white confrontation. The opening scene in *Call Me Charley* has the bigot, George, saying "Move on Sambo," and "We don't allow niggers around here." Charley responds by saying:

"My name is Charles. . . . Sometimes I'm called Charley. Nobody calls me Sambo and gets away with it." He dropped the paper he was rolling and moved closer to George. George swung back with the stick.[4]

The verbal exchange and the threatening gestures do not lead to physical combat either in the above scene or at any time in the book. When the white boys at school want to initiate Charley into their club, the fear of physical violence makes Charley run. It is not that Charley is a physical coward, but he knows there is a difference between fighting with the boys in his old neighborhood who belonged to his own race and fighting with white boys.

George tries very hard to make Tom Hamilton stop associating with Charley. The only time George and Charley are together is at the Hamilton house, and George usually finds a reason to go home soon after Charley arrives. George is not a likable boy. He is pampered, a victim of his parents' prejudices, and the parents are shown as not really class people: a little too loud, a little too pushy.

This idea that "class" people do not behave badly is a direct descendant of the slave attitude that masters were "quality" folk and the nonslave-owning population was "poor white trash." It is also related to the idea that "happy slaves" had good masters, while on occasion there was a bad master whose lack of good behavior caused the slaves to be unhappy.

A case of avoiding a black person, without name-calling, is found in *Bright April* when the Brownie troop is having a supper party. Phyllis, a girl from another troop, refuses to sit next to April. A bad storm comes up and the Brownies and their leaders are forced to spend the night at the farm where they are having the party. Late that night, April awakens to find Phyllis crawling into bed with her:

"It's me—Phyllis. I'm cold, and I'm *so* lonesome. Can't I stay here with you?" April was awake now.

"Of course," she answered, hugging Phyllis close.

Phyllis was quiet for a moment, then said hesitantly, "You know, at first I didn't like you. I never knew anyone just like you before. But Flicker told me about you and how nice you are. . . . When I touched your hand that time, I felt how nice and smooth it was. I saw that your dress was just as fresh and clean as mine, too." She stopped for a moment, then went on, "I like you now."[5]

DeAngeli is dealing here with a very complex problem in a very simple fashion. It is true that a white eight-year-old who had never met a black before would be curious about how black skin feels. It is also true that black is equated with "dirty," and the fact that April's dress is fresh and clean would influence Phyllis. But whether, given a small talk from the leader Flicker, Phyllis would select April's bed to crawl into to find solace is highly debatable.

Earlier in *Bright April* the author tells us that April is also concerned about "dirty" children:

> Some of the people in the block took no thought for the appearance of their houses inside or out. Some of them were not careful even of their own appearance. The children went to school in clothing that was not clean, with hair unbrushed and hands and faces unwashed. One of the children sat near April in school. She didn't like it.
>
> "Maybe the teacher will think I'm like that," she complained.[6]

While Mrs. Bright tries to explain to April the problems people face who live in houses without central heating and have the water pipes freeze in winter, the overall effect of the incident is the assumption that unclean children are not worthy of April's friendship or the teacher's attention. This attitude is what allows April to be susceptible to Phyllis' overtures based on the "fresh dress."

A nonracial type of name-calling is found in *Melindy's Happy Summer*, but the basis for it would appear to be racial. Melindy Miller is not on the Gray farm more than an hour or two when Mr. Gray labels her "Little Miss Brag." Melindy is a very bright, verbal, eager-to-please little girl, and Mr. Gray's reaction seems completely out of line. For a man with five children of his own, and who showed enough concern about racial problems to take three black children from the city into his home for the summer, Mr. Gray shows surprisingly little understanding and demonstrates no patience. One gets the feeling that Mr. Gray's annoyance with Melindy is based on his assumption that the three blacks would be properly appreciative of the opportunity being offered them. Melindy's natural exuberance is not humble enough.

Fortunately for Melindy, the smallest Gray girl, Peggy, falls into the water while on a picnic. Despite being frightened and not knowing how to swim, Melindy jumps in and saves Peggy. This makes everything all right; Mr. Gray now likes Melindy, and the rest of the visit will be a happy one for her.

In *Skid*, the hero faces a variety of antiblack situations, some of them quite subtle, others blatant. When Aunt Alice takes Skid shopping for a new suit, the storekeepers in the small Connecticut town bring out their least attractive and most gaudy suits to show him. While they are walking along the sidewalk, one white boy turns and says insolently, "How's everything in 'Jaw-ja?" Skid looks at the boy with the pale skin and light hair and mentally nicknames him "Flour Face." The boy's name is Allyn and he is Skid's tormenter throughout the book.

As noted *Skid* and *Call Me Charley* have many parallels: both boys are the only blacks in their area because their parents are live-in helpers in a white household; both have trouble being admitted to the white school, and both are faced with a single bigot to conquer. Allyn, like George, is eventually forced by group pressure to be civil to Skid. One major difference is that Skid reacts with more anger than hurt feelings to the insults and taunts of Allyn. In fact, Skid names his punching bag "Flour Face" and gives it a good pounding, thus getting a vicarious release for the anger within him.

Pony Rivers in *Little Vic* has two problems with white people. The first is with the jockeys on the backwater racetracks where Pony is trying to gain enough experience so he can ride his beloved Little Vic in a major race. His fellow jockeys do not like Pony, and the author says, "It was the first time in his life that Pony had ever had the feeling that people around him didn't like him."

Pony Rivers is sixteen years old, and it seems impossible that he could have lived in New York City and in Kentucky, Florida, and assorted other states without discovering that there are people who dislike blacks just because of their skin color. The jockeys are identified as farm boys, and not content to avoid Pony's company, they combine to cause an "accident" that hospitalizes Pony for weeks. This is one of the few cases of outright physical assault upon a black, but like so much of *Little Vic*, it is so subtly presented that many readers could miss the point entirely.

After release from the hospital, Pony hitchhikes to the Arizona ranch of Harry George, Little Vic's new owner. There he encounters Joe Hills, and he tells Joe how, when he was sick, he even got to thinking that he was a brother to Little Vic.

But Joe Hills didn't return the laugh, although a smile came to his face. It was not, however, the kind of smile that made you want to smile with him. As Pony looked at it, a strange fear came into his heart.

"Well," began Joe Hills slowly, "you *are* about the same color, for a fact." A mean look came into his face. "We don't want no colored riders around here. As I see it, there isn't no such thing as a colored jockey. And I don't even want no colored exercise boys on this place. We might be able to use you around the stables. But you can't never ride this horse or any other. Understand?"

Pony understood all too well. Joe Hills was like those boys who had caused his fall so many months ago. They had not liked him because he was colored. And now Joe Hills didn't want him to ride for the same reason. It made no sense at all to Pony. It only made him feel sick inside.[7]

Pony does ride Little Vic one memorable night, and the horse outraces a flash flood to save a family from drowning when they have foolishly pitched camp in a draw. Joe Hills is so angry at Pony riding the horse that he refuses to listen to Pony's account of how well Little Vic ran.

Convinced that Little Vic is now ready to run with the best, Pony hitchhikes to California where Mr. George is preparing another horse for the Santa Anita Handicap. Mr. George believes Pony's assessment of the horse, and he sends for Joe Hills and Little Vic. Pony rides Little Vic and wins the Santa Anita Handicap. Joe Hills offers his hand because he thinks Pony is "a great little guy," and we are left with the feeling that bigot and black will live happily ever after—or at least as long as Pony keeps winning races.

The Freed family's joy at moving onto its own farm is marred in *Lady-cake Farm* by the greeting awaiting them at one boundary line:

And then, at the southwestern edge of the pasture, they saw the high fence of barbed wire. They knew, by the peeled posts and shiny wire, that it was a brand-new fence. The barbs looked cruel in the spring light. And they were cruel. For on one of the posts was tacked a fresh shingle, and on the shingle were painted these words, "Niggers unwelcome. Keep out."[8]

In the world of children's books, fate is unkind to bigots, and Mr. Carle, owner of the fence and sign, is seriously injured when a cyclone hits while he is on a ladder painting his barn. None of the other men are around, and Mr. Freed rescues Mr. Carle and takes him to the hospital. When young Bob Carle tries to pay Mr. Freed for having helped save his father's life, Mr. Freed says:

"Mr. Bob, for the sake of my children, could you Carles manage to get along without the sign on your fence you put up to tell us, as ugly as possible, that we weren't welcome in these parts? D'you think it would hurt you any to take that sign down?"

"I took that sign down exactly one hour ago," Mr. Bob declared. "When I was at the hospital this morning, and told Dad of the happenings yesterday, he ordered me to remove the sign first chance I got. My dad said, 'Guess I was a little hasty hot, putting up that sign against neighbors.' "[9]

Another bigot who is forced to recant is Major Kramer in *Little League Heroes*. Major Kramer is furious when Joel Carroll is accepted on the team, and when told that Little League rules prohibit discrimination, he tells the coach:

"I don't care what Little League rules provide. . . . My grandson doesn't have to wear the same uniform as a Negro boy. There are ways this could have been handled even if he does live in this league's area. I'm surprised at you, Frank, for letting such a condition come about."[10]

Deprived of the good influences of Little League baseball, the major's grandson, Dudley, gets into trouble. Dudley and his new friends burn down the Little League clubhouse, but Joel and his friend Rox save most of the equipment. The major pays for the rebuilding of the clubhouse and he allows Dudley to return to the team.

Rox Dugan is not Joel's friend at the beginning of the book, but his conversion is less dramatic than the major's. At the time Rox is encountered in the book, he is calling Joel "Burrhead." He harasses Joel at every opportunity—but Rox is not a real bigot. He is just an unhappy, angry boy who has a drunk for a father. Once this is understood, Joel and Mr. Carroll help Rox by giving him the attention he needs, and soon Rox is ready to be a good team member.

ANTIWHITE ATTITUDES

Only one book in the study contained strong expressions of animosity toward whites: *Great Day in the Morning* by Means. It is also the book that contains the most vivid examples of invoking the double standard in judging blacks as opposed to whites. The antiwhite attitudes are expressed by minor characters while the central character, Lilybelle Lawrence, is chief spokesman for the double-standard thinking.

One of the few occasions that Lilybelle expresses regret at the condition of the black in white America is within her own mind:

There were plenty of Negroes today, she had heard, who wouldn't be white if they could choose. And Doctor Carver would have found the idea trifling. Yet what a burden dark skin and tight-curled hair could be in a land where light skin and straight hair predominated.[11]

This thought follows an argument among the girls at the YWCA where Lilybelle is staying in Denver. One of the girls, Sandy, is in nurses' training. A second girl, Carrie, objects to Sandy's account of how she got into nursing school, claiming that Sandy makes it sound too easy when, in fact, it has taken years of fighting to open nursing to blacks. Sandy admits this is so, but counters that when a class was started "there weren't any girls eligible. Even the high-school seniors who'd been making such a squawk about being nurses hadn't bothered to take the required courses."

Another girl asks whether it is fair to expect people to qualify on an off-chance that they might finally be allowed into nursing school? Sandy thinks they should. Carrie then points out that when a hospital offered to take an "all-colored class of trainees," the girls said "they weren't going in for any Jim Crow business in nursing."

The argument, then, is that blacks must prepare themselves to be admitted to vocations not presently open to them and when the opening comes, must be ready to accept segregation. Certainly Lilybelle accepts this line of reasoning.

The ultimate outcome of this attitude, according to the author, is progress for the black. The reverse attitude is a setback, and she goes to great pains to prove her point.

The group from the Y is out walking when Dakie Bennett, an ex-soldier who has lost an arm in the war and who interests Lilybelle very much, suggests they stop for a soda.

Lilybelle came out of her bright daze. "White Dime Store?" she asked uneasily.

"Sho' 'nough!" crowed Frankie May. "They've got a law in this state, gal. Got to serve everybody that wants to be served. We help things along when we goes in and stands up for our rights."[12]

The waitresses appear to be ignoring the group, and Dakie goes up to where they are standing together and asks for service. They get their sodas, feeling their waitress has skimped on both syrup and ice cream. Despite Lilybelle's discomfort, the group proceeds to "sit-in" for an hour, occupying needed seats. Eventually, Lilybelle refuses to stay, and Dakie leaves with her. He says:

"But they've got the law on their side," argued Dakie.
"Law! Be all right to go in and act mannersable. But when they behave like hoodlums they hurt the whole lot of us."
"Lilybelle, it's the times," Dakie said reasoningly. "White young folks act loud and crazy too."
"That makes me no never-mind," Lilybelle retorted, stamping along toward the Y. "White or black, there's manners and there's no-manners. You ever see quality act that way?"
"If it was white boys and girls, folks would overlook it," Dakie protested. "But a colored kid—it's not fair."
"Who said it was fair?" Lilybelle asked scornfully. "It's the way things are."[13]

Lilybelle is right, of course. It does not matter whether invoking double standards is fair, it is the way things are. She finds it out, to her sorrow, when she applies for a job in the same Dime Store. The manager tells her "stiffly":

"We've tried to be broad-minded in this store. . . . About race and all that. But I regret to say we've been obliged to revise our policy. As regards colored persons."
Lilybelle stood frozen by the hurt that never did wear out—frozen and scorched at once. The aching humiliation was like a living thing in the small office, and even the man seemed to sense it.
"Last Saturday," he said, "a young colored gang came to our soda fountain. Our girls waited on them. That's the law. And how did the young punks repay us? By talking and laughing like hyenas and keeping their seats for an hour while other folks waited."[14]

In the language of the 1970s, Mrs. Means is a bleeding-heart liberal. She does understand the hurt black people feel; she consistently zeroes in on the inequality of black life as contrasted with white life, and yet the message she delivers is that patience and good manners will eventually carry the day. One is tempted to ask the author if good manners will bring Trudy back from the grave she occupies because the hospital would not take "colored."

Shortly after Lilybelle is refused the job, Means has her say, "We crave to be treated like white folks, but if we act like the worst of them how we expect to be treated like the best of them?" It is, by literary standards, a lovely sentence, but the more appropriate question would be, "Why aren't all whites judged by the worst members of their race?" The answer, of course, is simple: the ruling group is not held accountable for all members of its race. Accountability is the province of the "inferior" group looking to raise itself "up" to the level of the boss-man.

BLACK ON BLACK

Time and again, throughout the preceding chapters and within the previous pages of this chapter, we have seen numerous examples of the black's dilemma in developing self-pride. The overall impact of being taught to "think white" is to degrade being black. The idea that all blacks are judged by one example of the race has encouraged black people to dislike or look down upon other members of their race who do not meet white standards.

It is not strange, then, that there are few examples of racial pride in these books. In fact most of the black characters are condescending toward their fellow blacks. Harriet Freeman's attitude in *Shuttered Windows* is typical. As a northerner, Harriet is constantly appalled by the southern blacks, but never is it seen more clearly than when she is visiting Booker School to play a basketball game. The occasion is rather like a homecoming game in college football: there are many events for the parents and relatives of the students.

Richie Corwin has just finished telling Harriet that he wants to get away to where things are different (an idea Harriet has planted in his mind):

"I should think you would want to get away!" Harriet responded vehemently. Her eyes frowned at the humanity that surged around her. White headkerchiefs, sometimes topped with disreputable hats, round, black heads, rags, rags; a rank smell of tobacco, though pipes were hidden here; a gabble of talk almost unintelligible.

Joan Senter [a white teacher] had been almost lifted from her feet and carried along by the human tide. She was washed up against Harriet, and her breathless laughter was sobered by Harriet's somber face.

"Don't take it so hard!" she said swiftly. She drew Harriet, and Richard, with her, into a cove behind a rack of dresses. "Harriet, remember it's like this with any part of *any* race that has no education and no higher contacts.

Weren't you ever down in the slums of a big city? Wouldn't you a lot rather have the island people's life and chance? And what about our white mountaineers?"[15]

Lack of education may be part of the problem, but basically the question is not one of "higher contacts," whatever that means, but of economics. Lacking running water, one does not bathe daily. Ignoring the reality of the conditions of an isolated people, one can still ask why the explanation is put in the mouth of a white person instead of the black.

The only truly strong statement on racial pride is found in Ovington's *Zeke*, a 1931 publication. Given the acuity of Ovington's observations on the status of being black in white America, it probably was no accident that she put the defense of blackness into the mouth of her African character Natu. It seems likely that she understood that a black who had been subjected all his life to white brainwashing would not be able to see the situation as clearly as a man who did not have to question his racial heritage.

Tolliver, like all boarding schools the world over, offers the students a film night now and then. Zeke and Natu go to the show, which is obviously an early *Tarzan* movie, although not so identified in the book. Natu has no objections to the scenery or the photographs of the wild animals, but the pictures of the natives make him angry: "They are the ugliest people they can find, and the stupidest. It's not fair."

Zeke agrees with Natu and:

They talked on the same theme after they were home, and both agreed that white people seemed to want to show the Negro at his worst. They liked to show ugly savages and the newspapers chiefly featured Negro crime.

While the boys are talking, Junior, a happy-go-lucky boy, arrives. Junior believes that everyone wants to be boss, and given the chance, Natu would treat whites as whites now treat blacks. He says that when Garvey becomes President of Africa one of his first steps will be to put the whites on the chain gang. Junior then imitates Garvey lording it over the whites. Natu points out to him that Garvey is a West Indian and does not talk like Uncle Remus.

"An' you hyar," Junior went on, paying no attention to the interruption and pointing his finger at Natu, "you is eddicated, eh? I disremember you' name, sah, but I see you hol' you' head high. You go to dat desk dar, what belon' ter me, de fust president ob de Republic ob Africa, an' you cac'late how I kin get mo' taxes f'om des hyar lazy niggers. Dere ain't so many chicken come dis month as de president kin eat. See dat I git mo'.''

Natu did not laugh. "You are without race pride," he said.

"Oh, beat it, you and your race pride. . . . My father went to college and my mother teaches in high school. They printed a picture of our house in the *Crisis*. 'One of the leading colored homes in Texas.' Shoot it! We ain't any better than the next fellow. And the next fellow ain't any better or worse than the white man who lives out by the country club. We're all alike. Some can shoot straighter, some can swear louder. That's all. As for our skins—the Lord made 'em to suit the climate where we were going to live. Black goes with palm trees, and yellow with desert, and white with ice and snow. What reason have you got to be proud because your skin goes with palms?"

"Truth and falsehood are mixed in all that you say," Natu replied. "People are different, and we ought to recognize differences, but not differences of color."

"They're the easiest to pick out." And Junior tumbled into bed.[16]

Certainly Junior is right in saying that color differences are the easiest to pick out. However, Natu's comment that differences should be made, but not on the basis of color, is the message that ought to have been carried in all the books.

14

AFTERWORD
A PERSONAL
VIEWPOINT

Whether one likes or dislikes, approves or disapproves, the image of the black that emerges from the sample of children's books analyzed, the fact is that the image does reflect a high degree of reality in terms of how a great part of white America viewed black America. It is perhaps mundane to observe that the content of the books is directly related to the society in which the books are produced. The observation is necessary because there is a strong tendency on the part of children's librarians and children's book critics to ignore that books are not produced in a vacuum.

The situation is circular: the society dictates the content and attitudes within the books and the books serve to perpetuate the societal attitudes from one generation to the next. When a book breaks the circle, whether in terms of literary style or deviation from accepted content, it is a landmark book in literary history. The book does not have to survive as great literature, but literary scholars of the future cannot ignore its influence upon the literary scene. In the field of children's literature about blacks analyzed here, there are no landmark titles. (In books published since the study ended, June Jordan's *His Own Where* is, in my opinion, a landmark title.)

Theoretically, there could have been four types of books in the study: (1) outright racist books; (2) condescendingly racist books; (3) traditionally liberal, do-gooder books, and (4) incisive, insightful books that lay bare the essence of humanity. In point of fact, the children's books analyzed within the study primarily fall into the second and third categories. There are individual incidents that certainly can be categorized as outright racist, but the overall impact, even of a book like *Diddie, Dumps and Tot*, is more condescendingly, than aggressively, racist.

The only discernible difference among the authors and books analyzed for this study in terms of whether they fit category two or three is that the liberal do-gooder authors present as their central black character an exceptional example of the black race. For example, Pomp, in *Cudjo's Cave*, is a paragon in ebony skin.

The basic literary problem with the books stems from the authors' preconceived ideas of what black people are like. Few of the authors allowed their characters to develop. Rather, early in each book the black was assigned a role to play, and with single-minded determination, the authors did not let the black step outside the role assigned to him or her. Again, this role-assigning is a reflection of societal attitudes. In the early days, blacks were happy or unhappy slaves; later they became faithful family servants with no distinguishing characteristics to differentiate them from happy household slaves.

The fact that the blacks were important only as workers can be seen by the difference in focus of the books from the Blanck bibliography and those coming from the *Children's Catalog*. Fifty-five books from the Blanck bibliography yielded some data for the study, either in the form of comments or in the actual presence of black characters. With the exception of Herman and Verman in *Penrod* and *Penrod and Sam*, all major black characters are adults. There are children present in books set on plantations, e.g., *Diddie, Dumps and Tot*, and in such titles as *Miss Minerva and William Green Hill* and *The Little Colonel*, but the black children do not play any significant role.

This pattern held for the three nineteenth-century titles in the *Children's Catalog* sample: *Cudjo's Cave*, *The Complete Tales of Uncle Remus*, and *King Tom and the Runaways*. With the exception of *Journey Cake* and *Hit and Run*, all remaining titles from the *Children's Catalog* sample have children or young adults as their central black characters.

The shift in focus required a new set of categories for role assignment and resulted in blacks being depicted as "quaint and curious pickanninies," as found in such books as *Frawg*, *Epaminondas and His Auntie*, and the *Nicodemus* books. This role was supplanted by the "missionary for his race" characters who either devote their lives to uplifting "their" people, e.g., *Shuttered Windows*, or serve as ambassadors of goodwill to show white people that black people are really very nice, e.g., *Melindy's Happy*

Summer. Finally, there is the type of book that pretends that black people are exactly like white people, e.g., *Strawberry Roan, Gooseberry Jones, Who's in Charge of Lincoln?*

Only in the role of missionaries for their race do the blacks find themselves in conflict situations, and as often as not, the conflict is not that of black-white but either internal conflict (should Harriet Freeman give up her dream of being a concert pianist and stay on Gentlemen's Island and uplift her people?), or conflict between blacks (is Lilybelle Lawrence right in pacifying whites or is a more militant stance called for?). When the black finds him/herself in a black-white-conflict situation, the odds are overwhelming that he or she will have to face only one bigot (*Call Me Charley, Bright April, Little Vic, Skid, A Cap for Mary Ellis, Little League Heroes*, and *Ladycake Farm*).

If by chance the black finds himself in a genuinely explosive situation, as in *The Empty Schoolhouse*, the trouble comes from "outside agitators" and the good folks of the area rally round as soon as the violent nature of the agitators manifests itself. The attitude is the reverse of the opinion held by some whites that racial conflict is caused by "Communists."

Only in *Mary Jane* does the character face a reasonably realistic situation with a reasonably realistic resolution. In *Mary Jane*, only the smallest step is taken toward improving black-white relationships, and it is unfortunate that Mary Jane is provided with such a thoroughly upper-middle-class pedigree.

The major problem with the books in the study and most of the black books published and accepted since its cutoff date, is that they personalize the race issue instead of recognizing it as the social-economic-political problem it is. A composite plot summary can illuminate this point. In such a plot, the black character moves out of the black world and meets in the white world *one* bigot. Some disaster, of varying levels of intensity, occurs, and the black proves himself adequate to the challenge presented. This action on the part of the black then leads either to the reformation of the bigot or to his becoming neutralized. End of problem.

The bigot is never a group leader. He is an insecure, pampered child, as in *Call Me Charley*, a bully, as in *Skid*, or a selfish neurotic, as in *A Cap for Mary Ellis*. If in real life persons of goodwill outnumbered the bigots in the same proportion as they do in children's books, there would be no racial conflict in society. But we know that the Ku Klux Klan and the White Citizens Council contain within their membership doctors, lawyers, businessmen, and teachers. The bigot is not always a "red-necked cracker" as William Armstrong's *Sour Land* would have us believe.

It would be very pleasant, in real life, if every black who is faced with a bigot had the opportunity to perform heroically and, magically, convert the bigot. And in real life being talented and successful does not assure the black man acceptance, either. We know from books by Sammy Davis, Jr., Dick Gregory, and other performing artists that being a star is not a shield against discrimination.

Finally, when racism is institutionalized and woven into the fabric of daily existence, a person of goodwill is severely limited in what actions he or she can take and what changes he or she can bring about. By having Pony Rivers ride in the Santa Anita Handicap, Doris Gates took first prize in this category of wishful thinking.

Little Vic illuminates several points that need understanding if the quality of books about blacks is to improve. First, to reiterate, is that a single white person cannot be shown to change a power structure. If this point is doubtful to some, ask the head of a building corporation who would gladly hire blacks, but is limited to those with the proper union credentials. Second, it is time to stop making the white individual the all-understanding benefactor of a single black. And third, books about blacks must depict the blacks in control of their own lives and fighting their own battles. The battles being fought must be those that are being fought—not one black against one white bigot, but the black community fighting the structure of white society, whether that fight concerns the right to go to a school of one's choice, or the right to eat at a lunch counter, or the right to work at a job of one's preference.

Perhaps most important of all, the blacks must be seen as fighting these battles, not to improve the lot of their race, but because as human beings they are entitled to these rights taken for granted by whites. We do not need any more books like William Armstrong's *Sounder*, where a black child who watches his father destroyed by racism overcomes the horrors of childhood to attain the lofty position of being allowed to sit in the white man's kitchen and help the white man's children become intellectually stimulated.

It would be pleasant to be able to end with a blueprint for magically changing the content of children's books about blacks. To do so, however, would be to assume the same stance the children's book authors of the past have assumed—namely that there is an easy way out, a solution to the whole racial problem. There isn't, and there isn't likely to be for a good long time.

First of all, let us look at the idea that only blacks should write about blacks. The racism in that veiw is no better than the view held up by white southerners that they were the only whites who "knew" blacks because they lived so closely with them. All black people are not alike, any more than all white people are alike. All black people do not have a single point of view on any subject, not even when they use the same words. Take, for example, two black adults saying to their respective children, "Why do you want to go to a white school? We don't need to be messing around with white folks." One man can hold this attitude because he is so conditioned to his situation as outsider that he cannot conceive of black-white "mixing." The second man may hold the opinion because he is a committed separatist.

It is understandable how the view came to be held, but it is a simplistic answer to the problem and must be rejected. There are more blacks writing and illustrating today than seemed possible a decade ago. Some of the black authors now writing and those in the future are not going to want to be limited to writing exclusively about blacks. If black authors and illustrators box themselves into a literary ghetto they will create another problem situation that will have to be resolved at some point in the future. Far better to keep the doors open and fight the battle in the open marketplace through reviews, recommended lists, and the high-quality articles found regularly in *Interracial Books for Children*. We must label racism when and where it is found and try to influence the potential purchasers of the material and the publishers who produce it.

Improving the quality of reviews and the selections made for standard bibliographies is something that can be accomplished with an expenditure of effort. The problem here is not limited to books about blacks: it is endemic to the children's book field. While more and more reviewing periodicals do require solid background knowledge for reviewing nonfiction books, they continue to act as if fiction were a homogeneous category in which one person can be expert. When this assumption is made what is evaluated is the readability of the book and little else. Reviewers of children's books should be experts in the fields in which they review and be made to demonstrate when dealing with a fiction title about blacks that they have read widely in the adult materials considered standard in the field. No one who has not read Malcolm X, Julius Lester, and Eldridge

Cleaver, to name just three of the more eloquent spokesmen, is in any position to make a judgment about any juvenile novel about blacks. This applies to black reviewers as well as whites who think they have read what it is all about if they have read Martin Luther King.

The failure to keep knowledgeable about current attitudes produces a serious time lag in children's books. At a time when the most important black voice in literature was Richard Wright's, juvenile authors were giving us *Melindy's Medal* and *Bright April*.

Literary purists view this concern with content analysis with alarm and see in it a conspiracy to make books propaganda weapons. Actually the opposite is true since knowledge accompanied by thoughtfulness *can* bring about insight. Without knowledge, we end up with the kind of books found in this study: mindless in terms of intellectual content *and* literary disasters. Good books, whether labeled realism or fantasy, are good precisely to the degree they offer insight into the human condition, and neither ignorance nor good intentions are renowned for their contributions to mankind.

Within the children's field, the critics of analysis in social terms are even more upset. They want children's books to be happy, to offer the readers hope and belief that they can aspire to anything they want to do. They forget, or don't know, that happiness is a relative condition and must be measured against unhappiness—in other words, happiness is the satisfactory resolution of a conflict.

Most of these critics, being white, have never had to think about aspirations in terms of what society would "let" them do, but only in terms of what they want to do. So they applauded (and some continue to applaud) books that tell the black person to work hard, wash regularly, find a white patron (to replace the good master of slave days), and you will reach the top and live happily ever after. Maybe that is true on another star in our universe; it is not true on Planet Earth.

While most of us survive the discovery that there is no Santa Claus or Easter bunny, few of us have the strength to spend a major portion of our lives working toward a goal only to discover it is not attainable. Not because we are not qualified—but because the power structure says we are not wanted because of what we are. Yet that is precisely the condition perpetuated by children's books that substitute wishful thinking for reality.

APPENDIX
Children's Catalog Listings

This table shows the editions and supplements of the *Children's Catalog* in which the books analyzed were listed. The sample included books found under the headings: Negroes—Stories; Negroes—Fiction; Slavery—Stories; and Slavery in the United States—Fiction. The table has been updated from the original cutoff date, 1968, to identify titles retained in the 1971 edition.

Author, Title, and Publication Date	*Children's Catalog* Edition
Bishop, C., *Little League Heroes.* 1960	1966
Bontemps, A., *Chariot in the Sky.* 1951	1951, 1956, 1961
Bontemps, A., *Sad-Faced Boy.* 1937	1941, 1946, 1951, 1956, 1961, 1966
Bontemps, A., *You Can't Pet a Possum.* 1934	1936, 1941, 1946, 1951
Bryant, S. C., *Epaminondas and His Auntie.* 1938 (original copyright, 1907)	1956
Burgwyn, M. H., *River Treasure.* 1947	1951
Carlson, N. S., *The Empty Schoolhouse.* 1965	1967*ᵃ, 1971
Credle, E., *Across the Cotton Patch.* 1935	1936
Credle, E., *The Flop-Eared Hound.* 1938	1941, 1946
Credle, E., *Little Jeemes Henry.* 1936	1941, 1946
De Angeli, M., *Bright April.* 1945	1951, 1956,* 1961,* 1966**
Decker, D., *Hit and Run.* 1949	1966
Evans, E. K., *Araminta.* 1935	1936, 1941, 1946, 1951, 1956
Evans, E. K., *Jerome Anthony.* 1936	1941, 1946, 1951, 1956
Faulkner, G., *Melindy's Happy Summer.* 1949	1951, 1961, 1966

ᵃ Single asterisk indicates book received the single-star recommendation; double asterisk indicates book was double starred.

183

Author, Title, and Publication Date	Children's Catalog Edition
Faulkner, G. and Becker, J., *Melindy's Medal*. 1945	1946, 1951, 1956,* 1961,* 1966*
Fife, D., *Who's in Charge of Lincoln?* 1965	1966, 1971
Fritz, J., *Brady*. 1960	1966, 1971
Gates, D., *Little Vic*. 1951	1956,* 1961,* 1966, 1971
Gerber, W., *Gooseberry Jones*. 1947	1951
Harris, J. C., *Complete Tales of Uncle Remus*. 1955[b]	1956, 1961, 1966
Hayes, F., *Skid*. 1948	1951, 1956,* 1966, 1971
Hogan, I., *Nicodemus and His Little Sister*. 1932	1936, 1941
Hogan, I., *Nicodemus and the Houn' Dog*. 1933[c]	1936
Hogan, I., *Nicodemus and the Little Black Pig*. 1934	1936
Hunt, M., *Ladycake Farm*. 1952	1956, 1961
Jackson, J., *Call Me Charley*. 1945	1956, 1961, 1966, 1971
Justus, M., *New Boy in School*. 1963	1966
Lang, D., *On the Dark of the Moon*. 1943	1946
Lang, D., *Strawberry Roan*. 1946	1951, 1956, 1961
Lattimore, E., *Bayou Boy*. 1946	1951, 1956, 1961
Lattimore, E., *Indigo Hill*. 1950	1951
Lattimore, E., *Junior, A Colored Boy of Charleston*. 1938	1941, 1946, 1951, 1956, 1961, 1966
Levy, M., *Corrie and the Yankee*. 1959	1968
McMeekin, I., *Journey Cake*. 1942	1956,* 1961, 1966, 1971
Means, F., *Great Day in the Morning*. 1946	1951, 1956
Means, F., *Shuttered Windows*. 1938	1941, 1946, 1951, 1956,** 1961
Newell, H., *A Cap for Mary Ellis*. 1953	1966, 1971
Newell, H., *Steppin and Family*. 1942	1946, 1951
Nolen, E., *A Job for Jeremiah*. 1940	1941, 1946
Ovington, M., *Hazel*. 1913	1916 II[d]
Ovington, M., *Zeke*. 1931	1936, 1941, 1946

[b] Harris, J. C., *The Complete Tales of Uncle Remus* (Boston: Houghton Mifflin, 1955) was used for the investigation, rather than the individual titles which are included for information at the end of this table.

[c] Noted here for information, but not included in final sample because a copy of the book was never located.

[d] Roman numeral indicates *Children's Catalog* supplement.

Author, Title, and Publication Date	Children's Catalog Edition
Pendleton, L., *King Tom and the Runaways*. 1890	1909, 1916 II, 1917, 1925, 1930
Sharpe, S., *Tobe*. 1939	1941, 1946, 1951, 1956*
Shotwell, L., *Roosevelt Grady*. 1963	1966, 1971
Sterling, D., *Mary Jane*. 1959	1961, 1966, 1971
Tarry, E., *Hezekiah Horton*. 1942	1946, 1951, 1956
Tarry, E., and Ets, M., *My Dog Rinty*. 1946	1951, 1956,* 1961, 1966, 1971
Taylor, M., *Jasper the Drummin' Boy*. 1947	1951
Trowbridge, J., *Cudjo's Cave*. 1864e	1916 II, 1917
Weaver, A., *Frawg*. 1930	1936, 1941
Harris, J., *Aaron in the Wildwoods*f	1917, 1925, 1930
Harris, J., *Daddy Jake, the Runaway*g	1916 II, 1917, 1925, 1930, 1936
Harris, J., *Little Mr. Thumblefinger and His Queer Country*	1917, 1925, 1930, 1936, 1941, 1946
Harris, J., *Mr. Rabbit at Home*	1917, 1925, 1930
Harris, J., *Nights with Uncle Remus*	1916 I, 1916 II, 1925, 1930, 1936
Harris, J., *On the Plantation*	1917, 1925, 1930, 1936
Harris, J., *Plantation Pageants*	1916 II, 1917, 1925
Harris, J., *Story of Aaron*	1917, 1925, 1930
Harris, J., *Uncle Remus and His Friends*	1916 I, 1916 II, 1917, 1925, 1930, 1936
Harris, J., *Uncle Remus and the Little Boy*	1917, 1925, 1930
Harris, J., *Uncle Remus Book*	1936
Harris, J., *Uncle Remus: His Songs and Sayings*	1916 I, 1916 II, 1917, 1925, 1930, 1936
Harris, J., *Uncle Remus Returns*	1925, 1930, 1936

e Included in Blanck sample, but noted here for information.

f See footnote b.

g 1936 *Children's Catalog* has title: *Daddy Jake, the Runaway and Short Stories Told After Dark*.

NOTES

CHAPTER 1

1. Benjamin Brawley, "The Negro in American Fiction," *Dial*, May 11, 1916, pp. 445–450.
2. George Greever, "Communications," *Dial*, June 8, 1916, p. 531.
3. John H. Nelson, *The Negro Character in American Literature* (Lawrence: University of Kansas Press, 1926), pp. 14–15.
4. Sterling A. Brown, "Negro Character As Seen by White Authors," *Journal of Negro Education* (1933), p. 180.
5. *Ibid.*, p. 192.
6. Sterling A. Brown, *The Negro in American Fiction* (Washington, D.C.: Associates in Negro Folk Education, 1937), p. 167.
7. David K. Gast, "Characteristics and Concepts of Minority Americans in Contemporary Children's Fictional Literature," (Ed.D. diss., Arizona State University, 1965), pp. 154–155.
8. Vine Deloria, Jr., *We Talk, You Listen* (New York: Macmillan, 1970), p. 26.
9. Morris Beja, "It Must Be Important: Negroes in Contemporary American Fiction," *Antioch Review*, 24 (1964), p. 336.
10. Laura Lee Hope, *The Bobbsey Twins* (New York: Grosset & Dunlap, 1904), pp. 56–57.
11. Malcolm X, *The Autobiography of Malcolm X* (New York: Grove Press, 1965), p. 36.
12. Eleanor Frances Lattimore, *Junior, A Colored Boy of Charleston* (New York: Harcourt, Brace, 1938), p. 129.
13. William H. Grier and Price M. Cobbs, *Black Rage* (New York: Basic Books, 1968).
14. Louisa Shotwell, *Roosevelt Grady* (New York: Grosset & Dunlap Tempo Books, 1964), pp. 70–71.

CHAPTER 2

1. LeRoi Jones [Imamu Amiri Baraka], *Blues People: Negro Music in White America* (New York: William Morrow, 1963), p. 2.

2. Samuel Griswold Goodrich, *The Tales of Peter Parley About America* (Boston: S. G. Goodrich, 1827), pp. 47–48.
3. Louise-Clarke Pyrnelle, *Diddie, Dumps, and Tot* (New York: Harper & Bros., 1882), pp. v–vi.
4. *Ibid.*, pp. 226–227.
5. Jean Fritz, *Brady* (New York: Coward-McCann, 1960), pp. 126–127.
6. Louis R. Pendleton, *King Tom and the Runaways* (New York: D. Appleton, 1890), p. 21.
7. Amelia Edith Barr, *The Bow of Orange Ribbon* (New York: Dodd, Mead, 1886), pp. 71–72.
8. Fritz, *op. cit.*, p. 122.
9. Mark Twain [Samuel Langhorne Clemens], *The Adventures of Huckleberry Finn* (New York: New American Library, 1959), p. 209.
10. *Ibid.*, pp. 209–210.
11. Florence Crannell Means, *Shuttered Windows* (Boston: Houghton Mifflin, 1938), p. 162.
12. Susan Warner, *Queechy* (New York: George P. Putnam, 1852), 2, pp. 84–86.
13. John Townsend Trowbridge, *Cudjo's Cave* (Boston: J. E. Tilton, 1864), pp. 133–135.
14. Dale Van Every, *The Disinherited: The Lost Birthright of the American Indian* (New York: William Morrow, 1966), pp. 263–264.
15. Fritz, *op. cit.*, p. 38.
16. William Dean Howells, *A Boy's Town* (New York: Harper & Bros., 1890), p. 11.
17. *Ibid.*, p. 126.
18. *Ibid.*, pp. 130–131.
19. *Ibid.*, p. 228.
20. John Hope Franklin, *From Slavery to Freedom: A History of Negro Americans*, 3rd rev. ed. (New York: Alfred A. Knopf, 1967), p. 183.
21. Edward Everett Hale, *The Man Without a Country* (New York: Franklin Watts, 1960), p. 30.
22. Paul Belloni DuChaillu, *Stories of the Gorilla Country* (New York: Harper & Bros., 1868), p. 175.
23. *Ibid.*, p. 392.
24. *Ibid.*, p. 113.
25. *Ibid.*, p. 117.
26. Hale, *op. cit.*, p. 33.
27. *Ibid.*, p. 34.

CHAPTER 3

1. Kenneth M. Stampp, *The Peculiar Institution: Slavery in the Ante-Bellum South* (New York: Alfred Knopf, 1956), pp. 192–236.

2. Georgene Faulkner and John Becker, *Melindy's Medal* (New York: Washington Square Press, 1967), pp. 40–41.
3. Stampp, *op. cit.*, p. 341.
4. Isabel McLennan McMeekin, *Journey Cake* (New York: Julian Messner, 1942), p. 25.
5. *Ibid.*, p. 36.
6. *Ibid.*, p. 50.
7. *Ibid.*, p. 68.
8. *Ibid.*, p. 115.
9. *Ibid.*, p. 82.
10. *Ibid.*, p. 60.
11. Thomas Nelson Page, *Two Little Confederates* (New York: Charles Scribner's Sons, 1932), p. 42.
12. Louise-Clarke Pyrnelle, *Diddie, Dumps, and Tot* (New York: Harper & Bros., 1882), p. 26.
13. Francis Robert Goulding, *The Young Marooners on the Florida Coast* (Philadelphia: William S. Martien, 1852), p. 199.
14. *Ibid.*, p. 206.
15. *Ibid.*
16. Martha Finley, *Elsie Dinsmore* (New York: Grosset & Dunlap, n.d.).
17. Thomas Bailey Aldrich, *The Story of a Bad Boy* (Boston: Houghton Mifflin, 1951), p. 6.
18. Page, *op. cit.*, p. 66.
19. *Ibid.*
20. Amelia Edith Barr, *The Bow of Orange Ribbon* (New York: Dodd, Mead, 1886), p. 50.
21. Arna Bontemps, *Chariot in the Sky: A Story of the Jubilee Singers* (Philadelphia: Winston, 1951), p. 75.
22. Eleanor Weakley Nolen, *A Job for Jeremiah* (New York: Oxford University Press, 1940), pp. 25–26.
23. *Ibid.*
24. *Ibid.*, pp. 61–62.
25. *Ibid.*, pp. 73–74.
26. Pyrnelle, *op. cit.*, p. 18.
27. Aldrich, *op. cit.*, p. 7.
28. Pyrnelle, *op. cit.*, p. 126.
29. *Ibid.*, p. 141.
30. *Ibid.*, p. 37.
31. *Ibid.*, p. 124.
32. Louis R. Pendleton, *King Tom and the Runaways* (New York: D. Appleton, 1890), p. 17.
33. Pyrnelle, *op. cit.*, p. 210.
34. *Ibid.*, p. 213.
35. Page, *op. cit.*, p. 277.

CHAPTER 4

1. Eleanor Weakley Nolen, "The Colored Child in Contemporary Literature," *Horn Book*, 18 (1942), pp. 348–355.
2. Quoted in Julius Lester, *To Be a Slave* (New York: Dial Press, 1968), pp. 62–63.
3. Arna Bontemps, *Chariot in the Sky: A Story of the Jubilee Singers* (Philadelphia: Winston, 1951), pp. 77–78.
4. Thomas Bailey Aldrich, *The Story of a Bad Boy* (Boston: Houghton Mifflin, 1951), p. 271.
5. Mark Twain [Samuel Langhorne Clemens], *The Adventures of Huckleberry Finn* (New York: New American Library, 1959), p. 50.
6. Dorothy Sterling, *Mary Jane* (Garden City: Doubleday, 1959), pp. 22–24.
7. John Townsend Trowbridge, *Cudjo's Cave* (Boston: J. E. Tilton, 1864), pp. 136–137.
8. *Ibid.*, pp. 125–131.
9. Louis R. Pendleton, *King Tom and the Runaways* (New York: D. Appleton, 1890), p. 9.
10. *Ibid.*, p. 52.
11. *Ibid.*, p. 269.
12. *Ibid.*, p. 271.

CHAPTER 5

1. John Townsend Trowbridge, *Cudjo's Cave* (Boston: J. E. Tilton, 1864), p. 105.
2. *Ibid.*, pp. 132–133.
3. Arna Bontemps, *Chariot in the Sky: A Story of the Jubilee Singers* (Philadelphia: Winston, 1951), p. 158.
4. Benjamin Quarles, *The Negro in the Making of America* (New York: Collier Books, 1964), p. 93.
5. Sterling A. Brown, "Negro Character As Seen by White Authors," *Journal of Negro Education*, 2 (1933), p. 186.
6. Louise-Clarke Pyrnelle, *Diddie, Dumps, and Tot* (New York: Harper & Bros., 1882), p. 29.
7. Louis R. Pendleton, *King Tom and the Runaways* (New York: D. Appleton, 1890), p. 56.
8. William Dean Howells, *A Boy's Town* (New York: Harper & Bros., 1890), p. 230.
9. Susan Warner, *Queechy* (New York: George P. Putnam, 1852), 2, p. 210.
10. Trowbridge, *op. cit.*, pp. 31–32.
11. *Ibid.*, p. 51.
12. *Ibid.*, p. 494.
13. Sophie May [Rebecca Sophia Clarke], *Little Prudy* (Chicago: M. A. Donohue, n.d.), pp. 124–125.

14. *Ibid.*, pp. 126–128.
15. Isabel McMeekin, *Journey Cake* (New York: Julian Messner, 1942), pp. 38–39.
16. *Ibid.*, pp. 122–123.
17. Bontemps, *op. cit.*, pp. 34–35.
18. *Ibid.*, p. 53.
19. Jean Fritz, *Brady* (New York: Coward-McCann, 1960), pp. 69–70.
20. Trowbridge, *op. cit.*, p. 239.
21. Charles Austin Fosdick, *Frank on the Lower Mississippi* (Cincinnati: R. W. Carroll, 1867), p. 146.
22. *Ibid.*, p. 96.
23. Jean Poindexter Colby, "How to Present the Negro in Children's Books," *Top of the News*, 21 (April 1965), pp. 191–192.
24. John Hope Franklin, *From Slavery to Freedom: A History of Negro Americans*, 3rd rev. ed. (New York: Alfred A. Knopf, 1967), p. 273.
25. Mimi Cooper Levy, *Corrie and the Yankee* (New York: Viking, 1959), p. 10.
26. *Ibid.*, pp. 183–186.

CHAPTER 6

1. John Hope Franklin, *From Slavery to Freedom: A History of Negro Americans*, 3rd rev. ed. (New York: Alfred Knopf, 1967), p. 331.
2. Charlemae Rollins, ed., *We Build Together*, 3rd rev. ed. (Champaign, Ill.: National Council of Teachers of English, 1967), p. xix.
3. Joel Chandler Harris, *Uncle Remus: His Songs and His Sayings*, in *The Complete Tales of Uncle Remus*, ed. Richard Chase (Boston: Houghton Mifflin, 1955), pp. xxvi–xxvii.
4. Harris, *Nights with Uncle Remus*, op. cit., pp. 209–210.
5. *Ibid.*, p. 119.
6. Harris, *Uncle Remus: His Songs and His Sayings*, op. cit., pp. 87–88.
7. Alice Hegan [Alice Caldwell Hegan Rice], *Mrs. Wiggs of the Cabbage Patch* (New York: Century, 1901), pp. 100–101.
8. Edgar Rice Burroughs, *Tarzan of the Apes* (Racine, Wis.: Whitman, 1964), p. 135.
9. *Ibid.*, p. 141.
10. *Ibid.*, pp. 196–197.
11. *Ibid.*, p. 219.
12. Josephine Diebitsch Peary, "Ahnighito," *St. Nicholas* (March 1901), p. 415.
13. Susan Coolidge [Sarah Chauncey Woolsey], *What Katy Did* (Boston: Roberts Bros., 1873), pp. 96–97.
14. Peter Newell, *The Hole Book* (New York: Harper & Bros., 1908), n.p.
15. Kirk Munroe, *Fur-Seal's Tooth* (New York: Harper & Bros., 1894), p. 73.
16. *Ibid.*, p. 82.

17. Florence Crannell Means, *Shuttered Windows* (Boston: Houghton Miffllin, 1938), p. 45.
18. *Ibid.*, p. 29.
19. *Ibid.*, p. 50.
20. Arna Bontemps, *Chariot in the Sky: A Story of the Jubilee Singers* (Philadelphia: Winston, 1951), p. 94.
21. *Ibid.*, p. 104.
22. *Ibid.*, pp. 189–191.
23. *Ibid.*, p. 234.
24. Sterling A. Brown, "The American Race Problem As Reflected in American Literature," *Journal of Negro Education* (1939), p. 275.

CHAPTER 7

1. Booker T. Washington, *Up from Slavery* (New York: Bantam Books, 1956), p. 84.
2. *Ibid.*, pp. 142–143.
3. Mary White Ovington, *Zeke* (New York: Harcourt, Brace, 1931), pp. 14–15.
4. Washington, *op. cit.*, p. 90.
5. *Ibid.*, pp. 156–158.
6. W. E. Burghardt DuBois, *The Souls of Black Folk* (Greenwich, Conn.: Fawcett, 1961), pp. 42–43.
7. Gunnar Myrdal, *An American Dilemma: The Negro Problem and Modern Democracy*, rev. ed. (New York: Harper & Row, 1962), pp. 888–889.
8. William H. Grier and Price M. Cobbs, *Black Rage* (New York: Basic Books, 1968), pp. 62–63.
9. Florence Crannell Means, *Shuttered Windows* (Boston: Houghton Mifflin, 1938), pp. 189–190.
10. *Ibid.*, p. 204.
11. Florence Crannell Means, *Great Day in the Morning* (Boston: Houghton Mifflin, 1946), p. 59.
12. *Ibid.*, p. 22.
13. Washington, *op. cit.*, p. 90.
14. Means, *Great Day in the Morning*, *op. cit.*, pp. 76–77.
15. *Ibid.*, p. 166.
16. Mary White Ovington, *Hazel* (New York: Crisis Publishing, 1913), p. 107.
17. Jonathan Kozol, *Death at an Early Age* (Boston: Houghton Mifflin, 1967).
18. Eleanor Frances Lattimore, *Junior, A Colored Boy of Charleston* (New York: Harcourt, Brace, 1938), pp. 8–9.
19. Marguerite DeAngeli, *Bright April* (Garden City: Doubleday, 1946), p. 42.
20. Doris Gates, *Little Vic* (New York: Viking, 1951).
21. Don Lang, *Strawberry Roan* (New York: Henry Z. Walck, 1946).

22. John P. Davis, ed., *The American Negro Reference Book* (Englewood Cliffs, N.J.: Prentice-Hall, 1966), p. 792.
23. May Justus, *New Boy in School* (New York: Hastings House, 1963).
24. Natalie Savage Carlson, *The Empty Schoolhouse* (New York: Dell, 1968), p. 20.
25. Judith Thompson and Gloria Woodard, "Black Perspective in Books for Children," *Wilson Library Bulletin*, 44 (December 1969), pp. 419–422.
26. Margaret Taylor, *Jasper, the Drummin' Boy* (New York: Viking, 1947), p. 9.
27. Florence Hayes, *Skid* (Boston: Houghton Mifflin, 1948), p. 176.
28. Jesse Jackson, *Call Me Charley* (New York: Harper & Bros., 1945), p. 87.
29. *Ibid.*, pp. 76–77.
30. Dorothy Sterling, *Mary Jane* (Garden City: Doubleday, 1959), p. 18.
31. Louisa R. Shotwell, *Roosevelt Grady* (New York: Grosset & Dunlap Tempo Books, 1964), pp. 59–61.
32. Thompson and Woodard, *loc. cit.*
33. Robert Coles, *Uprooted Children: The Early Lives of Migrant Farm Workers* (Pittsburgh: University of Pittsburgh Press, 1970).

CHAPTER 8

1. Clarence L. Barnhart, ed., *American College Dictionary* (New York: Random House, 1963), p. 962.
2. Samuel Griswold Goodrich, *The Tales of Peter Parley About Africa* (Boston: Grey and Bowen, and Carter and Hendee, 1830), ch. 20, n.p.
3. Barnhart, *op. cit.*
4. Paul Belloni DuChaillu, *Stories of the Gorilla Country* (New York: Harper & Bros., 1864), p. 20.
5. *Ibid.*, p. 50.
6. *Ibid.*, p. 208.
7. *Ibid.*, p. 191.
8. John Townsend Trowbridge, *Cudjo's Cave* (Boston: J. E. Tilton, 1864), pp. 257–258.
9. *Ibid.*, p. 271.
10. Edgar Rice Burroughs, *Tarzan of the Apes* (Racine, Wis.: Whitman, 1964), p. 78.
11. *Ibid.*, p. 87.
12. *Ibid.*, p. 92.
13. *Ibid.*
14. *Ibid.*, p. 99.
15. *Ibid.*, p. 204.
16. *Ibid.*, p. 205.
17. Thomas Nelson Page, *Two Little Confederates* (New York: Charles Scribner's Sons, 1932), p. 84.

18. Louis R. Pendleton, *King Tom and the Runaways* (New York: D. Appleton, 1890), p. 54.

19. Isabel McLennan McMeekin, *Journey Cake* (New York: Julian Messner, 1942), p. 69.

20. Annie Vaughan Weaver, *Frawg* (New York: Frederick A. Stokes, 1930), p. 11.

21. Booth Tarkington, *Penrod* (Garden City: Doubleday, Page, 1914), p. 240.

22. *Ibid.*, p. 242.

23. *Ibid.*, p. 245.

24. *Ibid.*, p. 151.

25. Booth Tarkington, *Penrod and Sam* (Garden City: Doubleday, Page, 1916), pp. 177–198.

26. Frances Boyd Calhoun, *Miss Minerva and William Green Hill* (Chicago: Reilly & Britton, 1908), p. 169.

CHAPTER 9

1. Georgene Faulkner, *Melindy's Happy Summer* (New York: Julian Messner, 1949), pp. 160–161.

2. *Ibid.*, p. 173.

3. *Ibid.*, p. 178.

4. Francis Robert Goulding, *The Young Marooners on the Florida Coast* (Philadelphia: William S. Martien, 1852), p. 41.

5. Marshall Saunders, *Beautiful Joe* (Philadelphia: American Baptist Publication Society, 1894), p. 18.

6. John Townsend Trowbridge, *Cudjo's Cave* (Boston: J. E. Tilton, 1864), p. 122.

7. *Ibid.*

8. A. H. Keane, "Negro," *Encyclopaedia Britannica*, 9th ed. (Chicago: R. S. Peale, 1890), 17, pp. 316–317.

9. Jane Andrews, *The Seven Little Sisters Who Live on the Round Ball That Floats in the Air* (Boston: Ticknor & Fields, 1861), pp. 73–74.

10. Eleanor Frances Lattimore, *Bayou Boy* (New York: William Morrow, 1946), pp. 17–18.

11. Arna Bontemps, *You Can't Pet a Possum* (New York: William Morrow, 1934), pp. 104–105.

12. Arna Bontemps, *Sad-Faced Boy* (Boston: Houghton Mifflin, 1937), p. 19.

13. Florence Crannell Means, *Shuttered Windows* (Boston: Houghton Mifflin, 1938), pp. 78–79.

14. Florence Crannell Means, *Great Day in the Morning* (Boston: Houghton Mifflin, 1946), p. 9.

15. *Ibid.*, p. 157.

16. Natalie Savage Carlson, *The Empty Schoolhouse* (New York: Dell, 1968), p. 2.

17. Stella Gentry Sharpe, *Tobe* (Chapel Hill: University of North Carolina Press, 1939), p. 11.
18. Ellis Credle, *Across the Cotton Patch* (New York: Thomas Nelson, 1935), n.p.
19. Hugh Lofting, *The Story of Doctor Dolittle* (New York: Frederick A. Stokes, 1920), p. 100.
20. *Ibid.*, p. 106.
21. Frances Boyd Calhoun, *Miss Minerva and William Green Hill* (Chicago: Reilly & Britton, 1908), pp. 70–76.
22. Joel Chandler Harris, *The Complete Tales of Uncle Remus*, ed. Richard Chase (Boston: Houghton Mifflin, 1955), pp. 109–111.
23. Trowbridge, *op. cit.*, p. 117.
24. *Ibid.*, p. 122.
25. William Dean Howells, *A Boy's Town* (New York: Harper & Bros., 1890), p. 230.
26. Louis R. Pendleton, *King Tom and the Runaways* (New York: D. Appleton, 1890), p. 2.
27. Mary White Ovington, *Zeke* (New York: Harcourt, Brace, 1931), pp. 19–20.
28. Means, *Shuttered Windows, op. cit.*, p. 6.
29. Means, *Great Day in the Morning, op. cit.*, p. 5.
30. Marguerite DeAngeli, *Bright April* (Garden City: Doubleday, 1946), p. 9.
31. Duane Decker, *Hit and Run* (New York: William Morrow, 1949), pp. 73–74.
32. Booth Tarkington, *Penrod* (Garden City: Doubleday, Page, 1914), p. 62.
33. Georgene Faulkner and John Becker, *Melindy's Medal* (New York: Washington Square Press, 1967), p. 45.
34. Thomas Bailey Aldrich, *The Story of a Bad Boy* (Boston: Houghton Mifflin, 1951), p. 64.
35. Louise-Clarke Pyrnelle, *Diddie, Dumps, and Tot* (New York: Harper & Bros., 1882), p. 228.
36. *Ibid.*, p. 106.

CHAPTER 10

1. Malcolm X, *The Autobiography of Malcolm X* (New York: Grove Press, 1965), pp. 162–163.
2. Martha Finley, *Elsie Dinsmore* (New York: Grosset & Dunlap, n.d.), pp. 107–108.
3. Francis Robert Goulding, *The Young Marooners on the Florida Coast* (Philadelphia: William S. Martien, 1952), p. 247.
4. Louise-Clarke Pyrnelle, *Diddie, Dumps, and Tots* (New York: Harper & Bros., 1882), pp. viii–ix.
5. *Ibid.*, p. 74.

6. Mary White Ovington, *Hazel* (New York: Crisis Publishing, 1913), pp. 20–22.

7. *Ibid.*, pp. 75–83.

8. Ellis Credle, *Little Jeemes Henry* (New York: Thomas Nelson, 1936), n.p.

9. Florence Crannell Means, *Shuttered Windows* (Boston: Houghton Mifflin, 1938), p. 30.

10. Isabel McLennan McMeekin, *Journey Cake* (New York; Julian Messner, 1942), p. 164.

11. Jesse Jackson, *Call Me Charley* (New York: Harper & Bros., 1945), pp. 19–20.

12. Georgene Faulkner, *Melindy's Happy Summer* (New York: Julian Messner, 1949), pp. 132–133.

13. Kenneth M. Stampp, *The Peculiar Institution: Slavery in the Ante-Bellum South* (New York: Alfred A. Knopf, 1956), p. 375.

14. Booth Tarkington, *Penrod* (Garden City: Doubleday, Page, 1914), p. 213.

15. Mark Twain [Samuel Langhorne Clemens], *The Adventures of Huckleberry Finn* (New York: New American Library, 1959), p. 13.

16. *Ibid.*, pp. 26–27.

17. Goulding, *op. cit.*, pp. 236–237.

18. Annie Fellows Johnston, *The Little Colonel* (Boston: Joseph Knight, 1896), pp. 53–61.

19. *Ibid.*, p. 61.

20. McMeekin, *op. cit.*, pp. 69–73.

21. Hope Newell, *Steppin and Family* (New York: Oxford University Press, 1942), pp. 41–43.

22. Joel Chandler Harris, *The Complete Tales of Uncle Remus* (Boston: Houghton Mifflin, 1955), pp. 103–104.

23. Mebane Holomon Burgwyn, *River Treasure* (New York: Oxford University Press, 1947), pp. 83–84.

24. *Ibid.*, pp. 86–97.

25. Means, *op. cit.*, pp. 169–170.

26. Johnston, *op. cit.*, pp. 79–80.

27. Don Lang, *On the Dark of the Moon* (New York: Oxford University Press, 1943), p. 22.

28. *Ibid.*, p. 95.

CHAPTER 11

1. Kenneth M. Stampp, *The Peculiar Institution: Slavery in the Ante-Bellum South* (New York: Alfred A. Knopf, 1956), pp. 368–369.

2. Mebane Holomon Burgwyn, *River Treasure* (New York: Oxford University Press, 1947), p. 7.

3. Dorothy Sterling, *Mary Jane* (Garden City: Doubleday, 1959), pp. 87–88.

4. LeRoi Jones [Imamu Amiri Baraka], *Blues People: Negro Music in White America* (New York: William Morrow, 1963), p. 186.

5. Joel Chandler Harris, *The Complete Tales of Uncle Remus* (Boston: Houghton Mifflin, 1955), p. 105.

6. Louis R. Pendleton, *King Tom and the Runaways* (New York: D. Appleton, 1890), p. 23.

7. Eleanor Frances Lattimore, *Junior, A Colored Boy of Charleston* (New York: Harcourt, Brace, 1938), p. 85.

8. Mabel Leigh Hunt, *Ladycake Farm* (Philadelphia: J. B. Lippincott, 1952), p. 80.

9. *Ibid.*, p. 84.

10. Arna Bontemps, *Sad-Faced Boy* (Boston: Houghton Mifflin, 1937), pp. 99–106.

11. Louise-Clarke Pyrnelle, *Diddie, Dumps, and Tot* (New York: Harper & Bros., 1882), pp. 114–115.

12. *Ibid.*, pp. 115–116.

13. Amelia Edith Barr, *The Bow of Orange Ribbon* (New York: Dodd, Mead, 1886), p. 74.

14. Alice Hegan [Alice Caldwell Hegan Rice], *Mrs. Wiggs of the Cabbage Patch* (New York: Century, 1901), pp. 145–146.

15. Mary White Ovington, *Zeke* (New York: Harcourt, Brace, 1931), pp. 161–165.

16. Hope Newell, *Steppin and Family* (New York: Oxford University Press, 1942), pp. 54–81.

17. Louisa May Alcott, *An Old-Fashioned Girl* (Cleveland: World, n.d.), p. 27.

18. Sarah Orne Jewett, *Betty Leicester* (Boston: Houghton Mifflin, 1890), p. 290.

19. Lattimore, *op. cit.*, p. 65.

20. Eleanor Frances Lattimore, *Indigo Hill* (New York: William Morrow, 1950), p. 88.

21. May Justus, *New Boy in School* (New York: Hastings House, 1963), p. 52.

CHAPTER 12

1. Booker T. Washington, *Up from Slavery* (New York: Bantam Books, 1956), p. 156.

2. John Townsend Trowbridge, *Cudjo's Cave* (Boston: J. E. Tilton, 1864), p. 423.

3. Florence Hayes, *Skid* (Boston: Houghton Mifflin, 1948), pp. 100–101.

4. Mark Twain, *The Adventures of Tom Sawyer* (New York: New American Library, 1959), p. 173.

5. W. E. Burghardt DuBois, *The Souls of Black Folk* (Greenwich, Conn.: Fawcett, 1961), p. 44.

6. Louise-Clarke Pyrnelle, *Diddie, Dumps, and Tot* (New York: Harper & Bros., 1882), p. 183.

7. Dorothy Sterling, *Mary Jane* (Garden City: Doubleday, 1959), p. 39.

BIBLIOGRAPHY

The Bibliography is divided into three parts: the General Bibliography; the Sample from Jacob Blanck's Bibliography, and the Sample from Wilson's *Children's Catalog*.

GENERAL BIBLIOGRAPHY

ALCOTT, LOUISA MAY. "M.L.," *Journal of Negro History* 14 (1929), pp. 495–522.

ARMSTRONG, WILLIAM H. *Sounder*. Illus. JAMES BARKLEY. New York: Harper & Row, 1969.

———. *Sour Land*. New York: Harper & Row, 1971.

BAKER, AUGUSTA. *Books About Negro Life for Children*. New York: The New York Public Library, 1963.

BARAKA, IMAMU AMIRI. See JONES, LEROI.

BARBOUR, FLOYD B., ed. *The Black Power Revolt*. New York: Collier Books, 1969.

BARNHART, CLARENCE L., ed. *American College Dictionary*. New York: Random House, 1953.

BEARD, DANIEL CARTER. *What To Do and How To Do It: The American Boys Handy Book*. New York: Charles Scribner's Sons, 1882.

BEJA, MORRIS. "It Must be Important: Negroes in Contemporary Fiction," *Antioch Review*, 24 (1964), pp. 323–336.

BERELSON, BERNARD. *Content Analysis in Communication Research*. Glencoe, Ill.: Free Press, 1952.

BLANCK, JACOB. *Peter Parley to Penrod: A Bibliographical Description of the Best-Loved American Juvenile Books, 1827–1926*. New York: R. R. Bowker, 1938.

BRAWLEY, BENJAMIN. "The Negro in American Fiction," *Dial*, 60 (May 11, 1916), pp. 445–450.

BROOKS, PHILIP. Review of Jacob Blanck's *Peter Parley to Penrod: A Bibliographical Description of the Best-Loved American Juvenile Books, 1827–1926*. *New York Times*, September 25, 1938, p. 32.

BROWN, STERLING A. "The American Race Problem as Reflected in American Literature," *The Journal of Negro Education*, 8 (1939), pp. 275–290.

———. "Negro Character As Seen by White Authors," *Journal of Negro Education*, 2 (1933), pp. 179–203.

———. *The Negro in American Fiction.* Washington, D.C.: Associates in Negro Folk Education, 1937.

Children's Catalog, 1st ed.–11th ed. Minneapolis and New York: H. W. Wilson Company, 1909–1966.

Children's Catalog: 1967 Supplement to the Eleventh Edition, 1966. New York: H. W. Wilson Company, 1967.

Children's Catalog: 1968 Supplement to the Eleventh Edition, 1966. New York: H. W. Wilson Company, 1968.

COLBY, JEAN POINDEXTER. "How to Present the Negro in Children's Books," *Top of the News*, 21 (April 1965), pp. 191–196.

COLES, ROBERT. *Uprooted Children: The Early Lives of Migrant Farm Workers.* Pittsburgh: University of Pittsburgh Press, 1970.

DAVIES, DAVID. Review of Jacob Blanck's *Peter Parley to Penrod: A Bibliographical Description of the Best-Loved American Juvenile Books, 1827–1926*, in *Library Journal*, 63 (November 1, 1938), p. 838.

DAVIS, JOHN P., ed. *The American Negro Reference Book.* Englewood Cliffs, N.J.: Prentice-Hall, 1966.

DUBOIS, W. E. BURGHARDT. *The Souls of Black Folk.* Greenwich, Conn.: Fawcett, 1961.

FORD, THOMAS W. "Howells and the American Negro," *Texas Studies in Literature and Language*, 5 (1964), pp. 530–537.

FRANKLIN, JOHN HOPE. *From Slavery to Freedom: A History of Negro Americans*, 3rd rev. ed. New York: Alfred A. Knopf, 1967.

GAST, DAVID K. "Characteristics and Concepts of Minority Americans in Contemporary Children's Fictional Literature." Ed.D. diss., Arizona State University, 1965.

GOODRICH, SAMUEL GRISWOLD. *The Tales of Peter Parley About Africa.* Boston: Grey and Bowen, and Carter and Hendee, 1830.

GRANT, JOANNE, ed. *Black Protest: History, Documents, and Analyses, 1619 to the Present.* Greenwich, Conn.: Fawcett, 1968.

GREEVER, GEORGE. Letter in "Communications," *Dial*, 60 (June 8, 1916), p. 531.

GRIER, WILLIAM H., and COBBS, PRICE M. *Black Rage.* New York: Basic Books, 1968.

GRIFFIN, JOHN H. *Black Like Me.* Boston: Houghton Mifflin, 1961.

GROSS, SEYMOUR L., and HARDY, JOHN E., eds. *Images of the Negro in American Literature.* Chicago: University of Chicago Press, 1966.

GROSS, THEODORE L. "The Negro in the Literature of the Reconstruction," *Phylon*, 22 (Spring, 1961), pp. 5–14.

HARDEN, J. W. "Louisa Alcott's Contribution to Democracy," *Negro History Bulletin*, 6 (1942), pp. 28–32.

HOWELLS, WILLIAM DEAN. *An Imperative Duty.* New York: Harper & Bros., 1891.

JONES, LEROI [IMAMU AMIRI BARAKA]. *Black Music*. New York: William Morrow, 1967.

———. *Blues People: Negro Music in White America*. New York: William Morrow, 1963.

KARDINER, ABRAM, and OVESEY, LIONEL. *Mark of Oppression*. New York: Basic Books, 1956.

KATZ, DANIEL, and BRALY, KENNETH. "Racial Stereotypes of One Hundred College Students," *Journal of Abnormal and Social Psychology*, 28 (October–December 1933), pp. 280–290.

KAY, HELEN. "Blackout of a Negro Child," *Top of the News*, 22 (November 1965), pp. 58–61.

KEANE, A. H. "Negro." *Encyclopaedia Britannica*, 9th ed. Chicago: R. S. Peale, 1890. Vol. 17, pp. 316–317.

KOZOL, JONATHAN. *Death at an Early Age*. Boston: Houghton Mifflin, 1967.

LARRICK, NANCY. "The All-White World of Children's Books," *Saturday Review*, 40 (September 11, 1965), p. 63.

LESTER, JULIUS. *To Be a Slave*. New York: Dial, 1968.

LOGAN, RAYFORD W. *The Negro in American Life and Thought: The Nadir, 1877–1901*. New York: Dial Press, 1954.

MALCOLM X. *The Autobiography of Malcolm X*. New York: Grove Press, 1965.

MILLENDER, DARTHULLA. "Through a Glass, Darkly," *Library Journal*, 92 (December 15, 1967), pp. 4571–4576.

MILLER, ELIZABETH W., ed. *The Negro in America: A Bibliography*. Cambridge: Harvard University Press, 1966.

MYRDAL, GUNNAR. *An American Dilemma: The Negro Problem and Modern Democracy*, rev. ed. New York: Harper & Row, 1962.

NELSON, JOHN H. *The Negro Character in American Literature*. Lawrence: University of Kansas Press, 1926.

NOLEN, ELEANOR W. "The Colored Child in Contemporary Literature," *Horn Book*, 18 (1942), pp. 348–355.

PARSONS, ELSIE C. "Joel Chandler Harris and Negro Folklore," *Dial*, 66 (May 17, 1919), pp. 491–494.

PLOSKI, HARRY A., and BROWN, ROSCOE C., JR., eds. *The Negro Almanac*. New York: Bellwether, 1966.

QUARLES, BENJAMIN. *The Negro in the Making of America*. New York: Collier Books, 1964.

ROLLINS, CHARLEMAE, ed. *We Build Together*, 3rd rev. ed. Champaign, Ill.: National Council of Teachers of English. 1967.

STAMPP, KENNETH M. *The Peculiar Institution: Slavery in the Ante-Bellum South*. New York: Alfred A. Knopf, 1956.

THOMPSON, JUDITH, and WOODARD, GLORIA. "Black Perspective in Books for Children," *Wilson Library Bulletin* 44 (December 1969).

VAIL, R. W. G. Review of Jacob Blanck's *Peter Parley to Penrod: A Bibliographical Description of the Best-Loved American Juvenile Books, 1827–1926*. in *Publisher's Weekly*, 134 (August 20, 1938), p. 521.

VAN EVERY, DALE. *The Disinherited: The Lost Birthright of the American Indian.* New York: William Morrow, 1966.

WASHINGTON, BOOKER T. *Up from Slavery.* New York: Doubleday, 1933. (Pagination for New York: Bantam Books, 1956 ed.)

WHITNEY, PHILLIS A. *Willow Hill.* New York: David McKay, 1947.

WORK, MONROE N. *A Bibliography of the Negro in Africa and America.* New York: H. W. Wilson Company, 1928.

SAMPLE FROM JACOB BLANCK'S BIBLIOGRAPHY

Fifty-five titles made up the final sample from Jacob Blanck's *Peter Parley to Penrod: A Bibliographical Description of the Best-Loved American Juvenile Books, 1827–1926* (New York: R. R. Bowker, 1938).

ALCOTT, LOUISA MAY. *Little Men.* Boston: Roberts Bros., 1871. (Pagination for Cleveland: World, n.d. ed.)

———. *Little Women.* Boston: Roberts Bros., 1868. (Pagination for Boston: Little, Brown, 1950 ed.)

———. *An Old-Fashioned Girl.* Boston: Roberts Bros., 1870. (Pagination for Cleveland: World, n.d. ed.)

ALDRICH, THOMAS BAILEY. *The Story of a Bad Boy.* Boston: Osgood and Company, 1870. (Pagination for Boston: Houghton Mifflin, 1951 ed.)

ANDREWS, JANE. *The Seven Little Sisters Who Live on the Round Ball That Floats in the Air.* Boston: Ticknor & Fields, 1861. (Pagination for Boston: Ticknor & Fields, 1887 ed.)

———. *Ten Boys Who Lived on the Road from Long Ago to Now.* Boston: Lee & Shepard, 1886.

BARBOUR, RALPH HENRY. *The Half-Back.* New York: D. Appleton, 1899.

BARR, AMELIA EDITH. *The Bow of Orange Ribbon.* New York: Dodd, Mead, 1886.

BENNETT, JOHN. *Barnaby Lee.* New York: Century, 1902. (Pagination for original publication in *St. Nicholas*, November 1900–April 1902.)

BURROUGHS, EDGAR RICE. *Tarzan of the Apes.* Chicago: A. C. McClurg, 1914. (Pagination for Racine, Wis.: Whitman, 1964 ed.)

CALHOUN, FRANCES BOYD. *Miss Minerva and William Green Hill.* Chicago: Reilly & Britton, 1909. (Pagination for Chicago: Reilly & Britton, 1908, Third Popular Edition [from the Wisconsin State Historical Society collection].)

COFFIN, CHARLES CARLETON. *The Boys of '76.* New York: Harper & Bros., 1877.

COOLIDGE, SUSAN [SARAH CHAUNCEY WOOLSEY]. *What Katy Did.* Boston: Roberts Bros., 1873.

DuCHAILLU, PAUL BELLONI. *Stories of the Gorilla Country.* New York: Harper & Bros., 1868.

FINLEY, MARTHA. *Elsie Dinsmore.* New York: M. W. Dodd, 1867. (Pagination for New York: Grosset & Dunlap, n.d. ed.)

FOSDICK, CHARLES AUSTIN. *Frank on the Lower Mississippi*. Cincinnati: R. W. Carroll, 1867.

GOODRICH, SAMUEL GRISWOLD. *The Tales of Peter Parley About America*. Boston: S. G. Goodrich, 1827.

GOULDING, FRANCIS ROBERT. *The Young Marooners on the Florida Coast*. Philadelphia: William S. Martien, 1852.

GRANT, ROBERT. *Jack Hall*. Boston: Jordan, Marsh, 1888.

HABBERTON, JOHN. *Helen's Babies*. Boston: Loring, 1876.

HALE, EDWARD EVERETT. *The Man Without a Country*. Boston: Ticknor & Fields, 1865. (Pagination for New York: Franklin Watts, 1960 First Book ed.)

HAWES, CHARLES BOARDMAN. *The Dark Frigate*. Boston: Atlantic Monthly Press, 1923.

HEGAN, ALICE [ALICE CALDWELL HEGAN RICE]. *Mrs. Wiggs of the Cabbage Patch*. New York: Century, 1901.

HOWELLS, WILLIAM DEAN. *A Boy's Town*. New York: Harper & Bros., 1890.

———. *The Flight of Pony Baker*. New York: Harper & Bros., 1902.

JEWETT, SARAH ORNE. *Betty Leicester*. Boston: Houghton Mifflin, 1890.

JOHNSON, OWEN. *The Tennessee Shad*. New York: Baker & Taylor, 1911. (Pagination for Boston: Little, Brown, 1945 ed.)

———. *The Varmint*. New York: Baker & Taylor, 1910. (Pagination for Boston: Little, Brown, 1945 ed.)

JOHNSON, ROSSITER. *Phaeton Rogers*. New York: Charles Scribner's Sons, 1881. (Pagination for New York: Charles Scribner's Sons, 1923 ed.)

JOHNSTON, ANNIE FELLOWS. *The Little Colonel*. Boston: Joseph Knight, 1896.

KELLOGG, ELIJAH. *Lion Ben of Elm Island*. Boston: Lee & Shepard, 1869.

KING, CHARLES. *Cadet Days*. New York: Harper & Bros., 1894.

KNOX, THOMAS WALLACE. *The Boy Travellers in the Far East*. New York: Harper & Bros., 1880.

LOFTING, HUGH. *The Story of Doctor Dolittle*. New York: Frederick A. Stokes, 1920.

MAY, SOPHIE. See Sophie May.

MUNROE, KIRK. *The Flamingo Feather*. New York: Harper & Bros., 1887.

———. *Fur-Seal's Tooth*. New York: Harper & Bros., 1894.

NEWELL, PETER. *The Hole Book*. New York: Harper & Bros., 1908.

PAGE, THOMAS NELSON. *Two Little Confederates*. New York: Charles Scribner's Sons, 1888. (Pagination for New York: Charles Scribner's Sons, 1932 ed.)

PEARY, JOSEPHINE DIEBITSCH. *The Snow Baby*. New York: Frederick A. Stokes, 1901. (Pagination for original publication, "Ahnighito," in *St. Nicholas*, March 1901.)

PECK, GEORGE WILBUR. *Peck's Bad Boy and His Pa*. Chicago: Belford, Clarke, 2 vols. 1883. (Pagination for Toronto: Musson Book, n.d. ed.)

PYRNELLE, LOUISE-CLARKE. *Diddie, Dumps, and Tot*. New York: Harper & Bros., 1882.

RICHARDS, LAURA ELIZABETH. *Captain January*. Boston: Estes & Lauriat, 1891.

SAUNDERS, MARSHALL. *Beautiful Joe*. Philadelphia: American Baptist Publication Society, 1894.

SCUDDER, HORACE ELISHA. *Doings of the Bodley Family in Town and Country*. New York: Hurd & Houghton, 1875.

SHUTE, HENRY AUGUSTUS. *The Real Diary of a Real Boy*. Boston: Everett Press, 1902.

SOPHIE MAY [REBECCA SOPHIA CLARKE]. *Little Prudy*. Boston: Lee & Shepard, 1864. (Pagination for Chicago: M. A. Donahue & Co., n.d. ed.)

STOCKTON, FRANK RICHARD. *The Floating Prince*. New York: Charles Scribner's Sons, 1881. (Pagination for original publication in *St. Nicholas*, December 1880.)

————. *Ting a Ling*. New York: Hurd & Houghton, 1870. (Pagination for New York: Charles Scribner's Sons, 1955 ed.)

TARKINGTON, BOOTH. *Penrod*. Garden City: Doubeday, Page, 1914.

————. *Penrod and Sam*. Garden City: Doubleday, Page, 1916.

TROWBRIDGE, JOHN TOWNSEND. *Cudjo's Cave*. Boston: J. E. Tilton, 1864.

TWAIN, MARK [SAMUEL LANGHORNE CLEMENS]. *The Adventures of Huckleberry Finn*. New York: Charles L. Webster, 1885. (Pagination for New York: New American Library, 1959 ed.)

————. *The Adventures of Tom Sawyer*. Hartford: The American Publishing Company, 1876. (Pagination for New York: New American Library, 1959 ed.)

WARNER, SUSAN. *Queechy*. 2 vols. New York: George P. Putnam, 1852.

WEBSTER, JEAN. *Daddy-Long-Legs*. New York: Century, 1912.

SAMPLE FROM THE *CHILDREN'S CATALOG*

Forty-nine titles made up the final sample from the various editions and supplements of the *Children's Catalog* (Minneapolis and New York: H. W. Wilson, 1909–1968).

BISHOP, CURTIS. *Little League Heroes*. Philadelphia: J. B. Lippincott, 1960.

BONTEMPS, ARNA. *Chariot in the Sky: A Story of the Jubilee Singers*. Illus. CYRUS LEROY BALDRIDGE. Philadelphia: Winston, 1951.

————. *Sad-Faced Boy*. Illus. VIRGINIA LEE BURTON. Boston: Houghton Mifflin, 1937.

————. *You Can't Pet a Possum*. Illus. ILSE BISCHOFF. New York: William Morrow, 1934.

BRYANT, SARA CONE. *Epaminondas and His Auntie*. Illus. INEZ HOGAN. Boston: Houghton Mifflin, 1938. (Original copyright, 1907.)

BURGWYN, MEBANE HOLOMAN. *River Treasure*. Illus. RALPH RAY. New York: Oxford University Press, 1947.

CARLSON, NATALIE SAVAGE. *The Empty Schoolhouse*. Illus. JOHN KAUFMANN. New York: Harper & Row, 1965. (Pagination for New York: Dell, 1968 ed.)

CREDLE, ELLIS. *Across the Cotton Patch*. Illus. AUTHOR. New York: Thomas Nelson, 1935.

————. *The Flop-Eared Hound*. Illus. (photographs) CHARLES TOWNSEND. New York: Oxford University Press, 1938.

————. *Little Jeemes Henry*. Illus. AUTHOR. New York: Thomas Nelson, 1936.

DEANGELI, MARGUERITE. *Bright April*. Illus. AUTHOR. Garden City: Doubleday, 1946.

DECKER, DUANE. *Hit and Run*. New York: William Morrow, 1949.

EVANS, EVA KNOX. *Araminta*. Illus. ERICK BERRY. New York: G. P. Putnam's, 1935.

————. *Jerome Anthony*. Illus. ERICK BERRY. New York: G. P. Putnam's, 1936.

FAULKNER, GEORGENE. *Melindy's Happy Summer*. Illus. ELTON C. FAX. New York: Julian Messner, 1949.

FAULKNER, GEORGENE, and BECKER, JOHN. *Melindy's Medal*. Illus. ELTON C. FAX. New York: Julian Messner, 1945. (Pagination for New York: Washington Square Press, 1967 ed.)

FIFE, DALE. *Who's in Charge of Lincoln?* Illus. PAUL GALDONE. New York: Coward-McCann, 1965.

FRITZ, JEAN. *Brady*. Illus. LYND WARD. New York: Coward-McCann, 1960.

GATES, DORIS. *Little Vic*. Illus. KATE SEREDY. New York: Viking, 1951.

GERBER, WILL. *Gooseberry Jones*. Illus. DUDLEY MORRIS. New York: G. P. Putnam's, 1947.

HARRIS, JOEL CHANDLER. *The Complete Tales of Uncle Remus*. RICHARD CHASE, ed. Boston: Houghton Mifflin, 1955.

HAYES, FLORENCE. *Skid*. Illus. ELTON C. FAX. Boston: Houghton Mifflin, 1948.

HOGAN, INEZ. *Nicodemus and His Little Sister*. Illus. AUTHOR. New York: E. P. Dutton, 1932.

————. *Nicodemus and the Little Black Pig*. Illus. AUTHOR. New York: E. P. Dutton, 1934.

HUNT, MABEL LEIGH. *Ladycake Farm*. Illus. CLOTILDE EMBREE FUNK. Philadelphia: J. B. Lippincott, 1952.

JACKSON, JESSE. *Call Me Charley*. Illus. DORIS SPIEGEL. New York: Harper & Bros., 1945.

JUSTUS, MAY. *New Boy in School*. Illus. JEAN BALFOUR PAYNE. New York: Hastings House, 1963.

LANG, DON. *On the Dark of the Moon*. Illus. NEDDA WALKER. New York: Oxford University Press, 1943.

————. *Strawberry Roan*. Illus. GERTRUDE HOWE. New York: Henry Z. Walck, 1946.

LATTIMORE, ELEANOR FRANCES. *Bayou Boy*. Illus. AUTHOR. New York: William Morrow, 1946.

————. *Indigo Hill*. Illus. AUTHOR. New York: William Morrow, 1950.

————. *Junior, A Colored Boy of Charleston.* Illus. AUTHOR. New York: Harcourt, Brace, 1938.

LEVY, MIMI COOPER. *Corrie and the Yankee.* Illus. ERNEST CRICHLOW. New York: Viking, 1959.

McMEEKIN, ISABEL McLENNAN. *Journey Cake.* Illus. NICHOLAS PANESIS. New York: Julian Messner, 1942.

MEANS, FLORENCE CRANNELL. *Great Day in the Morning.* Illus. HELEN BLAIR. Boston: Houghton Mifflin, 1946.

————. *Shuttered Windows.* Illus. ARMSTRONG SPERRY. Boston: Houghton Mifflin, 1938.

NEWELL, HOPE. *A Cap for Mary Ellis.* New York: Harper & Bros., 1953.

————. *Steppin and Family.* Illus. ANNE MERRIMAN PECK. New York: Oxford University Press, 1942.

NOLEN, ELEANOR WEAKLEY. *A Job for Jeremiah.* Illus. IRIS BEATTY JOHNSON. New York: Oxford University Press, 1940.

OVINGTON, MARY WHITE. *Hazel.* Illus. HARRY ROSELAND. New York: Crisis Publishing, 1913.

————. *Zeke.* Illus. NATALIE H. DAVIS. New York: Harcourt, Brace, 1931.

PENDLETON, LOUIS R. *King Tom and the Runaways.* New York: D. Appleton, 1890.

SHARPE, STELLA GENTRY. *Tobe.* Illus. (photographs) CHARLES FARRELL. Chapel Hill: University of North Carolina Press, 1939.

SHOTWELL, LOUISA R. *Roosevelt Grady.* Illus. PETER BURCHARD. Cleveland: World, 1963. (Pagination for New York: Grosset & Dunlap Tempo Books, 1964 ed.)

STERLING, DOROTHY. *Mary Jane.* Illus. ERNEST CRICHLOW. Garden City: Doubleday, 1959.

TARRY, ELLEN. *Hezekiah Horton.* Illus. OLIVER HARRINGTON. New York: Viking, 1942.

TARRY, ELLEN, and ETS, MARIE HALL. *My Dog Rinty.* New York: Viking, 1946.

TAYLOR, MARGARET. *Jasper, the Drummin' Boy.* Illus. AUTHOR. New York: Viking, 1947.

WEAVER, ANNIE VAUGHAN. *Frawg.* Illus. AUTHOR. New York: Frederick A. Stokes, 1930.

INDEX